ZERO KNOWLEDGE

ARNAUD PASCOLO

WARRINGTON
PUBLISHING

DANBURY, CONNECTICUT

Zero Knowledge
Copyright © 2025 by Arnaud Pascolo

Published by Warrington Publishing
Danbury, CT
www.warringtonpublishing.com

Printed in the United States of America
First Edition
ISBN: 978-1-944972-61-5 (paperback)
978-1-944972-62-2 (hardcover)
978-1-944972-60-8 (ebook)

Cover designed by Aleksandar N.
Edited by Carey Giudici, Tory Hunter, and Brent Howard

NOVELS BY ARNUD PASCOLO

An Open Shift

Zero Knowledge

For Marina

Without you, this book would have remained great ideas in my head

CHAPTER 1

WEDNESDAY, 18 SEPTEMBER 7:45 A.M.

Today is her birthday and tomorrow she is dead. These were Duan Ripa's first thoughts when he looked at his awakening wife, Mina. Trying to imagine what it would be like to go on without her.

They no longer discussed replacing the aging wallpaper in their bedroom; just six months ago, they quarreled for weeks if it should be off-white or aquamarine. Now, it looked permanent. And the grotesquely smiling Amazon box, full of summer clothes that Mina had once planned to organize, would never be opened again.

Just before they fell asleep yesterday, Mina admitted she was looking forward to waking up. She'd been as bright-eyed and bushy-tailed as someone enthusiastic about a holiday or a new job. Full of sincere, honest, unfiltered excitement about the end of her life. Mina was at peace with her situation and ready to see it through to the end. Her positive attitude lifted a world of weight from Duan's shoulders, and he couldn't help smiling as he wondered what she was up to. What could make someone in her dire straits so cheerful?

Yet, he knew the momentous words of her specialist were still haunting her: *I'm sorry, but it does not look good.*

This had all begun with the nagging pain in Mina's body a few months earlier. Initially, she suspected to be suffering from back problems, but when the pain started radiating throughout her body without an obvious source, she got worried. Ultimately, Duan could no longer face the suffering of his wife and made an appointment with a specialist at the local clinic. After one look at Mina's x-ray, they sent her for more extensive tests at the University

Hospital of Zurich in Switzerland. First an ultrasound, then a CT scan. Next, an MRI, and finally, a biopsy.

Duan would always remember the funereal silence in the car as they drove to get the test results. Stepping out of the car, they paused briefly, looking into each other's eyes, desperately seeking solace. The hospital was always considered a House of Hope by Duan. Now, that was hope mixed with fear.

The doctor's office had a surprisingly inviting ambiance. Gone were the sterile white walls and the cold, minimalist clinical décor. Soft, upbeat music drifted from hidden speakers, adding to the comfort of the space. Was all this designed to cushion the impact of impending bad news?

Mina and Duan solemnly took seats in two comfortable armchairs. A matronly doctor came next to Mina, laid her hand on Mina's arm, and gave them the dreaded news.

"I'm sorry, Mina, but it does not look good."

It felt as if a heavy curtain had fallen over the waiting room's large window. Duan glanced sideward at his wife and saw how she swallowed and kept staring at the Buddha statue in the corner. She turned her gaze in his direction, desperately seeking answers to questions that were unanswerable.

The oncologist quietly explained Mina was suffering from a blood cancer named Myeloma, where the cancer is formed in plasma cells. Over time, the cancerous plasma cells had accumulated in the bone marrow and crowded out her healthy blood cells. The doctor pointed at an MRI scan to show how the cancer had spread throughout her body. There was no chance she'd survive this.

Duan would always remember asking the doctor weakly what options they had. He knew the answer before she replied.

"None."

"How many months do you expect, doctor?"

"Four at max. However, be prepared for tough months ahead."

The doctor's unequivocally harsh response snuffed out their last spark of hope.

These five words—"it does not look good"—kept echoing. Their once hopeful future was now staring down a dismal destiny. The excruciating pain she had endured over the past weeks, the sleepless nights, her growing difficulty in walking—it all should have prepared him for this moment. Of course, he had sensed that something wasn't right, but Mina's unwavering determination had always carried her through every challenge. In her eyes, anything wrong could be fixed: a wrong lover, the wrong job, injustice in life, or even a lost youth.

Their trip home felt unreal. Halfway there, Mina finally broke the ponderous silence.

"This sucks big time. I feel so sorry for you. You don't deserve this! I don't fear death, but I do fear what's coming for you."

Still struggling with his thoughts, he did not know how to respond. Instead, he gently placed his right hand on her left thigh and kept his eyes on the road. Mina continued while she grabbed his hand.

"Will I become completely dependent on you? I know the doctor can manage the pain with heavy medication, but what kind of life will that be? You don't deserve this, Duan. I don't want my pain to destroy your happiness."

As she spoke these words with determination, he felt how the grip on his hand intensified.

When they got home, he noticed Mina's pale face and saw how her watery eyes had lost their usual intense focus. Expressionless, she looked at him and kissed him.

"I need to be by myself for a while to process all this."

She went up the stairs toward their bedroom. He kept looking at her till she left his sight. He knew his wife well enough to know she needed this time alone to do a meditation session. Meditation and mindfulness more than once had helped her in such a situation. After fifteen minutes, she came down. She looked as if nothing had happened.

"So, what's for dinner?" she blurted out. "You know what? I'd love to go out. If there's ever been a perfect moment to enjoy life, this is it! Come on, darling, let's spoil ourselves at our favorite restaurant, *Tong Thai*. Oh, and let's ask Gail and Luc to join us. They have to be at this special occasion." Mina sounded enthusiastic.

It was amazing to see how Mina acted as if nothing had happened. Duan wondered how she'd made peace with her tragic situation so quickly. Was it her meditation session? Or had the painkillers kicked in? They hadn't been out for weeks because of her condition, but Mina was clearly excited to see her best friend, Gail.

While driving to the restaurant, they discussed when to break the news to their friends. Right at the start, or was it better to wait? They decided on the latter and agreed Duan would start the discussion.

Tong Thai had won several prizes as the best Asian restaurant in town. Its exquisite interior, dominated by dimmed light and red colors, provided a mysterious Asian atmosphere. The staff and cooks were all Thai and spoke Swiss German with an entrancing Thai accent. Like chicken-satay dipped in a Lindt chocolate sauce.

When they stepped into the bar, Gail and Luc were already there. Gail jumped up when she saw them.

"Mimi! What a great, unexpected idea to meet each other. I like these unplanned events."

Mimi had been her nickname from early in the days they met. Mina always called her *Gaily*. That first meeting was over thirty years ago. They were more like sisters than friends. They shared everything. They could spend three hours gossiping at lunch and, next, talk to each other for another two hours on the phone.

After a round of drinks, the server took them to their table. Once seated, Duan looked at both Gail and Luc with a serious face. They immediately realized something was off. Gail realized the heaviness of the moment.

"What's up guys? Is there something?" She looked straight at Duan, prompting him to respond. He glanced at Mina, who gave him a gentle nod as permission for him to start sharing the news.

"Friends, we are here not for fun. We have something serious to share." Duan's gaze shifted to Mina, his voice faltering despite his best efforts, and his quivering Adam's apple betrayed the intense battle raging within him as he fought to keep his emotions in check.

Mina noticed Duan's difficulty and smoothly took over. "I have terrible news. This afternoon, we went to see the doctor. I have an aggressive form of blood cancer, and she gave me a life expectancy of four months. Sorry, I have to say it that bluntly, but there's just no gentle way of sharing this devastating news."

After a brief stunned silence, Gail grabbed her hand and shrieked, "Oh no!"

Out of shock, she dropped her glass of wine. With an echoey sound, it smashed into pieces on the tiled floor. Wine was all over, and people around started pushing themselves out of the way.

"No, No, No!" she screamed louder, followed by intensive crying,

Gail's dramatic response stopped every conversation in the restaurant. Two waiters, who'd just come in from the kitchen with trays, stopped and looked around in confusion. Even a pet macaw, perched in a bird cage just inside the door, was stunned into silence. And even the usually unemotional Luc was shocked; his mouth fell open.

Mina maintained her poise. "The doctor told us it does not look good. It may be impossible, but please, let's try to enjoy this dinner together. No drama." She raised her glass and toasted to good health without irony. Confused and hesitant, the other three followed and raised their glass. While they toasted, it was obvious Gail and Luc were too shocked to enjoy the meal.

"Come on, Mina, I'm in shock. It isn't fair to ask us to toast to good health after this. As if nothing has happened. I just can't." Gail continued her soft crying.

Mina remained calm, "I'm the most impacted, but trust me, I intend to deal with this in the only way that makes sense to me. Please, let's celebrate life."

The food they usually wolfed down was picked at and pushed around. Three of them were at a loss. Only Mina seemed at ease. She kept the evening going with her lively, radiant personality. Duan was falling in love with her all over again. Gosh, would he miss her!

Three months had passed since that dinner and the day their life had taken such a sudden dramatic turn. Duan had seen Mina coping well with her dire situation. They agreed Mina would step out of their cyber security consultancy company and focus on whatever she felt like doing. It appeared to Duan that she had found a new daily routine, and she started walking a lot. She could be gone for hours. As she explained to him, "To walk the cancer out of my body."

The pain, however, grew steadily worse. During their last visit to the specialist, the doctor confirmed her cancer had continued to spread. They were barely home when Mina looked at him and started the unavoidable discussion without any hesitation.

"Duan, it is clear this is not a battle I will win. The pain over the past two weeks has become unbearable, and I have concluded it is better I end my suffering."

Duan was shocked. Not because his wife brought up euthanasia; no, he was taken by the firm, unemotional way she formulated her words. It was clear she had been thinking this over. She was determined and did not leave any room for discussion; she introduced the subject as a statement, not a question.

Mina contacted the EXIT organization and completed the paperwork. An end-of-life attendant interviewed her, and her case was approved.

The day before, that same attendant had brought them the drug. Mina would take it today and end her suffering. Mina had chosen today, her birthday, as the day she would die. Practical as ever, she explained to Duan that it would spare him the burden of remembering yet one more date.

They spent their last morning in bed as normally as possible. Mina's calm mindset made it easier for Duan to accept what was coming. With their heads on the pillows, looking at each other, she whispered, "Darling, I know the coming period will not be easy for you, but please take your time, grieve, and focus on your future."

Although he knew this couldn't be possible, she seemed calmly expectant.

When Duan stepped into the shower, he could no longer hold his emotions. He allowed his tears to flow as the water poured down his head. He cried for several minutes.

Duan, usually outwardly calm, suffered from regular emotional depression, and Mina was the one who kept him in check. How would he handle this without her around? How much he feared a future without Mina, this was not the right moment to let his emotions dominate. No, he would not mention how much he was going to miss her or ask if she was sure about what she was going to do. These discussions were closed, and this last morning should be a moment to remember, filled with love and tenderness.

At 11:25 a.m., they went up to the bedroom and got on the bed. Soft music was playing on Mina's pink speaker, with many candles lit around the bed. To be as close as possible, they undressed.

Duan was lying on his side next to Mina. He had his eyes locked on hers. They stayed like that for several minutes without saying a word. Finally, it was Duan who broke the silence. "Darling, thank you so much for all you've done for me and for all the support you have given me over the past years. You shaped me into who I am today. Thank you."

"Oh no, Duan. You did this all yourself. You are such a wonderful person. I feel so proud of having spent these years with you."

They started kissing passionately, held each other tight, and let their emotions take over. One last time, they thanked each other for the exceptional moments of love and the glorious years they'd enjoyed together. It was a peaceful moment filled with transcendent love. He took his time to look at Mina one more time. Her typical Italian nose, her abs, her beautiful smile; none of the internal pains seemed to have affected her external beauty.

Then Mina decided it was time. She emptied the little bottle in one gulp, and they held each other tightly.

Only now did he notice that she had put on some makeup and was wearing his favorite perfume. They kept looking at each other. He kissed her softly on her forehead. She returned it with a wide smile.

After a few minutes, he noticed she closed her eyes. *Was this it?* He kept looking at her while his thoughts browsed through the many wonderful memories they shared.

He whispered, "I love you."

Unexpectedly, she opened her eyes. With a soft but determined voice, she said: "I'm ready, darling. All that had to be said is said, all that had to be done is done…."

With a final tender smile, Mina peacefully died in Duan's arms.

FIVE WEEKS LATER

CHAPTER 2
TUESDAY, 22 OCTOBER 10:52 A.M.

Two days ago, Luc Starck received a mysterious invitation for a meeting. Intriguingly, that invitation was part of a message included in a relatively small Bitcoin transfer. The message read:

> *Please meet me this coming Tuesday at 11 a.m. on the terrace*
> *of Hotel Loewen Am See in Zug. Trust me, you won't regret*
> *it. I will wear a red 'RF' Roger Federer cap.*

At 10:45 a.m., he received a text message to remind him about the meeting, stressing to be there exactly at eleven a.m.. Luc walked at a fast pace from the office to his appointment. It was a bit more than one kilometer. He kept looking at his watch. 10:52 a.m., he should be able to make it on time. The strong, chilly wind hit him straight in the face. It was cold because it originated from the nearby Swiss Alps and humid as it had gusted the past few kilometers over Zuger Lake.

In the distance, he could see the historic clock tower and compare its time with the time on his watch. Both showed 10:53 a.m. Precision was not for nothing called Swiss.

Zug is a midsize city just south of Zurich, at the edge of the world-famous Swiss Alps.

Luc had been traveling to Zug a few days every week on business. His start-up company, BionTic, had offices in Zug's Crypto Valley Labs building near downtown.

Early last century, the city was transformed into a tax paradise thanks to a generous law that allowed companies to pay no income tax, only capital gains tax.

The attractive tax regime, the city's stability, the steady growth, its commitment to innovation, and the region's stunning natural beauty proved a perfect match for the emerging crypto and blockchain movement. So, when cryptocurrency took off, blockchain entrepreneurs flocked to Zug as an ideal base for their operations.

Luc Starck was among the first to move.

10:55 a.m., Luc increased his pace as he passed the arcade of boutiques at the *Bahnhofstrasse*. He did not register the shops because his mind was fully on this upcoming meeting. It had completely dominated his thoughts from the moment he received the message.

He felt his phone ringing in his inner coat pocket. He took it out and saw it was Duan, the husband of his wife's best friend, Mina. Despite being pressed for time, he answered the call. Before Duan could say anything, Luc started.

"Sorry, Duan, but I'm on my way to an important meeting. I can't talk right now. I'll call you back later." He hung up before Duan could say a word and sped up his determined pace.

When Luc received the invitation for this meeting, he mumbled, "Is someone pulling my leg?" As an introvert, he often spoke to himself when alone. There were days when the only person he talked to was himself.

The Bitcoin transfer attached to the message got his immediate attention. He straightened his back, sat upright in his chair, and moved closer to his desk. Franticly, he started typing on his keyboard.

Identifying the details of that transaction only took him a few mouse clicks. When he realized the uniqueness of the sender's wallet, he leaned back in his chair in disbelief. He pushed himself away from his desk and rolled a few meters backward until he hit the book closet behind him. "This is incredible! It can't be true."

He moved back to his desk. To be one hundred percent sure, he redid the trace and confirmed what he saw was correct. Wow!

In 2008, on the heels of the economic recession that followed the banking crisis, the concept of cryptocurrencies like Bitcoin was proposed by someone using the name Satoshi Nakamoto.

Nakamoto, whose identity is still a mystery, believed that financial institutions had too much control over global financial systems. Unlike almost everyone else, Nakamoto took decisive action and published a paper that described the Bitcoin concept. That document shook up the world of finance and sparked the 'crypto madness' era.

Luc's disbelief when he traced the transaction came from the fact that the originating wallet from the transaction contained 19,000 virgin Bitcoins. It was not the millions of American dollars in that wallet. No, these were 19,000 *virgin* Bitcoins!

Virgin Bitcoins are freshly mined, never-used Bitcoins, like banknotes stored in a safe right after being printed. A wallet with 19,000 virgin coins could only belong to someone who started mining in the early days and had never used these coins.

Luc was well-established in the world of crypto. He knew all the big players. Yet, he had no clue who the wallet's owner might be. Had Satoshi himself reached out to him? If so, why? If not, then who? He couldn't wait to meet this mysterious stranger.

Collaborating with someone so wealthy could solve all his problems. Business had recently not gone well for Luc. While he had a filled wallet, the issues he faced may have him soon lose all his crypto wealth. That idea of losing all he had gained over the past years was his worst nightmare.

No, things were not going well for Luc and he desperately needed good news in his life.

The *Landsgemeindeplatz*, a picturesque public square at the lake, was one of the most idyllic squares in Switzerland.

On this chilly October morning, with the sun shining brightly, the square was filled with a diverse mix of tourists, crypto-entrepreneurs, and ostentatiously rich Swiss ladies. Restaurants, hotels, and entertainment spots were doing a brisk business.

The clock tower had just started chiming eleven bells as Duan stepped onto the square toward *Hotel Loewen Am See*. Curious and excited, he carefully scanned the square. It seemed busier than usual for a Tuesday morning. A group had gathered around a podium to hear an announcement. Everything seemed normal, and on the left, two families were enjoying the perfect weather and reliving yesterday's ice hockey match. Straight ahead, outside the terrace of the hotel, two gaggles of matrons were squealing with laughter like naughty schoolgirls. Then, Luc spotted somebody with a red cap sitting quietly at a table on the outer row of the terrace. As the man was looking away from him, Luc wasn't positive, but he guessed it was a Roger Federer cap. It must be the man he was supposed to meet and who had invited him!

When Luc tapped his shoulder, the stranger turned around and looked into Luc's eyes. He did not recognize the stranger.

"Hello, my name is Luc Starck. If I'm not mistaken, we have an appointment?"

"Indeed, I'm your man." The man stood up. "Nice to meet you, Mr. Starck. Can I invite you to take a seat here?" He spoke with a staccato voice as if reading from a script. "I'm sorry, but for security reasons, I cannot give you my name." He was about thirty-five years old with a worried look and a Mediterranean complexion. Probably Latino or North African.

Luc took his seat and prepared himself for the momentous conversation to begin. He raised his eyebrows expectantly, inviting the man to say something. He did, after a pregnant pause.

"Thanks for coming, Luc. You must be wondering why I invited you. Before I explain, let me give you this envelope. Please do not open it until I have left."

Luc took the envelope from the stranger and turned it over. There were two words printed on the front.

Clue One.

Clue One? He was tempted to open it. Did this mean more clues would follow? What could that possibly mean?

But he carefully followed the directions, slipping the envelope into his inside pocket. His palms began to sweat. He looked the stranger in the eyes. The guy kept silent. The suspense was killing him. Suddenly, a loud explosion broke the ponderous silence. Both looked around at what happened.

A confetti bomb had popped in the middle of the square, showering the fountain with multi-colored scraps of paper. The crowd around the podium started cheering and applauding. A sigh of relief calmed Luc down.

The stranger resumed his speech impassively as if he'd been practicing all morning. His voice was so low Luc could hear the old ladies chattering gaily nearby.

"I'm here to give you a message," the man said tonelessly.

Luc was confused. This wasn't getting any clearer. He glanced around the square.

"A message from who?" Luc tried. He looked the guy in the eyes, willing him to give a concrete answer.

"Sorry, I cannot tell you. However, what I can tell you is that this will be the most important meeting of your life. This will change your future beyond your wildest dreams."

Luc got the impression he was being toyed with like a cat touching a mouse with its paw. He wondered if he should have kept this appointment, although it didn't feel the man was threatening him. The man just seemed to recite a script. Somewhat annoyed, he tried, "For God's sake, tell me more about why you wanted to see me. Or will the message in the envelope explain it all?"

"No, I have more. Much more…." He paused. This conversation had a mysterious vibe. Luc had no clue what was happening.

Just as the guy opened his mouth to speak, his phone rang in his jacket pocket.

"Sorry, I have to take this." Apparently, he did not want Luc to overhear his conversation, so he took three steps away from the table toward the lake.

"Hello…." was all Luc could hear.

He felt the envelope burning in his inner pocket.

"What the heck was going on?"

Trying to relax, Luc smiled a little and mumbled a line from Alice in Wonderland. "Curiouser and curiouser."

Looking around, he checked to make sure nobody had heard him talking to himself.

The stranger walked toward the aviary on the lake side of the square, still talking on his phone, in no apparent hurry to finish the conversation.

Luc waved at the server to order a cappuccino while waiting for the guy to return. The server approached the table to take Luc's order. Just as Luc opened his mouth, he felt a weird bowling ball-sized pain deep in his gut. It doubled him over until his right shoulder was on the table. When he tried to ask for help, no words came out. Just a deep gurgling sound.

The server was shocked. He'd never seen anything like this before. "Mister, what's wrong? Can I help you? Sir?"

Luc put his hand on the table and tried to stand up but couldn't. Every muscle was suddenly seizing up. His sight was going fast as well. Luc's upper body started shaking, and those weird noises became louder. The old ladies stopped talking and looked at him in horror. A flock of birds overhead escaped to branches in a tree. Everyone around the podium stopped and stared at Luc as if in slow motion.

He collapsed convulsively, blood pulsating from his mouth in violent spurts. At last, Luc came to a standstill, hunched over the table.

The server ran inside to call emergency services, but by the time the ambulance arrived five minutes later, it was already finished.

Luc Starck was dead.

CHAPTER 3
TUESDAY, 22ND OCTOBER, 11:05 A.M.

The puddle of sweat under the press bench steadily got larger at the local police gym in Zug. On it, Bernt Berg was puffing and making grunting sounds. With every push, the sounds got louder, and the sweat drops grew larger. He thought how glad he was to be exercising again. After twenty-five years of marriage, his uniforms were no longer comfortable, but he had put off getting a larger size. The annual police fitness test kept getting harder to pass, and his daily moment of truth on the bathroom scale was less of a priority than it had ever been. Action was required.

Bernt knew that being physically fit would keep him mentally alert. Daily squats and knee push-ups helped him feel optimistic and independent, which had always been a personal trademark. Three times a week, he visited this gym to boost his fitness.

While physically not in top shape, mentally, Bernt was quite fit. Every police officer called him *Bernie the Hawk. Bernie the Hawk* was 'hyper-observant' and 'hyper-informed.' The first was a natural talent, and the second was a skill acquired over years of study and experience. He once made an educated guess, just by looking, that bloodstains on a suspect's shirt were from two different victims. This proved to be right.

Bernt Berg had served in the Zuger police for thirty years. Most recently, as an inspector with the Zuger regional police, the *Kantonspolizei*. It had never been a stressful job. Zug is a quiet city, with little excitement at its police headquarters, certainly compared to nearby Zurich.

That wasn't the case in 2001 when a mentally ill man in a police uniform named Friedrich Leibacher shot fourteen people in Zug's parliament. He finally turned the gun on himself in what became known as the *Zuger Massacre*. Investigating Leibacher's background had been Bernt's first major assignment.

Compared to that dramatic day, the call Bernt was about to receive about the death of a gentleman on the terrace of *Hotel Loewen Am See* was quite routine.

Bernt, fifty-eight years old, was counting down the days until an early retirement from the Zuger police force. A few years ago, he divorced his wife Hedwig, but he was still struggling to adjust to his new life as a bachelor. He had mixed feelings about ending his active career at the Zuger Police. Being single and unemployed could become a perfect excuse for alcoholism.

Three weeks ago, he asked for a meeting with his superior, Captain Tell Schmidt. In anticipation of his upcoming retirement, he had a special request.

Schmidt held office in the historic Zuger police station. His wooden desk on the squeaking wooden floor fitted perfectly with the rest of this historic part of town.

"How many more weeks, Bernt?" Schmidt asked him just after Bernt sat down.

"Thirty-one weeks, four days, twenty-three minutes, and twelve seconds," Bernt responded jokingly.

Schmidt, curious about the purpose of the meeting, tried, "Well, if you wish to stay in service some months longer, you are, of course, very welcome." Schmidt checked Bernt's reaction.

"No, that is not why I am here, Tell."

Schmidt was even more curious about what was coming.

"I have a special request to make."

"I'm all ears."

"My daughter Lisa-Lotte just graduated from the police academy, the *Polizeischule Ostschweiz* in *Amriswil.* I know it is uncommon for family members to serve together, but I hope my impeccable reputation," Bernt gave Schmidt a funny face, "and my upcoming retirement would allow you to accept my request for Lisa-Lotte and me to work together till my retirement."

He could see Tell Schmidt was taken by surprise by this unusual request. However, it did not take him any hesitation to accept it.

"Of course, Bernt. I know how special Lisa-Lotte is to you, and how happy you are she is joining the police force. I'm sure it is the best apprenticeship we can offer her."

While leaving Schmidt's office, Bernt called his daughter to share with her the good news about the upcoming partnership.

"I have good and bad news," Bernt said with a mysterious undertone. Before she could ask anything, he continued.

"The good news is that I have found you an apprenticeship at the Zuger Police Department."

"Great, Dad! Thank you so much. That is exactly what I was hoping to get. What is the bad news?"

"I'm going to be your mentor for the remaining time till my retirement."

"Hmm, I'm not sure what to say. How will mom react?"

"What does she have to do with this? Your mother should be happy I work with my own daughter rather than with another gorgeous blond." He knew his ex was still very much struggling with their divorce.

He realized that despite his wealth of police knowledge and experience, his old-fashioned manner could be hard for some younger officers to accept. His grandfather-style sense of humor included sometimes inappropriate and sarcastic jokes, which he considered amusing but were often just confusing. Just last week, he embarrassed everyone with one.

"What do you call a prisoner taking his mugshot in jail?" he exclaimed, interrupting what had been a serious discussion in the break room among fellow police officers. Visibly annoyed, they stopped their conversation and looked at him. "A cell-fie!" he blurted out.

Afterward, Lisa-Lotte tactfully suggested that she'd hoped he'd behave more like a mentor and inspiration to the officers so she could be proud of him.

"You don't seem to take anything seriously," she complained.

"I was just joking! Nowadays, some of these young officers take everything so seriously, they hardly ever laugh!"

Bernt looked at the clock on the wall. He had to rush. His duty would start at noon and before, he wanted to grab a quick lunch. He showered and went to the canteen.

He had just started his tomato soup when Lisa-Lotte arrived.

"Mind if I join you?"

"Of course not. But not too close. As you know, I'm a very messy eater."

She affectionately smiled as she pulled back her chair and sat down. His notorious messiness was not being missed at home. "Good thing you're wearing a red shirt when eating tomato soup, isn't it?"

"No, I'm not wearing a red shirt. It was white before I started my soup." Bernt laughed loudly at his silly joke. Lisa-Lotte hoped nobody had noticed his outburst.

Just then, his mobile phone emitted its distinctive Swiss "cow-moo" ringtone. He excused himself and answered. After listening and nodding briefly, he told her, "We'll need to eat later. Some guy just stopped breathing in the middle of the *Landsgemeindeplatz*. Apparently, there is a lot of blood at the scene, and they asked us to have a look."

Lisa-Lotte stood up and walked toward the exit behind her father, only now noticing his ridiculous white cow motif socks.

The square was just around the corner from the police station. When Lisa-Lotte and Bernt arrived, fellow officers had already fenced off half the square with yellow tape and were waiting for the coroner and forensic services.

The body had fallen off the wrought-iron table without disturbing any dishes. It was splayed onto the terrace in what would have been a very uncomfortable position. It must have just happened as blood was still dripping from the table.

Bernt got onto his right knee and briefly examined the body without touching it. No obvious signs of a crime, although that bloody mouth was not normal. The dead man appeared to be in his forties.

The face looked familiar, although it always surprised Bernt how death changes people. Classic detective novels sometimes suggested that the face of a murder victim was frozen in a telltale expression, but over the past thirty years, Bernt had seen enough bodies to know that faces all relaxed into the same impassive mask.

"You know him?" He looked at his daughter.

"Isn't that this crypto guy named Luc Starck?"

"Now you say so. You may well be right."

Bernt stepped onto the terrace and glanced around the square for anything out of the ordinary. It looked like any other Tuesday morning. In the middle of the square, there was a podium he hadn't noticed before. He'd check it later. Nothing seemed out of place in the buildings around the square.

Lisa-Lotte and Bernt started interviewing the server at a discreet distance. He described, with a tremble in his high-pitched voice, how his guest had collapsed.

"Initially, the dead man was with someone else. That other person wore a red Roger Federer cap. When I approached their table to take their order, the man with the cap stepped away for a phone call. I wanted to wait, but the dead guy signaled me to take his order. As I approached him, he just froze and, a few seconds later, collapsed. All these years here at the hotel, I've seen nothing like that!"

The server moved to a chair in the hotel lobby and began gazing blankly into space. This kind of intense excitement seemed to be more than the nervous server could handle.

"I tried to help him, but it was already too late!"

"What do you remember of that man with the cap?" Lisa-Lotte asked.

"He was tanned and was wearing a black leather jacket with dark blue jeans. He had darker hair. I guess he might have been Mediterranean, Tunisian, or Moroccan, but it could also be Italian. I'm sorry I cannot give you a clearer description." Suddenly, he recalled something.

"The man with the cap didn't return to the table after taking the call, which I found weird. He must have seen what happened to his friend, but when I started looking for him, he was already gone."

Lisa-Lotte looked across the terrace and noted the security cameras. She knew the square was actively monitored by several, and their colleagues were already checking the recordings.

While they had been interviewing the server, the Zuger Cantonal Forensic team arrived and identified the dead person as Luc Starck, 46 years old. His last known address was in Baar, a small city near Zug. Starck was married, his wife was named Gail, and they had no kids.

"Check this out," Bernt said, scrolling on his mobile phone. "Our dead friend apparently was not a stranger to the police."

"Really?" asked Lisa-Lotte, her ears perking up.

"Little over a year ago, Mr. Starck was a suspect in a criminal investigation of his crypto company. Some customers had accused him of stealing all their Bitcoins. Several victims filed a case against him but couldn't prove anything. Mr. Starck claimed his company had been the victim of a massive cyber theft."

Bernt continued, "More recently, Mr. Starck's wife, Gail, filed several complaints against her husband for domestic violence."

"Why don't we pay Mrs. Starck a visit and see how she reacts to the news of her husband's death?"

CHAPTER 4
TUESDAY, 22ND OCTOBER, 1:27 P.M.

Luc Starck's home in Baar was a large free-standing villa with a spectacular view over Zuger Lake. This part of town was home to many rich people, with its streets crowded with luxury cars. Bentley, Porsche, and Maserati all had dealerships in nearby Zug. Any of those cars would look right on the villa's gently curving driveway, set artfully into a well-manicured lawn. Even for this posh neighborhood, the house was remarkable. Beverly Hills in the Swiss Alps.

Bernt peeked through the gate, counting numerous security cameras and reinforced windows. Whatever was inside, the Starcks protected it well.

"Why don't you start the conversation?" Bernt whispered to Lisa-Lotte. Since they started working together, this was their first death, and Bernt was keen to see how his daughter would handle such a delicate conversation.

Lisa-Lotte double-checked Mrs. Starck's first name before pushing the intercom button, set tastefully into the front gate. A woman's voice answered the intercom.

"Frau Gail Starck?"

"That's me," the voice said. "How can I help you?"

"My name is Detective Lisa-Lotte Berg, and I'm here with my colleague Bernt. We are with the Zuger Police. Would you mind opening? We have something important to tell you."

Bernt noticed Lisa-Lotte spoke with a firm voice and without any hesitation. At the police academy, such conversations were actively role-played. "Well done," he told to her.

With a buzz, the gate opened, giving them a full view into the inner court with space for several cars.

As they approached the entrance of the luxury villa, they were greeted by massive white columns on either side of the front door. The radiating sun brightened the handle made of gleaming silver.

The front door opened. A gorgeous, dark-haired woman stepped into the doorway, obviously surprised to see police uniforms.

"Can we come in?" Lisa-Lotte asked.

The woman looked worried. "Is it about Luc?"

They could see her wondering what news they were about to share.

She led them into a luxurious kitchen and offered them seats at a round cutting-board table, positioning herself to look into the bright sunlight so her guests wouldn't have to. As they walked through the villa, Bernt observed every detail. Gail Starck had not been expecting them and it was a perfect opportunity to do a first quick inspection in his typical Starck-like manner.

Lisa-Lotte opened the conversation, carefully choosing her words.

"Frau Starck, we are extremely sorry to inform you that your husband Luc was found dead this morning just after eleven a.m. at the *Landsgemeindeplatz* in Zug."

Gail remained silent, gazing for a moment into her folded hands with a resigned expression. Both Bernt and Lisa-Lotte observed her intensively. First reactions to such a bad news message were always essential and could tell a lot. After a while, Gail started.

"This may surprise you, but I'm not devastated by your news. Surprised, yes, but shocked, no. Sorry if you were expecting a distraught wife, but I'm relieved he's dead."

This wasn't the reaction Bernt and Lisa-Lotte were used to getting from people when they heard about the death of their partner. Of course, they were aware of Gail's recent reports about her late husband's violence.

"If I may ask, what makes you say that?" Lisa-Lotte tried to keep Gail talking.

Gail ignored Lisa's question. "So, tell me, what happened exactly?"

"We don't know yet. The coroner is performing an autopsy this afternoon."

Gail tried again. "Was he shot? Was there a fight? You should know something."

Now, it was Bernt's turn to ignore her. "Mrs. Starck, why did you say you were relieved?"

"Luc is—uh, *was*—a *bastard*. I was in the middle of a very toxic relationship. A few months ago, he began having frequent outbursts that often turned very violent."

Gail lifted her shirt to show them blotchy blue bruises around her torso.

"I understand you reported this?"

"Yes, several times. These were not isolated events; it has been happening frequently and I'm glad it's finally over."

It was clear Gail expected follow-up questions, but Lisa-Lotte and Bernt remained silent.

She continued.

"Luc became someone different when he lost control. Unfortunately, I was always on the receiving end of his violence. After a few hours, he'd calm down and apologize."

The two officers listened carefully, with sympathetic expressions.

"Luc had been seeking help, but his violence intensified over the past few months. I was planning to leave him. I could no longer stand it."

Bernt took over the questioning from Lisa-Lotte. "Mrs. Starck, could you answer a few more questions?"

Gail nodded while straightening her shirt.

"Your husband met someone this morning on the terrace of *Hotel Loewen Am See*. Did you know about that meeting?"

"No, Luc never discussed his business."

"Did your husband have any health issues?"

"Not that I know of."

"You just asked if he was shot. Are you aware of any conflicts your husband was involved in or of anyone who may have wanted to do him harm?"

"Well. Luc's company, *CryptoSwap,* went bankrupt one year ago. It was one of the first crypto exchanges where individuals with Bitcoins and other cryptocurrencies could trade and store their digital assets. Like a bank, but all digital. Because of that bankruptcy, several *CryptoSwap* customers lost small fortunes when their wallets were emptied."

"So, what happened when his customers found their wallets emptied?" Lisa-Lotte took over.

"Luc reported the crime to the police, but his customers claimed it was Luc who had stolen their coins. Some of them were, uh… bad guys, if you know what I mean, and Luc got several threats. I tried to keep my distance, but there must be a link between Luc's business issues and his violence against me. It became too much for him and for me. I hope you now understand why I'm relieved. It's finally over."

"Mrs. Starck, I'm sorry to ask, but where were you this morning at around eleven a.m.?"

"I was here at home by myself."

"I see. Is there anyone you could stay with for a while? We can ask our police psychologist to stop by."

"No, I'm fine here, thank you. I'll call a friend." Gail Starck looked strong enough to be by herself.

While Lisa-Lotte was questioning Gail Starck, Bernt observed Gail deeply. Reading body language was one of his developed *Bernie The Hawk* skills. He noticed how she avoided eye contact with Lisa-Lotte when answering her questions. He saw how she touched her face several times and was fidgeting with her hands. All signs point to someone possibly lying. It was clear that Gail Starck had suffered a lot in her marriage. Could it possibly be that she could no longer stand it and had initiated action? She was not overly impacted. When they mentioned the death of her husband, she even seemed relieved. No, Gail Starck by no means was a sad widow.

"Okay, we'll get back to our office. Here's my card."

"Later today, we'll update you on what we found out." Bernt gently touched her elbow as a sign of support.

"Thank you very much." Gail was still very calm.

Back in the car, Lisa-Lotte looked at her dad.

"What does *Bernie The Hawk* think about this lady?"

"Something stinks!"

]

CHAPTER 5

TUESDAY, 22ND OCTOBER, 1:56 P.M.

After the police officers left, Gail returned to her kitchen table. She needed to think. She had not yet seen any news coverage about Luc's death, but it wouldn't be long before the story broke. The entire situation confused her, and feelings of sadness, followed by anger, dominated her thoughts.

As time passed, the reality of it all began to settle in. She had always relied on Luc for everything, especially managing their finances. With his recent bankruptcy behind them, she had little understanding of their current financial situation. She glanced around the house. *Could she afford to continue living here?*

Her mind then shifted to his crypto wealth. *What about his Bitcoins?* She wondered. *How could she access them?*

Her thoughts spun out of control. The uncertainty, the weight of everything crashing down on her—it was too much. Suddenly, feelings of panic combined with helplessness hit her. *What am I going to do?*

There were two people she had to call.

She grabbed her mobile phone and called the first number. It got picked up almost immediately.

"Hi, Duan, oh my God, so happy you answered."

The panic in Gail's voice was obvious.

"What happened?"

"Duan, it's Luc…" It was hard for Gail to keep her emotions in check. "Duan, Luc is dead!" she wailed. "Two police inspectors just told me."

"Do you know what happened, Gail?"

"He died just a few hours ago. The police told me they do not yet know how."

"Let me jump in my car and come over. I don't want you to be by yourself."

"That would be great!"

Next, Gail called Roberto Giobbi, CEO of Luc's current company, BionTic. He had to know about Luc's death.

"Hello, Roberto, Gail here." Before he could ask her anything, she blurted out. "Luc is dead!"

"What? How?"

"The police just came to tell me. That's all I know so far."

"Luc, dead? I just saw him yesterday! I'm so sorry, Gail. Do you want me to come over?"

"Don't worry, Roberto, I have a friend coming. Can we meet tomorrow morning? There is so much to discuss."

"Are you sure you're OK?"

"Yes, I'm fine. Don't worry. Let's meet tomorrow here in Baar, okay? Eleven a.m.?"

"Perfect."

Waiting for Duan, Gail returned to the kitchen in a state of shock and conflicting emotions. She was sad to learn of the death of a man she had once deeply loved, yet relieved the constant battles were finally at an end.

She thought about the previous evening.

Luc had been sitting in his easy chair, looking depressed. His hair was in disarray, shoelaces untied, and one shirt sleeve only partially rolled up.

She smelled an alcoholic miasma before noticing the bottle of whiskey on the coffee table.

"What's up, Luc? You look miserable."

"I'm fine," Luc said disconsolately. He obviously did not feel like talking, hanging halfway out of his chair, chin on his chest.

"Luc, you are not only ruining your own life but mine as well. For God's sake, something has to change!"

"You're right," he mumbled. "Maybe I'd better just end it."

"What's that supposed to mean?"

Luc grabbed the whiskey bottle and shakily poured himself another glassful. He sighed, looked at Gail sadly, and said, "Gail, it's way too much for me. I am a colossal failure and overwhelmed. Things at BionTic are falling apart, with that bastard Giobbi driving my company into the ground. To make things worse, a year after the bankruptcy, I'm still being chased and threatened by *CryptoSwap* customers. I'm afraid they might even go after you." Luc looked and sounded broken. He sobbed. "I guess suicide is my only way out."

Gail was suddenly scared. This was the first time Luc mentioned suicide. She thought she knew what had happened at *CryptoSwap* but was less aware of BionTic.

"Come on, Luc. There must be another way."

"If I'm no longer around, everything will be taken care of. All my fucking issues will magically disappear!"

"Luc!" she shouted, trying to snap him out of his miserable mood.

"Maybe I'll finally get the respect I deserve."

As his voice began rising again, Gail could see he was talking himself into another emotional dead end.

He stood up and smashed his whiskey glass against the wall.

"Nobody fucking understands me!" he shouted, his face filled with anger and dread. "I'm so bloody done with everything. Yes, maybe I should just disappear. But you know what? My death will be a big fucking surprise to everyone!"

His dilated pupils and rapid, involuntary eye movements showed her how alcohol was fully controlling his behavior.

"For God's sake, Luc. Stop this! Now you're seriously frightening me!"

Somehow, that connected. Luc leaned back wearily into his chair and calmed down. Staring off into space.

Gail was shocked and pensive as Luc fell silent. She had to admit that Luc's disappearance would bring much-needed tranquility into her life. The past year had been so miserable, one continuous tsunami of negativity.

Thinking back about the evening before, Gail wondered if she should have mentioned this conversation to the police officers. Maybe. She was surprised when they'd showed up, and only now she realized the relevance of that conversation with Luc's death. Anyway, the police mentioned they would contact her later in the day. She would definitely tell them.

Even having decided to reveal Luc's threat, she could not stop thinking about it. It was very relevant. Just twenty-four hours after she'd heard Luc talking about suicide, he was dead!

CHAPTER 6
TUESDAY, 22ND OCTOBER, 2:58 P.M.

The *blogchain.ch* office was housed in the attic of a residential building in Zug's Old Town. Carl Coppen had started his blog to cover all the exciting blockchain and crypto activities happening in what had become known as Crypto Valley.

Over the years, it has become one of the most popular blogs in the industry, with many daily site visitors from all over the world. It covered both the technology and human-interest side of the industry. With that many people concentrated in such a small area, there was no shortage of content to fill his blog.

Carl had become financially independent after a short yet hectic career in commodity trading.

He realized that continuing his eighteen-hour working days as a trader for another couple of years could prove disastrous for his health, so he stepped out of the corporate rat race and started his blog.

Last year, he'd hired two younger staff members. Misha Weitz was handling the advertisements and sales, and Ilse Bamberg helped him chase down the latest news stories. Carl had promised them twenty percent ownership of the blog if they reached the tough performance targets he had set. The first one was to reach one million visitors to the site in a single day. The second one was to achieve two million Swiss Franc in advertising revenue, and finally, the last target was to reach hundred fifty thousand registered users. Ilse and Misha had fully signed up for that challenge.

Ilse was a drop-out from the university in Zurich, where she had attended 'Journalism and Digital Media.' For her, the never-ending desire to find and publish scoops was professional revenge for not completing her studies. Her parents were disappointed and concerned when she informed them about dropping out. Every time she published an article that reached over 100,000 hits, she would take a screenshot and send them a copy, often with a small note like, "You See!" or "Told You So…".

At this moment, *blogchain.ch* was her only option to achieve personal success.

Misha Weitz was still studying. He attended the university in Lugano, where he was pusuing a bachelor study 'International Marketing Management'. Every day he would be present for a few hours in the *blogchain.ch* offices, where he was the full Sales and Marketing team. When he joined last year, he had written the marketing plan for Carl's blog, which he had been implementing step by step. Carefully, he had picked prospective advertisers from a long list of start-up blockchain players in the valley. Many of the advertisement contracts included a bonus payment if they reached one million visitors.

Misha had approached each of them personally and so far, he was very pleased with his hit rate. Four out of the seven prospects he approached had signed up for an advertising deal.

While he enjoyed his role in the company, he always had a latent eye for potential news stories. Without intending to upset Ilse, he had published a few scoops.

Carl got tipped about Luc Starck's death by a witness at the square who'd recognized Starck as the victim. When Luc's body wasn't immediately taken to a hospital and covered with a cloth, it was clear Luc Starck was dead.

Carl had an extensive network of 'blogchain spies,' as he called them, active in trading, blockchain, and crypto communities around Zug. He usually was only one WhatsApp message away from anything happening in Crypto Valley. His ambition was to make *blogchain.ch* the most authoritative crypto resource in the world. Shortly after receiving the news about Luc's death, he published the news on the blog's homepage and pushed notifications to his subscribers. Thousands of phones in the area started beeping when they received the news.

Luc Starck's shocking death reminded Carl of the long article he wrote about *CryptoSwap's* bankruptcy one year ago. It was his first cybercrime story. He followed up with several juicy stories on his blog for several weeks. That bankruptcy had helped his blog become successful. Almost overnight, the unique visitor count to his blog increased tenfold, and it was being quoted by various national media, hungry for news but too lazy to put their reporters on a story.

The three of them were sitting around the large round table in the middle of the office, as they would so often do during major news stories. Carl started.

"Team, Luc Starck's murder is juicy enough to become our *Cow Story of the Year.*"

Carl always referred to major cases as *Cow Stories* because they were ideal for being milked over several weeks. First, the breaking news. Next, the obituary, followed by several background stories with theories of what could have happened.

"Time is of the essence. Once the police figure out what happened and hold a press conference, the story is as dead as Luc Starck. Until then, we need to draw new eyeballs to our site and to do that, we need angles no one else has. This has all the potential to become the story that gets us a million visitors. The news of Luc's death alone generated 450,000 visitors, and the obituary I wrote another 350,000. 800,000 in total. We are getting there!"

"What else can we do?"

Ilse started.

"We need to know more about Luc's death. Of course, he could have died a natural death, but to die that young is odd. Let's see what the police report is on this. I'll contact the police about their progress. Also, I suggest I call his wife to get a first reaction."

Carl intervened. "No, I suggest you see her personally. The Starcks live in Baar. It's not that far."

"OK, I will first call my contact at the police and go to Baar first thing in the morning. I'll pass there on my way into the office."

"A good plan."

Misha also offered help. "I wouldn't mind knowing a bit more about his current company, BionTic. It is not uncommon for a business dispute to get out of hand."

Carl energized the team. "Up to a million!" They stacked their right hands, one on top of the other, in the middle of the table

CHAPTER 7

TUESDAY, 22ND OCTOBER, 3:09 P.M.

The moment Duan hung up from Gail, he jumped into his car to drive to Baar. At this time of day, it should take him twenty-five minutes to reach her house.

His relationship with Luc was odd; how much he tried, he could not establish a solid relationship with the guy. At times, he wondered if Luc was suffering from Asperger's syndrome. It certainly would explain his inability to make or maintain friendships. It could well be that because of that personality trait, he got involved in cryptocurrencies early, which paid off handsomely. Luc had long recognized the tremendous potential of the crypto coins industry and started the crypto exchange *CryptoSwap*. Within four years, it became a gigantic mess.

He knew that more recently, Luc had started a new crypto venture, BionTic. Duan had never figured out what BionTic was up to. Like many blockchain start-ups, it seemed to break new ground in established industries by creatively applying new technology.

Despite the intense dislike he felt for Luc, Duan couldn't deny a pang of envy for his entrepreneurial spirit. If he could only capture a fraction of Luc's relentless energy and fearless approach to risk, he would have been able to handle life with more emotional balance.

While Luc seemed to soar with unshakable self-confidence, Duan's life had been a turbulent emotional ride. Everything started to change for the better when Mina walked into his world.

Their paths first crossed at a client site where Duan was engaged in a security maturity assessment for his cybersecurity consultancy, which he had established a few years earlier. Mina was a security analyst at the company that had contracted him. From the moment he laid eyes on her, she captivated him. Whether it was her striking appearance or the proactive manner in which she handled the audit, he was enchanted. Her presence made this professional engagement very special.

One evening, Duan was caught off guard when Mina suggested they meet for drinks after work. They ended up at a cozy bar inside Pino, an Italian restaurant just a short walk from her office.

Seated on high stools at the bar, they each ordered a gin and tonic.

"So, tell me, who is Duan?" she asked, her deep, dark eyes locked on his.

A deep connection began to form between them before he realized it. In just twenty minutes, Duan found himself baring his soul, confessing his struggles with anger management, emotional turmoil, and a suspicion that he might be mildly autistic.

"Any idea where that might come from?" Mina asked gently.

Duan sighed, his voice tinged with frustration and sadness. "I have no clue. I remember having these intense outbursts in primary school, coming out of nowhere. My parents thought it might be because I was born prematurely. You wouldn't believe it, but I spent the first weeks of my life in an incubator in intensive care."

"Well, you seemed to have survived that pretty well," she said tenderly, placing her hand on his arm.

"Okay, my turn. What secrets does Mina hide?" he asked, eager to delve into her soul.

Mina swallowed and fell silent, clearly overthinking what to say.

"Sorry if this is getting too personal," Duan offered.

"No, it's fine. It's just... it's just that things are tough for me right now."

Duan leaned forward, showing her she had his full attention and creating a safe space for her to open up. Mina instinctively lowered her voice.

"For the past three years, I've been trapped in a relationship with a man who drains every ounce of my energy. He's a serious drug addict. Chris Engel is his name. Despite his countless promises to quit, he's nothing but a master of deception. When he's high, he transforms into someone I barely recognize—aggressive and terrifying. It's a nightmare that leaves me constantly on edge."

"Why not just leave him?" Duan asked, unable to resist the typical male response.

"I wish I could. I love him and feel imprisoned by the hope that I can help him stop his destructive behavior."

Her voice trembled as she spoke, revealing years of hardship, lies, and unfulfilled promises.

It was a memorable evening that stretched deep into the night. The next morning, when they met in a meeting room, she presented him with a napkin covered in scribbles.

"Were you serious?" she asked.

Faintly, Duan remembered that after several gin and tonics the previous evening, he had tried to convince her to join his cybersecurity company. Gradually, details came back to him, including his scribbled employment contract and proposed salary on the napkin. With a wide smile, she slid the napkin across the meeting table toward him.

"Was I serious?" he wondered, echoing her question in his mind. Of course he was. Changing his mind was not an option now.

"Yes, of course I was," he replied with a cheeky grin.

"So, is the offer still valid?" she asked.

"Yup," he confirmed.

She picked up a pen and signed the napkin. Two months later, Mina began working at Duan's cybersecurity consultancy.

As days turned into weeks, their casual conversations and shared moments began to take on a deeper meaning. There was an undeniable connection, one that neither of them could ignore. Slowly, almost imperceptibly, they started spending more time together, and before they realized it, they started an intense love affair. Finally, Mina found the strength to walk away from her abusive boyfriend, and Duan witnessed firsthand how Mina rebuilt her self-worth step-by-step. Jokingly, he often mentioned how he was her savior.

The beauty of their relationship was that it worked both ways. Mina helped him to counterbalance his emotional instability. With her in his life, he started managing his crises better; he recognized when anger was about to surface, and the breathing techniques she taught him helped him stay in control.

He recalled how, a few weeks before her death, they discussed this.

"Duan, I am so pleased to see how you have found your emotional stability in life. I'm proud of you."

"Well, all thanks to you, darling. You do not realize how much you help me to cope with my imperfections. What would I do without you?"

What would I do without you? Suddenly, these words echoed in his head. He remembered how he was scared like hell about Mina's imminent death during these days, worrying about how he would cope without her as his primary emotional stabilizer.

He was driving on autopilot, and his mind was not on the road.

It was that picture of her lying in his arms just after she had died that made a lasting impression on him. He felt her skin against his body and could smell her perfume. He wondered if he was imagining it, but in his thoughts, she appeared to have a smile on her face. Finally, he let his emotions go and cried intensely with her in his arms. What to do without her? He felt so lost.

They had planned for Mina's body to be picked up at one p.m., so he had almost ninety minutes with her alone in the house. It was so unreal. They had not discussed what to do during that time. He could not ignore her. He played her favorite playlist on the sound system in their house and found it hard to leave her by herself in their bedroom. He cleared the plates with the cake they had eaten for her birthday. Both cakes had barely been touched. His mood kept flipping between crying and happiness.

He started making several calls to family and friends to tell them *it* was done. He was calm and had to take some time for himself.

Motionless, he was sitting in an armchair in the bedroom, looking at her dead body. A sensation of loneliness and helplessness slowly started to descend on him. A feeling he had felt before.

Duan grew up as an only child. He was six years old when his mother died. She was Swiss and met his Chinese father while studying Mandarin at the Zhejiang University in Hangzhou. Once their studies were completed, they relocated to Switzerland. For the rest of his youth, he lived with his father. His dad patiently taught him strong Chinese values of harmony, benevolence, righteousness, courtesy, wisdom, honesty, loyalty, and filial piety, the traditional Chinese upbringing.

When his father died of a heart attack, Duan felt abandoned. It suddenly dawned on Duan that with Mina's death, it was the fourth time someone taking care of him had disappeared. His mother, his father, his granddad, and now his wife, Mina.

Duan suddenly realized that this time things were different; now, *he* was in charge. This unaccustomed feeling put him in conflict with his inner self.

The Duan that was used to be taken care of had to change. He would need to take the initiative and sort everything out on his own. He'd have to marshal all his strengths, experience, and determination in a whole new way.

After Mina's death, it took Duan several weeks to regain his normal rhythm.

Gail helped him move beyond his obsession with Mina's terminal pains and death so his mourning wouldn't last as long. She provided the support he needed and offered an emotional safety net, preventing him from falling into a black hole.

Over endless afternoons at her kitchen table, they relived wonderful memories and talked about his fears for a future without Mina. Little did he know that soon after, he would be helping Gail cope with the death of her husband.

Because Gail and Mina shared everything, Mina had briefly told Duan that Gail and Luc were having marital problems, but Gail never mentioned anything to him. Duan wondered how many details Gail had shared with Mina. Most likely, she did not want to burden Mina with more to worry about.

These recent meetings at Gail's kitchen table had brought Duan close to her. Gail reminded him so much of Mina, and the chemistry between him and Gail was undeniable.

Reflecting on it now, Duan realized he had always had feelings for Gail. Of course, his deep, fusional relationship with Mina had always kept him in check, and Gail appeared content with *her* Luc.

With Mina's death, that barrier was removed, and Duan found himself contemplating what might happen between him and Gail now that Luc was no longer in the picture. Yes, Gail was special to him, but at the same time, Mina was still so fresh and present in his head.

CHAPTER 8
TUESDAY, 22 OCTOBER, 3:35 P.M.

The twenty-five-minute trip went fast. At the exit Baar, the Zuger Lake showed up in full sight.

Duan entered the posh neighborhood where Gail lived. Formula One drivers Sebastian Vettel and Kimi Räikkönen both lived in this area, which was not too hard to imagine considering the size of the houses he was passing. At the end of the road, he saw the Starcks' residence. The gate was open. He turned into the driveway.

By the time he stopped the car, Gail came running out of the front door. As he stepped out, she fell into his arms.

"Just cry, Gail, let it all out." He folded her in his arms silently. Every time she wanted to start talking, the tears closed her throat.

Despite her emotional state, she looked gorgeous. He wondered if it was because of his thoughts for her in the car, but he observed a kind of beauty in Gail he had never noticed before. Her half-long dark hair and blue eyes immediately struck his attention. Gail exuded class, even on this sad day.

Gently, he guided her back into the house to the kitchen. The luxury designer kitchen of German origin featured a panoramic view over an abundant, well-maintained garden, with a full view of the lake and the Alps in the distance. Like the rest of the house, it had a contemporary design with many straight lines, much brushed steel, and cherry wood accents.

Duan filled a glass at the water dispenser and put it with a box of tissues near Gail.

"Did you hear from the police?" he asked quietly.

"No. Not yet," she stuttered.

Duan knew from personal experience that after the death of your partner, the presence of someone you trust calms you. No need for immediate discussions and talks. Tenderness, care, and an arm around you are the best medicine. That's why he had come.

He brewed and poured two cups of tea. Gail was pensively looking into her cup. This gave her time to catch her breath and organize her thoughts.

"I feel weird and twisted, Duan." As she spoke, Duan kept glancing sideways, watching her facial expressions. "It's been hell. I once loved Luc, but over the past months I started hating him deeply. It sounds weird, doesn't it?"

He moved his chair, pulled her closer, and asked, "What was going on between you two?"

"I have no idea what triggered it. As you know, Luc always kept his business activities private but was obviously under a tremendous amount of stress. It began getting bad a few months ago." She stared out the kitchen window.

Duan could see her reliving all that had happened over the recent weeks.

"He started drinking and got nasty. I hated being around him."

"Do you think he was stressed out about work?"

"I asked him many times, but he wouldn't tell me. There were only more violent outbursts. A few times, he turned so violent I called the police!"

When Gail raised her shirt, Duan could see several bruises. He could only imagine what she'd been going through and instinctively put his arm around her as a sign of support.

This started Gail's waterworks going again. She slumped over, exhausted but needing to talk. "I need to get these emotions out. It is not because of Luc's death. It's because this is finally behind me."

Sitting at her kitchen table, she continued. "A few months ago, Luc had another one of his rages. He kept hitting and kicking me and wouldn't stop. I felt like shit, was desperate, and had no clue what to do. I thought I would die. I left and called Mina. You were out on a business trip, so I stayed with her for two nights. I don't know how I could have survived otherwise."

Her crying became a wail. Duan held her tight. Finally, she ran out of tears and finished her story.

"I spoke for hours with Mina about all the violence. Despite being with her, it was so hard to relax. I was afraid that the monster would appear at any moment. Duan, I deeply, deeply hated him. I'm so glad that the bastard is gone."

When he looked at her face, he noticed her stressed jaw and her deep breathing. There was no doubt Gail had gone through an extremely tough period.

"He even mentioned my life was in danger."

"Your life in danger? Did he give any specifics?" Duan was shocked by what he heard.

"Well, yesterday he finally confessed he was being threatened by his *CryptoSwap* customers and was facing major issues with BionTic as well. He looked more depressed than I had ever seen him and was drinking a lot. Then, he threatened to commit suicide and got aggressive again. He threw his glass of whiskey there against the wall."

She pointed to the spot on the wall where the damage was still visible.

"Thank God he did not touch me this time. I was so bloody scared."

"Do you think Luc might have committed suicide?"

"Oh no. But he said, 'My death will be a big surprise.'"

"What could he have meant?"

"I have no clue." As she said these words, he noticed how she stared out of the kitchen without any focus in her eyes.

The two of them kept sitting like that for several minutes. Duan could feel and see Gail gradually calm down.

"You want soup? All these emotions make me hungry, and I have some leftovers in the fridge."

"Good idea. Let me do the table." Duan knew his way into the kitchen and prepared the table. He felt at home here. The smell of the pumpkin soup gave the place an extra homey feeling, especially with the rain that started hitting the window.

While enjoying their soup, they continued the conversation.

"Could it have to do with his crypto business?" Duan thought out loud.

"That's very well possible. During the *CryptoSwap* bankruptcy, some victims claimed to have proof that he had been behind the theft. Luc had been questioned extensively by the police and spent a fortune on lawyers. It killed his company, but in the end, they couldn't prove anything. Did one of them take revenge?"

"It is unreal, isn't it, that I'm here? Luc's death, Mina's death, who could have imagined that six months ago." Duan felt an upcoming lump in his throat and visibly struggled to maintain it; his underlip started quivering. He saw how Gail noticed it from across the table. Gently, she started caressing his arm.

"It's indeed weird how life is putting us to the test. How have you been? We have not spoken for almost two weeks."

"I'm fine. I'm sorry, but I did not come here to cry. No, I should be supporting you and not the other way around. The past weeks have not been easy. I still feel so empty without Mina at my side. Will things ever get back to normal?"

"Of course. It's okay to feel like that."

"Only now I realize how dependent I was on her. These days, I struggle to energize myself. Waking up is an effort, and working even more. With Mina, it was all so easy."

Her caressing suddenly stopped, and she looked at him.

"Duan, I need help to sort out Luc's affairs, could I count on you? It gives you a distraction. What do you think?"

The thought of being with Gail pleased him. She carried positive energy. That was exactly what he needed.

"Of course, with all pleasure. Although I'm not sure I can help you much with all his crypto coins, I will do my best."

"Talking about crypto, Do you have access to Luc's crypto wallet?"

"No, Luc kept his crypto business completely separate, but I must admit I have no clue about our current financial situation."

"Do you know his wallet's address?"

"I heard him talking about it, but I must admit I don't even understand what a crypto wallet is. Can you imagine? Me, the wife of a crypto entrepreneur. Sometimes, I feel so stupid when it gets to crypto coins and blockchain."

"Well, I'm no expert either, but let me try to explain. A cryptocurrency wallet is a digital online folder to store and organize cryptocurrency. It's called a wallet because, like a physical wallet, where you put cash and cards in, it stores the keys you use to sign up for cryptocurrency transactions and provides the interface to access your cryptocurrency. Every wallet has a unique address and requires a key to access what's in it."

"I think he may have shown me that once in his office. Wait a sec."

Gail came back with a piece of paper torn from a legal pad.

"Could this be it?"

"That indeed looks like a wallet address. Let me check." Duan grabbed his phone and logged onto a site that allowed him to check the balance of any bitcoin wallet. He entered the long number and pressed Enter.

"Bloody hell!"

"What's wrong?"

"Gail, this wallet contains 8,327 bitcoins!" He opened the calculator and showed it to her.

"What's that?

"Luc's wallet contains almost one billion dollars, Gail. One billion, can you imagine?"

"I remember him mentioning he had seven thousand Bitcoins, but that must have increased."

Gail was silent.

"That much money always means trouble."

"And you have no access?" Duan tried.

"There must be a way to open that wallet. Isn't there?"

"I'm afraid not. Crypto wallets are only accessible with the private key for that wallet. You don't have that?"

"No. And you know what? I don't want to have anything to do with his frickin' crypto coins!"

"Come on, isn't that a bit too harsh?"

"No, not at all. Luc has caused me nothing but misery, and I want nothing to do with anything that reminds me of him."

"Without that private key, these coins will be lost forever."

"Fine with me! Luc is gone, and so are his fucking coins. The bastard left me with enough misery!"

Her firm rejection took him by surprise.

"Come on Gail, please do not act under the influence of your emotions. These are now your coins and there's no need to feel any guilt about that. Let's have this discussion another time."

"Absolutely not. Each of those bloody Bitcoins will remind me of his violence, endless beatings, and cold eyes. For him, it was all about money, and he had been chasing wealth for years. See what it has done to him? Luc was chased by gangsters. Now he is dead, and I've endured endless stress. No, this is a unique opportunity for me to finally grab my independence."

"You are right; later, you may see Luc's death as the best thing that ever could have happened to you."

When he said that, Gail initially looked shocked, but gradually, her face turned to anger. With a loud voice, she reacted.

"How could you say that, Duan Ripa? Yes, I'm sad and disgusted by Luc, but you, more than anyone else, should know what it is to lose your partner. That was a completely inappropriate comment."

Duan was shocked and realized it was not the smartest thing to say.

"I'm sorry, Gail."

It was clear his apologies did little to Gail, and it was obvious his words made her feel extremely uncomfortable. He did not know how to react and kept staring in front of him.

CHAPTER 9
TUESDAY, 22 OCTOBER, 4:12 P.M.

Bernt followed his daughter into the conference room, where they were meeting with the team to discuss the investigation into Starck's death. The room on the top floor overlooked the historic old town. During major investigations, one large room would be reserved as a situation room. It was a functional room with plenty of wall space and whiteboards to monitor progress. The boards and walls were still empty.

Bernt was leading the meeting and was joined by eight other team members around a large table. The group included two inspectors, three detectives, a coroner, and two women from forensics. Except for the forensics team, everyone had worked with Bernt on other cases.

Before starting the meeting, Rudy, the inspector on his right, leaned toward Bernt and said, "I'm so glad you can work with Lisa-Lotte on this case. I'm looking forward to seeing you with her in action."

Bernt thanked him politely and started the session.

"Team, it has been almost five hours since Luc Starck was found dead. As you all know, these first hours are key, so let's see where we are."

He turned toward the coroner, Mr. Sumi, and invited him to give them an update.

The coroner, a well-dressed veteran officer, started. "Our autopsy just finished. Unfortunately, we could not pinpoint an obvious cause of death. For now, we're still calling it a heart attack. There are no signs of violence, no visible injections, nothing. Luc Starck appears to have died from natural causes, but we still have a few tissue samples to look at."

"How about the blood coming from his mouth?" Bernt asked.

"Well, he had severe internal bleeding," Sumi responded seriously.

"So, did he die a natural death or not?" Bernt looked at the coroner.

Rudy Kotkin, a middle-aged inspector with movie-star looks who'd been searching for the man with the red cap, raised his right hand.

"Bernt, I don't think so. We have some odd observations about the man with the red cap. We spotted him on public surveillance cameras around the square. Our first sight was of him leaving the train station. At 10:33 a.m., he arrived at the square and waited for a seat. As if he was waiting for someone or something. He sat with his back toward the camera, so the meeting with Mr. Starck was not completely visible. They were talking for four minutes. Then he stood up to take a call, and shortly after that, Mr. Starck collapsed. Oddly enough, the man ignored that and walked straight back to the station and took the first train to Zurich. Despite his cap, we have a decent picture of his face. We informed our colleagues in Zurich, and he was stopped at Zurich's main train station. They have his name and address and asked him to remain available for questioning."

"Great job, guys!" Bernt said. They'd captured the man in the red cap much faster than he'd anticipated.

Bernt noticed how Lisa-Lotte was closely observing his actions. He maintained eye contact with everyone around the table to keep them engaged and gave each person a chance to speak. When Bernt spoke, nobody fidgeted.

"So, the guy with the red cap arrives by train, walks directly to the square, talks to Mr. Starck for four minutes, stands up without noticing the collapse, and leaves Zug. This stinks! I don't like scenarios that make no sense!"

"Let's see if we can find better footage from other cameras. This was the last person he met, so we need to talk to him. Rudy, ask Zurich to bring him here first thing tomorrow for an interview."

While Bernt thought about his next question, he was surprised to see Lisa-Lotte taking over the discussion. "What do we know about Mr. Starck's belongings? Anything odd?"

Another detective referred to a list of what was found on Luc Starck. "The usual. On his phone, we found a calendar entry for an appointment at eleven o'clock at the main square, but it had no name. Only one word, *Invitation* at eleven a.m. The only odd item was an envelope in his inner coat pocket with 'Clue One' written on the front of it, but it was empty. Everything has been sent for further forensic tests."

The news of the envelope surprised everyone on the team, wondering what this could refer to.

Bernt continued. "One more thing." Looking at Patrick, a senior detective, he said, "Would you mind digging into Luc Starck's company, BionTic? They're in the Crypto Valley Labs complex. I want to know everything about that company. Were there unpleasant politics? How are things there financially? Anything that could have led to Mr. Starck's death?"

Patrick made a note on his pad.

Before Bernt could move on, Patrick spoke up.

"Digging into Starck's history, I found that seven years ago, he lost many Bitcoins himself when the crypto exchange he used ran away with all its customers' crypto assets. I guess it may have been the reason he started his exchange."

"Good catch, Patrick." Bernt moved on.

"Finally, about the Starcks, anything about their violent history?"

A female officer stood up. "I found three reports filed by Mrs. Starck about acts of violence by her husband. The first one was four months ago."

Bernt reacted. "Thanks, Caroline. Mrs. Starck hated him deeply and looked relieved when Lisa-Lotte and I informed her of his death. We need to take a serious look at her. She has the obvious motive."

"I have one last thing," Lisa-Lotte said just before Bernt wrapped up. "I've been contacted by a journalist from the online blog site *blogchain.ch*. She asked if we could issue a formal statement about Luc Starck's death, including any preliminary details about the probable cause of his death."

Bernt had been burned more than once when trying to share information too early with the media.

"Well, at the moment, I don't think we can say anything concrete. Tell them the initial report from the coroner suggests it was a heart attack, but we're waiting for the results of additional tests. We'll let them know as soon as we hear anything. Who wants to handle that?"

A junior officer with media experience raised his hand from the back.

Bernt wrapped up the first team meeting. "Guys, it's too early to call this a crime, but the suspicious behavior of our man with the red cap makes that seem likely. We need to find out *who* did this, *how*, and *why*."

CHAPTER 10
TUESDAY, 22 OCTOBER, 7:09 P.M.

After spending that very emotional afternoon with Gail, Duan drove home. Seeing his friend going through such a tough period affected him big time.

The past period had definitely intensified their bonding. The way she bounced jokes back and forth and how she teased him never failed to crack him up. Yet the Gail he met this afternoon was vulnerable. The fact she called him for help was a clear sign she trusted him. He had found it difficult to leave her.

His thoughts went back to something Gail told him shortly after Mina's death. It was about an intimate discussion between the girls that took place during Mina's last days.

Gail had been reading Dr. Viktor Frankl's worldwide bestselling book, *Man's Search for Meaning*. The more she read it, the more she could relate the book's message to the pain Mina was going through during these days. Gail explained how much Mina fit the profile of a survivor, with qualities that everyone who knew her admired.

"Dr. Frankl was a Jewish doctor who survived internment in three concentration camps and carefully observed how different prisoners were reacting to unbelievably difficult lives," Gail told Mina.

"The biggest difference between those who survived and those who perished, he decided, was that the survivors had identified their meaning of life."

"I know no one who's more of a natural survivor than you," she told Mina. "We've never discussed it before, but you must be very clear about your life's meaning."

After he heard Gail talk about the book, Duan immediately ordered it online, but so far, it was still unopened next to his bed. He hoped it could provide him with deeper insights and help him understand characteristics of his wife he had not yet realized.

He still hadn't come to grips with the loss of Mina, and thinking about her made it a double depressing drive home. The rain on his windshield being swept back and forth by the wipers was hypnotic.

Traffic in the rain slowed down, and he focused on the taillights of a bus in front of him. He replayed his discussion with Gail about Luc's crypto wallet. Having almost a billion dollars in his wallet was hard to get his head around. He appreciated Gail not wanting to have anything to do with it, but then again, *one billion*! Knowing all that money might be accessible blew his mind. It motivated him to dig deeper.

Duan, whose father was half-Chinese—hence his Chinese name—had always loved mathematics. He had a bachelor's in mathematics, a perfect background for his studies in cybersecurity, with a specialization in encryption techniques.

The world of crypto coins had gained Duan's special interest, but its erratic speculative nature, with exchange rates fluctuating several percent in a week, had kept him from becoming actively involved. He was convinced that the global financial infrastructure that Satoshi Nakamoto had conceived would revolutionize the financial world.

Several times, Luc had tried to convince him to buy Bitcoins, but Duan's conservative mindset had always prevailed.

The bus in front of him made a sudden stop. He reacted just in time to avoid an accident. He hated driving in the dark while it rained. There was so much going on in his mind that it was hard to focus on the road.

His thoughts went back to an explosive meeting he'd had three weeks ago with Luc. Luc had called to suggest they meet at a bar in downtown Zug. For weeks he had been trying to find the right moment to tell Gail about that curious meeting, but did not want her to learn about the dark side of her husband. After she showed him her blue marks all over her body, that meeting suddenly put Luc in the right perspective. He was in doubt telling

Gail about this during the afternoon, afraid it would have been too much for her to handle.

When Duan arrived at that bar, he could tell Luc hadn't waited for him to start drinking. His eyes were glazed, and his speech slurred. The setting sun was radiating through the window. The place had an appropriately melancholic vibe, with Pink Floyd's *Comfortably Numb* playing in the background, straight out of a Jim Jarmusch movie.

"Duan, I need your help. I'm in trouble. Deep."

Well, this was a first. Usually, the arrogant bastard would never ask for help.

"Do you remember when *CryptoSwap* was accused of stealing coins from its customers?"

"Yes."

"Well, the threats I've been getting from those ex-customers are getting more and more serious. The threats have continued for months, and they're from criminals who seem quite prepared to act on them. As you know, criminals love cryptocurrencies as the perfect way to hide illegal funds. I tried to tell them I'd never touched their coins and that they were victims of a cybercrime, but they said they'd found their coins in a wallet of mine."

Luc glanced back and forth nervously as he ordered another round of drinks.

"Then, two days ago, a huge guy was waiting by my car near the casino. He was solid muscle and looked Asian. A cabinet with feet. He stopped me, opened his jacket, and showed me the biggest revolver I've ever laid eyes on. It was the first time in my life I'd been threatened like that."

"I can imagine." Duan listened empathically, curious about what was about to come.

"He said I had three days and promised things would continue to escalate until I returned his coins. Sure enough, two days later, he was waiting at the Crypto Valley Labs exit. A Bruce Lee-kind-of-guy came out with him from behind a tree and punched me hard in the kidneys. They leaned over me and said I had one more day to return their coins. So, I realized how serious they were when they locked me in the trunk of my car. It took me almost thirty minutes to work my way through the back seat and get out."

"That sounds like a movie. Why didn't you go to the police?"

"He warned me three times not to tell anyone, or things would get worse. And, Duan, he was huge!" Luc seemed to be outlining a city bus.

"A cross between Rambo and Oddjob. You remember that Chinese bulldog from James Bond's *Dr. No?*"

Duan nodded but was getting annoyed with Luc's stereotyping Asians as bad guys in movies. After all, Duan was part Asian. He understood Luc was drunk, but his bad-mouthing of Asians was getting really old.

"So, what do you want me to do, Luc? What's your plan?" Duan looked around to make sure nobody was eavesdropping.

"Nothing. I just want you to know the pressure I am facing, just in case something ever happens to me. Life just sucks. Everybody's against me."

Luc talked louder and louder as he pounded the table with a muscular fist, like any other self-pitying drunk.

"Even my goddamned wife doesn't understand my shitty life!"

Duan tried again to reason with him.

"Luc, you better leave her out of this. She has nothing to do with your problems."

Luc inhaled and exhaled deeply, like a bull about to charge. As he continued to shout, people at other tables were listening despite the melancholic sound coming out of Roger Waters' guitar.

"You can't tell me what to do in my home. Mind your own business, Chink."

Duan got so fed up with Luc's ranting and struggled to maintain his temper.

Two days later, Duan got a call from Luc. He apologized and explained how the incessant pressure was affecting him.

"Duan, I'm so sorry about the other night. I'm in deep *kimchi* and feel surrounded, with no idea where to turn for help. In case something happens to me, please tell the police everything you know about who is threatening me and why."

Duan felt used. They had not spoken for weeks, and suddenly, it seemed like he was on speed dial with Luc as his closest buddy.

"Wow, that sounds like too much for you to deal with alone. Does Gail know what is going on with you?"

"Oh no, for God's sake, keep her out of this. I'm already causing enough trouble for her, and those gangsters threatening me have said she could be next. This pressure is too much for me, and it makes me explode at home. I feel so sorry for her.

"There's something else I need to tell you, Duan."

Typical. Just two days after Luc got angry in that bar, Luc was eager to confide again as if nothing had happened. His apology carried much less weight with Duan than Luc seemed to imagine.

"Duan, in case anything ever happens to me, please promise you will help."

"Of course." This was not the moment to ask for details.

Now Luc was dead, that discussion suddenly took on a completely different meaning.

CHAPTER 11
TUESDAY, 22 OCTOBER, 10:43 P.M.

Yong Chi finally arrived in Switzerland after a twenty-hour trip. He'd started his long journey the day before in Shenyang, China, just north of the border with North Korea. From Shenyang Taoxian International Airport, he flew to Frankfurt. Then took a train to Zurich.

He always enjoyed traveling by train in Europe. The cities that crowded near the train tracks showed culture and history much more than stations in China.

Zurich was famous around the world as Switzerland's largest city but only had half the population of his hometown. Perhaps that explained its more leisurely pace and abundance of historical and cultural sights.

He wandered a few blocks through the city's brightly lit downtown, crisscrossed by trolley tracks, to the nearest Globus department store. At the DIY section, he went through a list of items he would need for this trip. In the basement food arcade, he bought a pate pie and a small bottle of red wine for a light supper, which he could eat during the train ride to Zug.

Yong had spent several weeks preparing for this trip to find the guy who had betrayed and stolen from him.

Yong Chi, thirty-two years old, was born in Chengdu, China, but moved to Shenyang with his parents when he was ten. His father quickly found a job in Shenyang's booming rail industry. Yong got interested in IT and joined the local hacking community, dominated by North Korean hackers. The highly sophisticated internet infrastructure in Shenyang was far superior to what was available to North Koreans in their home country, where only a fraction of the population had access to the Internet.

With such a low presence of the internet, it was paradoxical that North Korea had produced some of the world's most elaborate hackers. Many North Korean hackers in Shenyang resided in the comparatively luxurious Chilbosan hotel. It had become known as the 'hackers hotel,' serving as the home base for several major cybercrime syndicates. North Korea supported multiple hacker teams to keep a close watch on South Korean intelligence, military, and business internet communities.

Yong struck up friendships with several expert hackers and picked up many tricks of the hacking trade. Recently, he'd learned that some hacking friends from the old days, Jon Chang Hyok and Kim Il, had formed the nucleus of the Lazarus hacking group until being convicted of the Sony hack several years earlier.

He was a quick learner and, in no time, had established himself as a skilled hacker in this very unusual community.

Yong - brave in Chinese - always had a strong interest in new and evolving untested opportunities.

As a young boy, Yong got himself involved in innocent criminal activities but gradually got dragged into more serious, hazardous crimes.

Yong saw himself as a modern-day Genghis Khan, never needing to regroup or retreat. Always forward, finding weaknesses and having his way.

That ferocious entrepreneurial mindset led him to be one of the first to set up a large-scale BitcoinBitcoin mining farm just outside Shenyang. Similar to gold, Bitcoins are 'mined,' not by digging into rock but by solving a complex mathematical puzzle on a computer.

He started mining with just a few servers, but when he saw the huge profits in Bitcoin mining flowing in, he scaled up his operations and soon established himself as one of China's largest cryptocurrency miners. In hindsight, Bitcoin saved his life; once he'd discovered the income he could generate from mining, he no longer found time for criminal activities. It pushed him onto the straight and narrow, if you will.

When the political climate in China turned against cryptocurrency, and the government cracked down on mining, Yong was forced to find foreign locations to store his Bitcoins. He decided to diversify his coin storage, known as custody, into various crypto exchanges around the world.

The decentralized nature of Bitcoin was also the Achilles heel of the system. For the crypto ecosystem to work, it required crypto exchanges where users could store their currencies and swap their digital currencies for cash or other cryptocurrencies. These exchanges were not regulated, and more than once it happened that owners of these exchanges walked away with all the crypto coins of their customers. Hence, Yong was extremely careful in selecting an exchange he could trust.

One of the most trustworthy exchanges he identified was *CryptoSwap*. It was based in Switzerland for more credibility. Switzerland seemed a less risky place to store his digital wealth than many of the other crypto exchanges that were popping up all around the world.

Yong moved 40% of his coins, a value of over 200 million dollars, into *CryptoSwap*. Unsure about how quickly the Chinese government would close his operations, he decided not to wait. He had to move without delay and move his coins before moving himself abroad.

Yong's troubles started the day he logged into his account at *CryptoSwap*, and the balance showed zero. He suspected *CryptoSwap* had suffered a technical glitch, but when he tried again thirty minutes later, and the balance was still zero, he got worried.

He contacted the *CryptoSwap* customer support team, asking for an explanation of his zero balance. Other than the standard confirmation mail, he did not get any immediate feedback. After twenty-four hours, he became even more worried.

Yong contacted a fellow miner who'd also stored his coins with *CryptoSwap*; to his surprise, his friend had the same experience; his wallet balance was also at zero.

The next day, *CryptoSwap* informed him that several customers had become victims of a cybercrime. Their message said:

> *Since encryption keys are very long and hard to remember, our customers often use the software program Notepad to store them. We discovered that hackers had modified the notepad program, so every time someone saved their private encryption key in the application, a copy would be sent to the hackers. Once the hackers had collected enough keys, they emptied our customers' wallets.*

Yong also used *Notepad* to store his private key.

His disbelief soon turned into anger. He couldn't have been hacked! When it came to his online presence, he was extremely careful; he anonymized his online surfing, encrypted any communication, and had his home network protected behind various firewalls.

After several days of investigation, he finally traced the origin of the virus that had infected his *Notepad* program. He discovered it was *CryptoSwap* that had planted the virus in the application. For weeks, he traced his coins and finally found the smoking gun; his coins had landed in an account owned by Luc Starck.

"I've got him. The bastard!" Yong screamed. Finally, he could link his lost coins to that malicious owner of the crypto exchange.

Yong confronted Luc with his findings, but Luc ignored him. After being nice a few times, he decided he needed to get out his Mongolian longbow.

Yong contacted some Chinese criminals based in Zurich and contracted them to apply serious physical pressure on Luc Starck. They went to see Luc in Zug, but he refused to cooperate. They reported how Starck resisted their intimidation and refused to return Yong's coins. Yong realized he'd have to travel to Switzerland and take care of it himself.

Fully packed with all the stuff he needed for the coming weeks, Yong stepped back into the Zurich main train station, *the Hauptbahnhof.* He checked the departures screen, looking for the next train to Zug and from what platform it left. To an ignorant bystander, Yong looked like just another tourist doing a standard Eurorail trip. However, if you paid close attention to the determination in his eyes and his focus, it made him look like anything but a tourist.

Yong lived by an old Chinese saying that said, *Those who do not offend will not be offended, and those who offend will be offended.* The time had come for him to go on the offensive.

In Zurich, he became Genghis Khan, determined to conquer his enemies.

CHAPTER 12
TUESDAY, 22 OCTOBER, 10:53 P.M.

That evening, Gail couldn't catch sleep. The events of the day kept replaying in her mind, each thought stirring up more anger, more resentment.

The last months had been a nightmare—a slow, suffocating descent into a relationship she had no longer wanted to be part of. She should've ended things long ago, but now it felt like she was trapped in a life that wasn't hers. She always saw herself as such a smart girl but rationally could not grasp why she had not given up weeks ago.

Her mind drifted to a Friday evening a few months ago. It was supposed to be a quiet night. She'd made Luc's favorite dinner, set the table, waiting for him to come home. She'd called him twice and texted him a few times, but there had been no response. She tried to tell herself it wasn't a big deal—maybe he was busy, maybe he just hadn't heard his phone. But the minutes stretched into an hour and then another.

At 9 p.m., she finally gave up. She warmed up the food, sat down, and started eating alone. Just as she raised her fork to take a bite, she heard the unmistakable sound of his car in the driveway.

The front door crashed open, followed by the heavy thud of his bag hitting the floor in the hallway.

"Gail!" His voice, slurred and thick, cut through the silence.

"Oh my God," she muttered to herself.

"Yes, I'm here," she called, trying to keep her voice steady though her heart was racing. "Where have you been? I've been trying to reach you."

He stumbled into the kitchen, leaning heavily against the doorframe, eyes glazed, his movements jerky and uncoordinated. He was drunk. Drunk like she'd never seen him before.

"You, uh…what are you doing?" His words were sluggish, disconnected. He looked at her, but it wasn't like he was seeing her. His eyes were unfocused, looking past her as though she wasn't even there.

Gail's stomach sank. She knew this look. She'd seen it a few times before—the kind of look that chilled her to the bone, the kind that meant nothing good.

"I'm having dinner," she replied, trying to sound casual, even though the tension in her chest was nearly unbearable.

"Dinner?" His voice grew louder, more hostile. "Dinner? You couldn't wait for me? You just gave up on me?"

The words hit her like a slap. No, not again.

His breath reeked of alcohol. It struck her hard, overwhelming her senses. He lurched forward, nearly knocking over a chair, his eyes wild, his movements erratic.

"Luc, please—" she started, but he cut her off, raising a finger to point at her, a dangerous glint in his eyes.

"You think you're so clever, huh? You think you can just ignore me and carry on with your little life like I don't matter? You think you're better than me?" His voice rose, each word dripping with accusation. He reached for the whiskey bottle in the cabinet, his hand shaking.

"I'm not saying that," she said quickly, but her voice was trembling now. She could feel the tension building like a storm cloud waiting to break.

He poured himself a drink, his hand unsteady, spilling some of the liquor onto the counter. "You should be on your knees, thanking me for everything I've done for you! You think this house, this life—you think it's yours? You think you earned it? No. You owe me, Gail. Everything you have, you owe to me."

These words were hitting her hard. Luc was standing there, angry and drunk, and everything she had feared about him—the rage, the entitlement, the disregard for her—was coming to the surface.

She took a deep breath, trying to keep calm. "Luc, this isn't you. You need to stop drinking. You're out of control." Her voice was barely more than a whisper, but she knew it was too late. The look in his eyes told her everything.

His face twisted, contorting in anger. "You don't tell me what to do!" He slammed his glass down so hard that it shattered on the counter, whiskey splashing across the floor.

Gail's heart hammered in her chest. This is it. She could feel the room closing in on her, the air thick and suffocating. He took another step toward her, and she instinctively backed away. But there was nowhere to go. He was closing in, and she was cornered.

"Look at me!" he shouted, his voice a mix of rage and something darker. "You think you're better than me? You think you can just walk away from me? You think you have the right to leave? This—this house, this life—I built it. You wouldn't have any of it without me!"

His voice was a roar now, a tidal wave crashing over her. She took a step back, trying to put some space between them, but the anger in his eyes burned through her. He was losing control—and she had no idea how far it would go.

"Luc, please, I just want to be left alone," she said, her voice shaking. "I don't want to fight. I just want to—"

But she didn't get to finish. He reached out, grabbing her by the arm with a grip so tight it felt like he was going to crush her bones. She gasped, the pain shooting up her arm.

"You think you can walk away from me? You think you can leave?" His voice was low, venomous. "I'll make you stay, Gail. You won't leave me."

"Let go of me!" Her voice broke as she tried to pull away, but his grip only tightened.

In a burst of panic, Gail shoved against his chest, pushing him back with all the strength she could muster. For a moment, he stumbled, and that was all she needed.

Her heart racing, she spun on her heels and ran for the door. Her feet slapped against the hardwood floor as she yanked it open, slamming it behind her with all her force.

Get out! Get out!

The bruises from his last assault hadn't yet faded. She had to get out!

She ran for the car, her breath coming in frantic gasps. The keys were in her hands, but her fingers fumbled, slick with sweat, and for a split second, it felt like she wasn't going to make it. Then, with a shaking hand, she unlocked the car and threw herself inside, slamming the door shut.

Her heart was pounding so loudly she could barely hear herself think. She hit the accelerator, the tires squealing as she sped out of the driveway, her eyes fixed straight ahead, not daring to look back.

The gate opened in front of her, and she shot through it, her car racing into the night.

Ten minutes later, she pulled into a gas station, her hands still shaking on the wheel. She sat there for a moment, taking deep, shaky breaths, trying to steady herself. But as the weight of the past hour pressed down on her, the tears came anyway—hot, desperate, uncontrollable. She buried her face in her hands, sobbing, her chest heaving with the force of it.

It was too much. Too much.

No way was she going back home. There was only one person she could call—and that was Mina. Her best friend, Mina. The last thing she wanted to do was burden Mina with her problems. After all, Mina had enough on her plate, fighting blood cancer. It had only been two weeks since their meeting at the Thong Thai, where Mina had shared the heartbreaking news with her and Luc about her terminal illness.

Twice, Gail reached for her phone, ready to call Mina. And twice, she hesitated. No, she didn't want to disturb her. But then again, they shared everything—*really* everything.

And then, suddenly, it hit her. Duan was out of town this weekend on a business trip. She'd even messaged her just this morning.

The phone rang. Mina picked up immediately.

"Mimi!"

"Gaily, what's up?"

"Oh, darling... I'm so done with that loser. Tonight, he came home completely wasted and started harassing me. I just... I couldn't stay. I had to leave. I can't be near him anymore. I'm done. I'm so sorry. I know you've got so much going on, and I didn't want to dump my mess on you."

"Gaily, for God's sake! You know you can always talk to me. You're coming over here. Duan's gone for the weekend. It'll do us both good to spend the weekend together, don't you think?"

Twenty-five minutes later, they were snuggled together under a blanket, each holding a glass of Pinot Noir.

"You know," Gail said quietly, "I feel so disappointed in myself. Why can't I just pack up and leave? Why am I still here, dealing with all this?"

Mina sipped her wine and gave a soft smile. "Have you forgotten my days with that drug addict, Chris Engel? We were together for four years, and most of that time, he was either high or intoxicated. Trust me, I know all about an extreme emotional dependency."

Gail sighed. "I know, but I feel like I've completely lost myself. I'm so dependent on Luc for everything. What have I really achieved in life? It's great I've started my studies, but what about everything else? I feel like I've wasted the last few years."

Mina set down her glass and cozied up to her. "Gaily, everything is a lesson. The trick is to see it that way. If you do, you won't be disappointed. Life doesn't always follow a perfect path, but it does teach you something every step of the way."

Gail paused, letting the words sink in. In the space of just ten minutes, they had fallen back into their familiar roles—Mina, the wise one who always knew just what to say, and Gail, full of doubts and fears. But tonight, it felt different. It felt like Mina was the calm in the storm, and Gail... well, Gail was trying to find her way out of it.

Over time, she'd learned how to cope with these moments of doubt. When fear or uncertainty crept in, she would close off—become quiet, distant, or shield herself behind a facade of confidence. She called it her survival mode.

It wasn't a perfect defense. Gail knew it could be off-putting to people who didn't know her well. They saw the tough exterior and assumed she was unapproachable, maybe even cold. But those who knew her, who'd spent enough time with her, understood that beneath the hard shell was a soft heart, one that cared deeply—maybe too much sometimes.

During that joyful weekend together, they also had serious conversations about Mina's cancer and life after death. Moments of tears and laughs alternated that weekend. A weekend they both desperately needed. Three empty bottles of Moët de Chandon and three empty boxes of Kleenex were the silent witnesses of their time together.

Still awake, lost in her thoughts about that memorable weekend, she stepped out of bed and took a sleeping pill.

Oh my God. How much did she miss Mina? Today, more than ever.

By 01:20 a.m., she finally fell asleep.

CHAPTER 13
WEDNESDAY, 23 OCTOBER, 8:01 A.M.

Lisa-Lotte arrived early that morning at the police station. Cases like the death of Luc Starck would keep any police officer busy, but in her situation, this was an extra-special case. She was determined to show her father what she was capable of as a police officer and would not disappoint him. She had barely slept. When she woke up, her smartwatch showed a sleep score of sixty-two, confirming her lousy night. However, that did not stop her from being super-awake because their day started with an important interview.

She met her father at the coffee machine where he was talking to his colleague Rudy, who had guarded the early morning transport of the man with the red cap from Zurich to Zug.

"He is ready for you. He is in room two. The poor guy looks confused and nervous. I would be the same if I were to be interviewed by you two." Rudy smiled as he stirred his cappuccino.

Lisa-Lotte looked at her father. "Dad, okay if I lead the interview?"

"Of course, I'm barely awake."

Rudy looked at Bernt. "Look at that, just from school and now already full of initiative. Just like her dad. A Berg-star is born!" Laughing, he hit Bernt on the shoulder, who barely managed to keep all the coffee in his cup.

Lisa-Lotte and her father walked down the stairs to interview room two, where the man was waiting.

The man with the red cap sat at a large table that had a set of handcuffs built into it, but he wasn't being detained. There was a microphone in front of him on the table.

Lisa-Lotte could not wait to start interviewing him. During her sleepless night, she had been playing the interview several times in her head. As from her younger years, she had learned from her dad that being prepared is half the battle won, certainly in this case. It was the first time her father witnessed her interrogation skills, and it was essential this went well. At this moment, he was their only lead in the mysterious death of Luc Starck. She could not mess this up.

In the cold, sterile interview room, Lisa-Lotte and Bernt sat on opposite sides of the table, both impassively studying the man and maintaining a grim silence for ten seconds. This was how Lisa-Lotte had usually seen Bernt start his interrogations. From her father, she learned how the power of silence is so often ignored. It can tell you a lot about people, as they fill it with often involuntary thoughts. The guy with the red cap, sitting in between them, remained silent and only looked confused.

Lisa-Lotte started the interview. "Good morning. My name is Detective Lisa-Lotte Berg, and this is my colleague Bernt. We have a few questions to ask. Your name is Franz Brucker, correct?"

"Correct."

Brucker still looked confused but not nervous. Like her father, Lisa-Lotte was trained to read body language. At the academy, they were presented with many pictures of individuals where they had to 'read' the person and tell in what state of mind they were in.

Brucker was leaning back in his chair with his arms crossed and raising his eyebrows. Her reading of him was that he was relaxed, curious to find out what they had to say, but his closed arms told her he was not going to talk easily.

"Mr. Brucker, yesterday morning, you met Mr. Luc Starck at the *Landsgemeindeplatz* on the terrace of *Hotel Loewen Am See*. Can you tell us why you were meeting him?"

Brucker sighed, relaxed even more, and put his arms on the table. Now he knew why he was at the police station.

"Someone asked me to meet Mr. Starck there yesterday at 11 a.m. sharp."

"Who asked you?"

"I have no idea."

"Really?" Lisa-Lotte responded. She silently looked Brucker straight in the eye, inviting him to keep talking.

"This is a long and embarrassing story, but I was forced to meet Mr. Starck yesterday at eleven a.m., say hello to him, hand him an envelope, and follow the script I'd been given."

Now Lisa-Lotte and Bernt looked confused. This narrative was not getting clearer.

"OK, Mr. Brucker, let's start from the beginning. Who forced you into this, and why did you agree?" Lisa-Lotte spoke with a voice showing authority and determination.

Embarrassed, Brucker lowered his voice.

"OK, it started two months ago. I received an anonymous email with the subject *Surprise* from an email address named *YourNightmare@mymail.com* with a compromising video of myself attached. It was indeed a nightmare." Brucker stopped, hoping that Bernt and Lisa-Lotte would not ask for details.

"What was compromising in that video, Mr. Brucker?"

"It was me enjoying, hmmm, how can I say that?" Brucker got more embarrassed. "OK, I was masturbating. It was a video somebody had taken with my mobile phone camera while I was visiting a porn site. They must have hacked my mobile and activated my camera. You can imagine how embarrassed I was."

Daughter and father both tried to put up an emphatic look.

"The email said that the video would not be distributed if I followed their instructions closely. If not, they'd post it on my Facebook and LinkedIn feeds. I was terrified, naturally."

Even the memory of it still scared him. Lisa-Lotte noticed how his hands were shaking slightly.

"What happened next?"

"I had to confirm receiving the email, but after that, they remained silent for a while. Then, one week later, I received a parcel containing an envelope, a phone, a page of instructions, and a red cap. I suspected our conversation this morning would be about this, so I brought along the instructions to show them to you."

It was a printed list titled "The to-do list that will rescue you."

- *Mr. Brucker, follow these instructions, and your video of pleasure will be destroyed.*

- *Confirm receipt of this letter with an email to YourNightmare@mymail.com. Just write in the mail body, Instructions Received.*

- *Tuesday, 22 October at 10:30 a.m., sit at the first table on the terrace of Hotel Loewen Am See in Zug. See the attached sketch. [It showed the terrace, with an arrow pointing to the table where he was supposed to sit].*

- *Please wear the red cap you find in this package.*

- *Bring the included envelope marked 'Clue One' with you.*

- *Set the alarm on your phone to ring at 11:05 a.m.*

- *At 10:45 a.m. use the included phone and send a text to number +41.79.2982789 with the text, Do not forget your 11 a.m. meeting!*

- *At 11:00 a.m., an unknown gentleman will approach you. He will introduce himself as Luc Starck. Tell him you cannot share your name.*

- *Please start a conversation as per the attached script. [A small envelope marked Script was included].*

- *When the alarm on your phone rings, act as if you receive a call and excuse yourself. Apologize you must take the call.*

- *Walk to the aviary near the lake, continuing to talk on your phone.*

- *Once you are out of sight, leave the square.*

- *When you are done, please reply to this email address with Done.*

- *Walk back to the train station and take the first train back to Zurich. Dump the phone in one of the garbage bins at the station.*

"That is exactly what I did. To the letter."

"Did you hear again from the person who sent you these instructions?"

"Yes, on the train. On my way back to Zurich, I already received an email thanking me for my help, confirming that the video had been deleted."

Lisa-Lotte and Bernt looked puzzled. Brucker appeared to be honest and relieved to share the secret he had carried with him for weeks.

"This is all for now, Mr. Brucker. Please be available in case we have more questions. I'll have one of my colleagues visit you later today to look at the emails you received. Do you still have the package in which your instructions were sent? We are keen to have this checked."

Brucker nodded. "I'll give it to the officer later. Can I go?"

"Yes, Mr. Brucker, you can leave. Thanks for your cooperation."

Pausing in the doorway, he turned around. "I hope Mr. Starck is doing well. Is he OK?"

"I'm sorry to tell you, Mr. Brucker, but Luc Starck died a few seconds after you left him."

"Oh, my God!" Brucker was shocked. He walked out of the room, continuously shaking his head. He was about to leave their sight when he stepped back inside. His relaxed look had instantly transformed into an extremely worried grimace.

"Hang on, you are not thinking I have anything to do with Mr. Starck's death, do you?"

Lisa-Lotte maintained her poise and did not react.

"For God's sake, can you please, for one minute, put yourself into my shoes?"

"OK, I should have been more careful with the sites I visit on the internet." He looked at Bernt. Lisa-Lotte did not want to think about what websites her father visited.

"I was bloody tricked into this. They hacked my phone. I had no choice. Can you imagine what would have happened if that video appeared on my social media feeds? For weeks, I've had sleepless nights about this." He started sweating, and his speech became more like a staccato stutter.

"How would I explain that to my wife? My kids? What would they hear at school? At work? Oh my god, this would have been a fucking disaster. This is the worst thing that ever happened to me." In despair, he looked at Lisa-Lotte, and when she did not react, he turned to Bernt. When he also remained silent, Brucker continued.

"And now that poor Mr——. Sack, uh, Starck. I have no clue what I have done, what could have caused his death. The poor guy. I feel so sorry, so fucked up!" Tears started running down Brucker's cheeks. With his head between his hands, he walked out of the door. They could hear him wailing in the corridor.

When Brucker was gone, Bernt and Lisa-Lotte discussed what they'd heard and seen.

"Wow, that was unexpected. It shocked him when we said Starck was dead. Don't you think?"

"I agree. He was set up. The question is by whom and why."

Bernt was silent for a moment. "Okay, let's go."

Lisa-Lotte was surprised by the assertive statement from her dad, who normally was very relaxed. "To where?"

"Let's go back to the *Landsgemeindeplatz*. We must have overlooked something."

CHAPTER 14
WEDNESDAY, 23 OCTOBER, 9:27 A.M.

Gail woke up late that morning but stayed in bed, still exhausted by her ongoing emotional roller coaster ride and the sleeping pill. She thought of the day she first met Luc on the ski slopes, their wedding in Verbier with Mina as her witness, their vacations, and their dizzying transition from being middle-class employees to a high-society couple awash in glamor and glitz.

When they met, Gail had just finished her study of English and had started a job as an editor with an international publisher. Within five years, she deeply regretted that study and detested the job.

When *CryptoSwap* started to flourish, she stopped working to start a study in business law. But before she realized it, she had a life as a lady of leisure and was filling her days playing golf, tennis, and reformer Pilates. Money was no longer an issue, and she kept postponing that study.

Soon, she realized she'd put her life in the hands of Luc and became completely dependent on him. She was stuck in a spinning wheel of life that was kept in motion by Luc Starck, and she desperately had to break out of it. Even now, knowing Luc was dead, it felt as if he was still pushing the pedal.

Gail had been living in a continuous state of doubt and uncertainty. Doubts about her husband and uncertainties about their relationship and herself. His crises and loss of self-control, which had occurred more and more frequently, were taking a huge toll on her. She was suffering from regular headaches, weight loss, and struggling to keep her own life on track. Often, she thought about divorce or suicide as her only way out and was embarrassed to talk about it all to anyone but Mina.

Finally, six months ago, she registered at the University in Zurich and started her study of international business law. It was her escape and, unconsciously, a preparation for a life after Luc. It had become clear they had no future as a couple, and she had to invest in herself. This week, the university was closed, and she had a study week. But with Luc's death, that study would have to slow down for some time.

Checking the wall clock, she realized she had to rush; it was getting late, and she'd promised to meet Roberto Giobbi, CEO of Luc's company BionTic, to discuss Luc's death and what it would mean to them and the business.

She rushed out of bed, took her shower, and threw on some casual clothes. Stepping out of the bathroom, Gail checked her phone for messages.

Hello Gail, hope you had a peaceful night and could get enough rest. Love Duan.

So sweet of him. He was such a comfort.

She walked downstairs, stepped into the kitchen, and switched on the automatic coffee machine. As she was putting an espresso cup under the machine, a strong, muscular arm grabbed her from behind. She instantly froze, unable to move a muscle.

"What the fuck! What's happening?" For one moment, she thought someone was joking, but it was clear this was serious.

A hand closed heavily around her mouth as the person whispered. "Keep quiet, and nothing will happen." Gail didn't recognize the voice but detected a foreign accent. She could hardly breathe. A needle jabbed her arm, and she fell unconscious.

When Gail woke up, she didn't know how long she'd been unconscious or where she was. She had goosebumps; she was in a chilly area. It smelled like a forest – as if someone had freshened up the room with a pine air freshener. A taped-up set of ski goggles blocked her sight, and noise-canceling headphones were playing an audio stream of white noise, like her grandparents' TV after midnight. Her hollow scream faintly echoed like she was in a small concrete room.

She was lying on a bed, her arms and legs bound tightly to its bare frame. She did not know where she was, but this had to be linked to Luc's death. Things went so fast at her home that she barely had time to get afraid, but in the quietness of this place, a deep sense of fear started to take control of her. *What the fuck had happened?*

Then, the white noise in her headset stopped, replaced by an electronically modified voice.

"Hello, Mrs. Starck. Sorry, I had to put you in such an uncomfortable position. I hope you are well."

"Who is this? What do you want?"

"Sorry, Mrs. Starck, but I cannot give you my name. For the time being, you can call me Mr. Satoshi. What do I want? Well, that's simple. I want my money back."

Gail recognized the name Satoshi as the first name of the mysterious inventor of Bitcoin. Of course, this couldn't be the famous Mr. Nakamoto.

"What money? Who are you?"

"The more you cooperate, the sooner I can take you home."

Gail remained silent to see what would come next.

A minute later, the voice continued.

"I can tell you this. Your husband has been playing games. He emptied several crypto wallets of *CryptoSwap* customers. For about six months, I've been in touch with him and given him ample time to return my coins, but the bastard refused to cooperate. Hopefully, with you in this delicate situation, he will become more responsive."

Gail was shocked. Did the man not know Luc was dead? Or was this just to confuse her? If so, it worked. She had no clue what was happening to her. She wondered how he would react if she told him Luc was dead. Would the man realize his mission was doomed, and would he kill her? She decided, for the moment, it was best not to mention Luc's death.

"I'm sorry, but I don't know what you're talking about. My husband never involved me in any of his business affairs."

"OK, I understand. However, I need your help. In a few seconds, you'll hear a beep on your headset. After the tone, please record a message to your husband explaining you are in the hands of a group named *CryptoJustice*. Tell him to read our demands on *www.CryptoJustice.org*. If he refuses, I'm afraid you may never see him again. You understand?"

"Yes. *CryptoJustice* on www.*CryptoJustice*.com…uh, sorry CryptoJustice.org."

"Okay, that's correct, here we go…."

After a few seconds, Gail heard the beep and began her message.

"Hello, Luc. I've been abducted from our house and don't know where I am. I'm taken by a group calling itself *CryptoJustice*. I understand you've been talking to them for a while, and it's related to *CryptoSwap*. You can find their demands on www.*CryptoJustice*.org. Once you honor their request, I will be released. If not, I am afraid something terrible may happen to me. Please, please, do whatever it takes to free me."

"Thank you," the electronic voice said.

Gail wondered how they planned to get this message to Luc. It was a wasted effort since Luc would never receive it. She suddenly realized that her decision to not mention Luc's death might put her in danger. How far would her perpetrators go to get what they were looking for? It was clear they were serious. What was next? She panicked; would they kill her? Was she shaking because of the temperature or was it fear of what was coming? Whatever was coming, it had to do with Luc. He had caused her enough pain while he was alive, but her resentment against him grew even bigger now the bastard was dead!

CHAPTER 15
WEDNESDAY, 23RD OCTOBER, 10:08 A.M.

Duan was about to have a call with a new client. He was contracted to run a security incident simulation for the company. He had to postpone the call the day before when he suddenly had to leave to see Gail.

Duan's office was structured and well-organized. Together with Mina, they'd shared a large office on the first floor of their house. On his desk, he had one standard laptop that he would use for office work and two high-power laptops used for heavy-duty encryption calculations. Mina's desk and her laptop have been left untouched since her death. Removing them felt odd.

When Duan started his own cyber security consultancy company, *AnyCrypt Inc.*, it was perfect timing. The demand for cybersecurity experts and services had exploded. Two years later, he hired Mina.

From the moment Mina joined his company, business started booming. Not only was she a skilled cyber expert, but she could also sell their business like nobody else. Any assignment she started was finished quickly and efficiently and would often result in a referral or repeat order. Mina was a born entrepreneur.

Mina's disappearance from the company made him realize how much he'd depended on her active involvement in day-to-day operations. They had anticipated the increasing business impact pressure, so as soon as Mina became ill, Duan stopped taking on new jobs. His priority became spending quality time together.

Only a few weeks after the funeral, he began accepting new contracts until things had returned to normal.

Normal? Fully back to normal, never. For the past nine years, Mina had taken care of things. Mina was his caretaker. Only now did he understand how much she had been running the show without him realizing it.

After his call, he started working through his emails. Suddenly, in the top right corner of his screen, a notification popped up. He had received a new message in his private email inbox. When he saw the sender, his breathing got stuck. The only word he could get out was, "huh?"

The mail he had received was from luc@hisdeath.com

He had no clue what was happening to him. He briefly wondered if he should call Gail so they could open it together, but didn't want to cause her more stress.

The subject read, *From Luc*. Short, but clear.

It had only three sentences.

The key is at the source.

P.S.
If anyone can figure it out, it will be you.

"What the fu—!"

Duan had no clue what this cryptic sentence meant. Was this possibly referring to the key to Luc's crypto wallet? It looked like some form of a riddle to be answered. As if he were being tested. He kept repeating the sentence, but the more he repeated the six words, the less sense it made.

Duan was aware of websites like *www.afteryourdeath.com*, which allow you to send customized emails to a list of personal contacts after your death. You had to check in regularly to let the system know you were still alive and well. If it did not receive your 'alive' signal according to an agreed-upon schedule, it would send prepared emails to a list of people you wanted to be notified. He guessed such a service had triggered the mail he just received.

He got himself another espresso. As he could not get that cryptic sentence out of his head, he decided to give it a try. If the words *The Key* meant the private key to Luc's crypto wallet, *The Source* could refer to the location of that key. What source could it be? He looked online for synonyms of the word source. But none of them rang a bell or made sense.

He wrote a few prompts to get his brain in gear:

Luc's birthplace.
Where Luc met Gail for the first time.
Where his company started.

He still had no leads. Maybe the commonsensical Gail could shed light on it. *The Key is at the source.*

He called her mobile number. No answer. He called her home number. Nobody was there either. He left a text message asking her to call him back ASAP. Gail was always fast.

"Wait…," he mumbled to himself. What if the key was not what he thought it was? What if this meant something different altogether? His encryption mind ran full speed. "Hang on…." He grabbed his computer and entered the riddle, receiving a list of one thousand anagrams of the sentence. From 'hate touchiest Yerkes' to 'AI retouch these tykes,' plenty of useless combinations.

He kept trying for almost an hour, but whatever combination he tried, none gave him any clue about Luc's private key.

To change his focus, he visited Luc's website, *www.cryptoluc.ch*, which he had built for Luc. He wondered if he should post anything on it about Luc's passing. Duan went to the *About Luc* page to at least add a sentence mentioning Luc's death and turn its background to black.

As it opened, he remembered some private keys he'd put on the server that hosted Luc's website so Luc could share encrypted files with others.

Duan connected with the website server, found the site's home folder, and opened the 'Keys' folder, where he had placed the private keys. In the folder, he suddenly noticed a folder named *_ForDuan* that he had not seen there before.

"Wow!" Could it be that 'The Source' referred to the server that hosted the website? Luc knew only Duan had access to this server, so it would be the safest place to leave confidential information.

Using his Unix programming skills, he changed the directory to the *_ForDuan* folder and listed all files in it. There was only one file. It was titled *ForDuan.txt*.

Duan's hands got sweaty. It was pure luck that he'd found the document so easily. He typed *type ForDuan.txt* to display the contents of the file and pressed *Enter*.

CHAPTER 16
WEDNESDAY, 23 OCTOBER, 10:42 A.M.

Duan had hoped that solving that first puzzle would have shown him a string of sixty-four characters that would make up the private key to Luc's crypto wallet. Unfortunately, that was not the case.

After he pressed *Enter*, another riddle appeared. It said:

De Witch: Train, my name and you're in the game.

Below that cryptic line, a link to a website was shown. It took him to *www.lucsprivatekey.ch*. The website that appeared was minimalistic. It was all blank and showed in the middle just a single input field. It was labeled *Enter Key here*. Underneath it was a *Submit* button.

Curious to know where he had landed, Duan entered some random numbers and pressed *Submit*. A spinning wheel appeared for a few seconds and next, a window popped up. It said: *0% correct*. He mumbled to himself, "I'm on track but still out in left field."

His first feeling was one of discouragement. How would he ever figure this out? Then he remembered what Luc had told him. "If there's one person who can figure it out, it will be you." Well, thank you, Mr. Starck.

Along with feeling mistrusted by Luc, Duan felt flattered that Luc had acknowledged his interest in cryptography.

Over time, Duan had come up with various personal methods to crack difficult codes. He closed his eyes and visualized absorbing the puzzle into his body, like Mina's body trips. Mentally, he spent five minutes studying the puzzle from all angles. If nothing came to him, he'd mentally take a step away and let the process continue in his subconscious. It could take hours or days, but an idea usually popped up that was likely to be the answer.

While Duan was deep in thought, his laptop pinged, announcing a new email. It was another one from Luc!

> *Dear Duan,*
>
> *When you receive this email, something terrible has happened to me. Congratulations on solving the first puzzle. Sorry, I cannot give you more direct instructions to access the private key to my crypto wallet, but I have got myself in trouble with dangerous people and cannot risk them getting hold of these emails. Please be very careful with those people. They are extremely dangerous.*
>
> *Best,*
> *Luc*

Luc had it all well planned.

Mentally, Duan returned to yesterday's conversation with Gail and that missing private key. He had to admit, the challenge of finding it intrigued him. Gail had been adamant about not wanting to have anything to do with 'Luc's fricking coins.' So why should he put effort into finding that key? If he found it, what would he do? These were not his coins.

The more he thought about it, the more he needed to talk to Gail. She should know about Luc's emails and the riddles. She ought to know. He called her again, but still no response. Then he tried her landline, but no answer there either. Something was wrong. Should he go to her house and check it out?

Restlessly, Duan paced through his house. From his study to the kitchen, sipping a fourth espresso, and back to his study to repeat the cycle five minutes later. Darn it. He missed Mina as his sparring partner at times like this.

The months before Mina's death had been so stressful that it felt like he was on autopilot. Recently, things got calmer, but in the past twenty-four hours it had all gotten messed up again. He obviously couldn't leave Gail by herself and had to help her get through this difficult period. Mina had usually taken the lead whenever things got hairy.

Thirty minutes later, he pulled into the parking area outside the Starcks' villa in Baar.

As he stopped in front of the house, he saw a woman waiting by the intercom as if she'd been ringing it. When Duan lowered his window, she said, "I think she's not here. I had an appointment with her."

He waited for a moment, assuming she would continue talking and explain who she was. When she didn't, he started.

"Nice meeting you. I'm Duan Ripa, a friend of the Starcks. It's odd that she isn't here, isn't it? I've also tried calling her all morning with no answer on her mobile or landline."

"Oh, I'm a friend of Gail's and was checking to see how she's doing after her husband's death." She reached out to shake hands.

Duan looked inquiringly at the woman. She noticed his surprised look.

"She told me she'd be home now. Any idea where she could be?"

"No clue," answered Duan, still wondering who this visitor might be. "I must admit, I'm kinda worried. She should be home."

The woman left, saying she'd call again in an hour. Duan waited for another twenty minutes. He tried the intercom several times while waiting and walked around the house. There was no sign of Gail, and he was getting worried. He decided to go to the police in Zug and report that Gail Starck was missing.

As soon as the woman was out of Duan's sight, she placed a call on her phone.

"Carl, Ilse here. As promised, I went to Mrs. Starck's house in Baar. She wasn't there.

"Are you sure?"

"Of course, I tried calling her and peeked into the house, but it looked like no one was home."

Carl sounded disappointed, fearing he missed the opportunity for a juicy story on the blog.

He did not give up and kept pushing. "You'd expect that right after her husband's death, it wouldn't be so difficult to find her. Please keep trying to contact her. Don't forget to try via her social media sites. If she doesn't answer over the next two hours, I say we should put an alert on the homepage, reporting we believe Gail Starck has gone missing."

Ilse heard the disappointment in his voice. "OK, will do, but I think I already may have a confirmation of her missing."

"How?" She heard hope coming back in Carl's voice.

"Well, for thirty minutes, I was waiting at the house, and two men came by who said they were worried they couldn't get hold of her. I got the names of these guys. The first one was named Roberto Giobbi, and the other one was named Duan Ripa."

"Great find, Ilse. I love how you never give up!" Carl responded. "As always, *blogchain.ch* beats the envious competition with breaking crypto news!"

In the world of blogging, it was all about being the first. Carl would never put any hot news on the back burner. Ten minutes later, *blogchain.ch* posted the scoop on its home page.

> *Gail Starck, wife of dead crypto entrepreneur missing?*
>
> *Blogchain.ch has received unconfirmed information that Gail Starck, wife of crypto entrepreneur Luc Starck, is missing. Starck was found dead yesterday in central Zug.*
>
> *Two of Gail Starck's close friends, Duan Ripa and Roberto Giobbi, CEO of Starck's company* BionTic, *expressed concerns about her sudden and unexplained disappearance. Is this the next chapter in the Luc Starck saga?*

CHAPTER 17
WEDNESDAY, 23 OCTOBER, 11:35 A.M.

Running down the stairs of the police station, trying to follow her rushing father, Lisa-Lotte's mobile phone rang. It was the front desk.

"Hello, Lisa-Lotte. A gentleman is here asking for the officer in charge of the Luc Starck investigation. I tried Bernt but couldn't get hold of him. Would you mind coming down?"

"Bernt is with me. We're on our way."

Downstairs, Lisa-Lotte and Bernt met the man who had been waiting for them. He was rather small, she guessed around five feet tall. His eyes revealed he was not one hundred percent Swiss. She guessed he had an Asian background.

"Hello, I'm Lisa-Lotte Berg, and this is my colleague Bernt." They shook hands.

"Nice meeting you. My name is Duan Ripa." Despite his non-Swiss appearance, he spoke Swiss German without accent.

Lisa-Lotte noticed the man looked surprised. People often assumed police inspectors to be older, overweight guys like her father. Not a blonde.

He started speaking without any delay. It was clear he was eager to tell them his story.

"I'm a friend of Luc and Gail Starck. You know the man who was found dead yesterday at the *Landsgemeindeplatz*. If I'm not mistaken, you are looking into his death."

"Indeed. Do you have relevant information for us?"

"Not about Luc Starck's death, but about his wife, Gail. I deeply suspect she has gone missing."

Lisa-Lotte raised her eyebrows and instinctively studied the man. His appearance seemed off; his eyes darted left and right, and he displayed fleeting micro-expressions that contradicted any signs of concern.

"Well, that would surprise me. We met her yesterday. How come you think she suddenly is missing?"

The man told them about his relationship with Gail and the fact he went to see her yesterday afternoon. He explained that for the past few hours, she had not returned any of his calls or messages.

"Well, there could be many reasons she did not react. Maybe the death of her husband became too much for her, and she needed time with herself. I suggest you give it another day. You'll see she'll show up again. There is no need for you to worry."

Mr. Ripa appeared to be shocked by her response and looked angry. With a raised voice, he said, "I think you're making a huge mistake, Miss Berg. You should take my concern seriously. I called Mr. Starck's company, BionTic, to ask if she was there. I learned the CEO also had an appointment this morning to meet Gail at her house, and she didn't show up. I'm worried about Gail's disappearance. This is not like Gail. Luc's death has brought us into close contact, and yesterday, I spent the full afternoon with her. She absolutely would have mentioned any plans to leave. Look what happened to Mr. Starck. And now his wife can't be found. It can't be a coincidence, can it?"

"Again, Mr. Ripa, I think we should give it another twenty-four hours. If you don't mind, we need to move." Lisa-Lotte was done with him. They were heading for an urgent meeting, and this guy was only delaying their work.

As she moved in the direction of the exit, pushing her father with her, she handed him her card with her contact details.

Bernt stepped in and said with a calm voice, "Mr. Ripa, I see you are getting agitated. Why don't you give it some time, and we'll speak later today?"

Lisa noticed how the man reacted confused about her dad's intervention. The guy hesitated for a moment but turned his attention back to her and continued, "You will regret this big time, and I will not accept your arrogant behavior. You are a bloody disgrace to the Zuger Police. You bloody…" It was obvious he realized that finishing his sentence could mean trouble, especially here in a police station.

Lisa-Lotte kept ignoring him, and while stepping out of the station, she could hear him stutter, "But… but…" The rest was inaudible as the heavy front door fell into its lock.

She looked at her father.

"Looks like Mr. Ripa is somewhat hot-tempered. I would not be surprised if we will hear more from him."

"Hang on." She saw her father stepping back into the station, to return one minute later.

"What did you do?"

Bernt looked at her with a serious face. "You can't leave that guy angry at the station. You never know what he is up to. I went in to apologize to him on your behalf and asked Rudy to talk to him. I also suggested Rudy to check Gail Starck's whereabouts."

She instantly felt belittled but realized her father was right in that she had been too harsh to the guy. Every day, she learned something from her father.

Finally, they could continue their way to the square. Lisa-Lotte could barely follow Bernt.

They had just left the station when she noticed the *blogchain.ch* alert, about Gail's possible missing. She showed it to her dad.

"Hmm, looks like Mr. Ripa indeed had a point. I will call him later."

Their first stop was at the police warehouse to go through Luc's belongings in search of clues.

Hans, the officer who had inspected Luc's possessions, welcomed them.

"Bernt, Lisa-Lotte, good timing for you to come here. We unlocked Luc's phone and are monitoring it for new messages. Look what we just received."

He showed them Luc's phone.

"What is it?"

"It's from his wife, Gail, and has an audio file attached. Listen to this." Hans played the message.

When the recording finished, they looked at each other, confused. Then he replayed the message.

"Very weird," Hans commented. "Mrs. Starck is in deep trouble since whoever is behind this is not aware that Mr. Starck has died. I'm sure they will soon find out. It is now front-page news."

Lisa-Lotte looked disturbed, realizing she had not taken Duan Ripa's report seriously.

"Did you visit that website www.cryptojustice.org?"

"Yes, I did. Here, look."

Hans showed her his laptop.

It was a very simple website with just a single string of text:

2,000 Bitcoins to be sent to
3J98t1WpEZ73CNmQvieavnyiWrnqRhWNLy

Below the text, a big countdown clock was counting down the seconds:

29 hours, 44 minutes, and 20 seconds.

Hans added, "Recently there has been intensive communications on Luc's *Telegram* channel with someone called *CryptoJustice*. These heated conversations had been about Luc's alleged involvement in the theft of Bitcoins at *CryptoSwap*."

"Thanks, Hans. Let our cyber forensics team look into this and see what we can find about who is behind that website."

Next, they reviewed the envelope that Luc Starck had in his inner pocket. After hearing Brucker's story, that message seemed even more significant.

"Someone would only write 'Clue One' if more clues are coming," Lisa-Lotte mused out loud.

"Or it may have been done to mislead us. Misdirection," Bernt argued. "Since it's the first clue, let's see if others pop up. As of now, we still haven't established a cause of death or motive, just a random set of questions. We have no other clues. Although? Maybe I have one. Let's go to the square. I need to check out something."

While walking to the square, the mystery of the Man with The Red Hat kept her busy.

"Do you believe that Brucker guy, Dad?"

"He sounded honest to me. I'm convinced he got dragged into this unwillingly."

"That story about him masturbating was really embarrassing. You'd better watch out next time you visit one of these sites." Lisa-Lotte grinned cheekily at her dad.

Her father had to laugh. Thank God the relationship with him was improving, so they were comfortable joking about such a touchy topic.

When her father separated from her mother, there were moments when their relationship was under much tension. She felt confused and no longer could give him full attention and care, afraid her mother would be affected.

Since they began working together, however, their interactions were becoming more productive every day. As if they'd been partners for years. They'd agreed to always do their thinking out loud. Her father had always been known as a strictly logical and analytical thinker. "I reason, therefore, I am." Hence, she followed his hunch to visit the square without any questions.

Five minutes later, Lisa-Lotte and Bernt were looking around the idyllic square again. She noticed her father doing his typical Hawk scan of the environment.

"Why did you want to get back so urgently, Dad?"

"I realized Brucker had been forced to meet Luc Starck and sit at a specific table on the terrace. Do you remember that drawing in his instructions? It specifically pointed to this location. I would like to have another look at that specific table."

As they approached the terrace, the table mentioned in Brucker's script was empty.

"Why not take a seat?" Bernt said with a wave of his hand. "I'll let the server know we have some follow-up questions."

Bernt ambled toward the server while Lisa-Lotte took a seat and looked around thoughtfully. "No clue what to look for," she mumbled. She felt under the table and looked through the plants on the low terrace wall. Nothing unusual.

Her father returned. "I ordered us each a cappuccino. They're delicious here."

"We're in luck. Our colleagues had asked the hotel not to remove the chairs and tables overnight."

"I've been looking around but don't know what we are looking for. This is a table and chair like all the others. I also checked out the plants here on the side but can't see anything there either."

Bernt also did another scan. He inspected the square in case there was anything suspicious in the buildings across the square.

"No. If they'd shot him, we would have found something. There were no bullet holes around here." Bernt was frowning in concentration.

"There has to be something. Brucker insisted he'd been told to meet Starck at this particular table. The drawing he'd received showed an arrow exactly to this chair. There must be a specific reason he wanted him to sit here. Let me check under the table again."

Bernt went on his knees. Lisa-Lotte looked embarrassed, hoping nobody would notice her dad on his hands and knees. Of course, the prime entertainment when sitting on a terrace is observing others, and Bernt's act got some discreet attention.

"Hmm, other than bubblegum, there's nothing down here to see." Bernt checked the bottom of the table, stood up, and even turned the table upside down to inspect its feet.

"Nope, nichts, nada," Bernt muttered.

"What next?" Again, that silence. Lisa-Lotte could hear him thinking.

"Please stand up." She stood up and Bernt took her chair and minutely felt and explored every inch.

Suddenly, he shouted, "Aya!!!"

Lisa-Lotte looked worried. "What happened?"

"There's something sharp here. Hang on, I feel something underneath the seat." He turned the chair over.

Everyone in the square was now focused on Bernt and his antics. "There you go!" Bernt beamed at her.

Bernt saw that underneath the seat, a small blue plastic box had been attached. He checked the other seat. No box.

"How the hell could our colleagues from forensics have missed this? I'll bet this is what we are looking for. No idea what this is, but I'm sure we will find out."

As Bernt turned the chair back over, he noticed something etched on the plastic box. It was barely visible. Only when he held it in the sunlight could he see something written on it.

"I'll be damned." Bernt raised his eyebrows at Lisa.

"What is it, Dad?"

"There's something written on the box!"

"Tell me!"

"Clue Two."

Lisa-Lotte frowned. This story got odder by the hour. She looked at her dad and noticed a weird look in his eyes.

"Dad, what's up?"

Bernt tried to talk but couldn't say anything. He crumpled slowly to the ground.

"Dad! Dad!" Lisa-Lotte kneeled beside him, applying CPR to fight her rising panic. She kept talking frantically. "Hang in there, Dad. This is Lisa-Lotte. Keep going. Help is on its way."

Within five minutes, the ambulance arrived. It took them a minute to get through the crowd growing from other tables and passersby. One medic checked Bernt's condition. When they noticed his blood pressure was dropping, they did not hesitate. They put him on the stretcher and pushed him into the ambulance. Lisa-Lotte joined him in the back and started praying.

CHAPTER 18
WEDNESDAY, 2 APRIL, 9:35 A.M.

Seven years earlier

The Berg family lived a quiet life in their apartment on the outskirts of Zug. Their children, Lisa-Lotte and Andi, were two years apart, with seventeen-year-old Andi being the older sibling. The two had extremely different personalities. Andi was extroverted, outgoing, and a bit of a thrill-seeker. Lisa-Lotte, a mirror image of her father Bernt, was modest and conflict-averse.

Although Andi shared much of his mother's adventurous spirit, he had been deeply influenced by his father since childhood. Every Wednesday afternoon, when school let out early, Andi would pick-up Bernt from the Zuger police station. The stories of ongoing investigations captivated him, and he would listen intently at the dinner table. From the age of five, Andi always had one dream: to follow in his father's footsteps and join the Zuger police force. Just last week, he received confirmation of his acceptance to the *Polizeischule Ostschweiz* in *Amriswil*, and he was counting the days until the program began that summer.

That weekend, a common debate unfolded at the breakfast table.
"Guys, the winter season is almost over. I wouldn't mind going skiing today," Hedwig said, glancing around the table to gauge interest. Predictably, the family was split; Hedwig and Andi were eager, while Bernt and Lisa-Lotte were hesitant.

Hedwig, twelve years younger than Bernt, had grown up skiing and often felt the call of the slopes. Bernt, on the other hand, wasn't an enthusiast.

Unlike many Swiss, he'd only taken up skiing later in life and preferred a relaxed pace. Still, he valued these outings as family time, knowing the kids would soon grow up and prefer to ski with friends.

"Okay, let's go," Bernt finally relented. "It may indeed be the last weekend."

Two hours later, the family stood at the top of the mountain, taking in the stunning view of the valley below, with Lake Zug faintly visible in the distance.

"Ready? Let's go!" Hedwig called out.

Once on the slopes, Bernt found himself enjoying the fresh air and physical activity. Andi, on his snowboard, took off immediately, performing a quick 360 on a small, steep hill. Hedwig chased after him while Bernt and Lisa-Lotte followed at a more measured pace. Gradually, mother and son disappeared from their view.

"You okay, Dad?" Lisa-Lotte asked, keeping a close eye on her father as they descended.

Five minutes later, the family regrouped at a fork where the slope split into two paths: a challenging black piste to the left and an easy green run to the right.

"We'll take the black!" Hedwig shouted, and she and Andi sped off, quickly gaining momentum and catching air on a ramp. From a distance, Lisa-Lotte could hear Andi's excited shouts.

Father and daughter chose the green path, moving at a relaxed pace. Part of the piste was flat, requiring them to ski-walk, but they knew this section well. After rounding a corner, the descent resumed, and they made their way to the lift station below.

"I don't see Mom and Andi," Lisa-Lotte said, scanning the area.

"Hmm, maybe they already went back up?" Bernt suggested.

The routine was always the same: ski down, split into pairs, and meet at the lift. Her mother and brother's absence felt unusual.

"Dad, I don't like this!" she said, grabbing his arm and pulling him close. "They're always here by now.

Bernt tried to reassure her. "Let's give them a few minutes. There are tight sections on that path—it wouldn't be the first time someone got held up."

His calm tone provided some relief, but just as he finished speaking, his phone rang with its familiar cow-moo ringtone. He answered, and even from a distance, Lisa-Lotte could hear her mother's panicked voice.

"Bernt, Bernt!" Hedwig cried.

"What's wrong, darling?" Bernt asked, his voice steady but concerned.

"It's Andi. Andi!" Her voice cracked with hysteria.

"What happened?" he asked urgently.

"Andi lost control on the tight section of the track… and fell off the mountain!"

Lisa-Lotte froze, her heart pounding in her chest as her mother's words cut through the air like a knife.

"How is he?" Bernt's tone had shifted, no longer calm but filled with fear.

"I don't know!" Hedwig sobbed. "It's so steep, and I can't see him. He's just… gone!"

The gravity of her mother's words sank in like a weight. Lisa-Lotte clutched her father's arm, her vision troubled with tears. In despair, she was looking at her dad. The winter world around her felt even more muted than normal, the vibrant white of the snow and the distant hum of the lifts replaced by a suffocating silence.

"We're coming up. Stay where you are."

Her imagination went into overdrive, filled with visions of Andi sprawled on jagged rocks far below, his snowboard twisted and broken. She turned toward her father, desperate for reassurance, but his expression—a mix of resolve and dread—offered none.

"Dad, please, we have to find him!" she pleaded.

Bernt didn't respond immediately. Instead, he grabbed her hand, gripping it tightly. "We will," he said firmly, though the tremor in his voice betrayed him.

As they rushed toward the lift, the cold mountain air stung Lisa-Lotte's face, but it was nothing compared to the icy fear clawing at her chest. Somewhere below, her brother was waiting—hurt, helpless, or worse—and the seconds stretched into an eternity. Just as the lift began to ascend, they caught sight of a ski ambulance speeding away from the station, a red rescue stretcher trailing behind it like a lifeline in the snow.

CHAPTER 19
WEDNESDAY, 23 OCTOBER, 3:24 P.M.

Bernt was in intensive care for three hours. Lisa-Lotte had been waiting the whole time in a family room, thanking a steady flow of police officers coming by to get news and gently express their concerns.

The waiting was unbearable. A series of doctors said her father was still unconscious and heavily medicated. They would have to wait for blood test results to know what had happened.

It was not the first time she had been sitting here. The last time was seven years ago when she and her parents spent long hours waiting for news about her brother Andi. After four hours, the specialist came walking in their direction through the long corridor. His body language did not promise any good news. His face and shoulders were down.

"I'm so sorry."

Her father grabbed both her and her mother with one of his arms. They stood there for some time. There were no tears left with any of them after they had shed so many over the past hours.

"The complications of his fall just were too much. We tried our best, but in the end, internal bleeding started again, and he died five minutes ago. I'm so sorry."

For Lisa-Lotte, the loss of her brother was a devastating emotional event, causing her to lose her feelings of safety and stability. However, it was the way her parents responded to the crisis that altered everything.

Her father, a usually stoic and emotionally distant man, became even more withdrawn and struggled to express his grief and failed to support his wife. He buried himself in work, avoiding any confrontation with the overwhelming sadness that had filled their home. In contrast, her mother, who always had been more expressive, showed a big need to mourn and often broke down in front of her. In lack of support from her husband, her mother now expected her daughter's shoulder to be there to cry on and was pressuring her to be strong. Her own sadness, combined with the opposing expectations from her parents, started to take a huge toll on her. For some period, she avoided being home.

As time passed, the cracks in the marriage of her parents grew deeper. She witnessed constant tension, heated arguments, and long silences between them. The couple couldn't communicate through their growing pain. Eventually, they separated, unable to repair the growing divide. Lisa-Lotte, devastated by the collapse of her family, became caught in the middle, torn between her parents' conflicting needs.

In the midst of this family turmoil, she found herself increasingly turning to her father. His quiet presence, though painful at times, felt right. Slowly, over time, she realized that her father's emotional distance was a shield he put up to survive the loss of Andi. He began to speak to her more openly, sharing moments of vulnerability, regret, and love. His presence gave her a sense of comfort, even if it couldn't replace the warmth of the family they had once been.

After her parents' divorce, Lisa-Lotte grew closer to her father. It became an unspoken connection, forged not only through their loss but also by their mutual determination to rebuild.

Was her decision inspired by love for Andi or respect for her father? Whatever the reason, the police academy felt like a natural path for Lisa-Lotte.

When she shared her decision with her father, he struggled to keep his emotions in check. The thought of the Berg name remaining active within the Zuger police force deeply moved him.

Her mother, however, reacted quite differently. On her way to a Maltese dog club meeting, she was far from impressed. Holding her white Maltese, Luna, in her arms, she frowned down at the dog, tugging at its meticulously coiffed hair with her bright red nails.

"One Lieutenant Columbo in the family is more than enough!" she declared sharply.

But Lisa-Lotte was resolute. Three years later, she graduated from the police academy cum laude and eagerly awaited the moment she would receive the white-and-blue chest emblem of the Zuger police.

While waiting in the quiet and comforting family room, Lisa-Lotte's thoughts turned to memories of her dad. Her earliest memories of him were when he took her hiking in the mountains, pushing her stroller. She mentally browsed photos of them together in the woods and during her first ski lessons, followed by hours of fun together on the slopes. She recalls playing board games and how she gradually learned to enjoy his classic jazz albums: Oscar Peterson, Coleman Hawkins, and Dave Brubeck. Yes, she was daddy's girl.

While getting herself another ristretto, hoping it would keep her awake, she continued to flip through memories of her father. Among all the good memories, one specific topic had always been a contentious one: her everlasting search for a perfect partner.

Introducing her first boyfriend came to mind. How would he react to seeing his daughter with another man? Her mother knew her daughter and husband well enough to reassure her. Bernt did not explicitly say anything but weighed the various pros and cons. His reactions to the youngsters were neutral, however, always ending with some remark about a minor defect with them. One ate with his elbows on the table, another didn't look at him when he was talking, and a third did not look in love with her. Always something.

The last one had unexpectedly been a hit. She'd met Anton in a bar and, after a few months, nervously introduced him to her parents.

The meeting started well but improved once the conversation with him switched to trains and trams. Her father's biggest passion. Anton turned out to be quite an expert. He knew all seventy-four railways in Switzerland by heart and knew details on types of trams and trains that even her father did not know. Her dad got visibly excited and even invited Anton to see his train collection in the attic.

"Poor guy," she said to her mom when her dad and Anton left the living room.

When Anton finally said goodnight, her father was singing Anton's praises. He was unlike any of the others. He had perfect manners. A definite keeper!

Soon after, she fell into an intense love affair with Anton and got married six months later. Once she and Anton started living together, it was obvious their relationship was not going to work. Their marriage didn't last long and ended eight months before her parents divorced. Afterward, she realized that she'd unconsciously been focused on finding someone as much as possible as her father. Oddly enough, shortly after her divorce, she read a study that reported significant facial correlations between a woman's long-term partner and her dad, especially around the nose and eye area. The theory was that girls form a 'mental map' of their father's appearance, which they seek in a spouse. The phenomenon even has a name, the Electra complex.

All these melancholic thoughts went through her mind while she was sitting in that waiting room, worried about her father's condition.

Finally, a nurse appeared. Her father was still unconscious, but she could visit him. Although she was asked to keep it short.

As she walked through the sterile, fluorescent-lit corridors of the hospital, her heart started pounding in her chest. Finally, she arrived at the door of the intensive care unit. When she saw him lying motionless, hooked up to a maze of machines and monitors, she started crying. He looked so helpless. As a reaction, she put her hand in front of her mouth and stood there for some minutes, staring at her motionless father. He was hooked up to a ventilator, his breathing labored and shallow.

Quietly, she stepped to his bed and reached out to take his hand. She was startled by the coldness of his skin. It was as if he was no longer there, lost in his unconsciousness. She whispered his name, hoping that he would stir, that he would hear her voice and wake up, but he remained still.

The beeping of the machines filled the room. It was a constant reminder of her father's fragile state. She looked at the numbers on the monitors, with her heart breaking as she saw his vital signs fluctuate. Her sadness was replaced by anger at how this could have happened, how the man she loved so much could suddenly be so helpless.

She tried to stay strong for her father, hoping that somehow her presence would bring him comfort.

"Hello, Dad, Lisa-Lotte here. I love you." She kissed him on the forehead.

She did not know if she was imagining it, but he appeared to show a gentle smile.

His condition was serious, and she was afraid of what the future would hold. She stayed by his side for several minutes, holding his hand and hoping for the moment that he would open his eyes and return to her.

The nurse entered.

"I think we should let your father rest."

Lisa-Lotte kissed her father once more on his forehead. "See you, Dad. Rest well and take care of yourself."

Outside the room, the nurse said, "Your father is still in very critical condition."

"Any results from the blood tests?" Lisa-Lotte asked.

"It makes little sense, but everything seems normal. We're doing additional tests to find out what exactly happened. We should know more tomorrow morning."

"Will he be okay?"

"We hope so. But we have one big concern."

Lisa-Lotte tried not to panic. "What's wrong?"

"During our initial tests, it appeared your father has no sensation in either leg. Your father's legs might be paralyzed."

"Oh, my God!" Her father is paralyzed? It could be no coincidence that within twenty-four hours, that chair killed a person and almost took a second one.

Thinking about her father lying crippled in his bed just before his retirement filled her with a mix of anger and revenge. But it's the determination to find whoever was responsible for this that dominated her mind.

CHAPTER 20
THURSDAY, 24TH OCTOBER, 7:15 A.M.

Waking up was difficult for Lisa-Lotte. It was two a.m. when she finally got home from the hospital. She set the alarm clock to be on time at the station in the morning.

She was struggling with the choice of going back to the hospital or to work. After she called the hospital and learned her father's situation was stable and they kept him asleep, she decided on the latter.

She pushed the daily briefing to eleven a.m. so she could get herself organized after the busy day yesterday.

While waking up, she wondered for a moment if she would be summoned to the office of Captain Tell Schmidt. Because of her dad's accident, she suddenly got emotionally involved in the ongoing investigation, so there was a chance her superiors would ask her to step away from the case. She was prepared for that discussion and was determined to stay on.

Lisa-Lotte was committed to learning who was behind this crime. Yes, in her mind, this was a crime. Although they lacked hard evidence, she was now convinced Luc Starck did not die a natural death. Someone was playing deadly games, and she wouldn't stop before closing this case.

Because of the hecticness the day before, she had not been able to follow the news, so only during her breakfast did she notice that local and national news outlets reported about her father's accident. The articles all quoted *blogchain.ch*. She went to the blog and found the article on its homepage.

Lead investigator in Luc Starck's case seriously injured.

> *Today, inspector Bernt Berg from Zuger police was seriously*
> *injured at the Landsgemeindeplatz. Berg has been taken to the*
> *hospital in Baar and is currently in intensive care. At this*
> *stage, it is unclear how this incident is related to Luc Starck's*
> *death two days ago, but it cannot be a coincidence that Berg got*
> *injured at the same location as Starck.*

She knew how these online publications were extremely unpleasant for the police. It gave the impression to the public eye they were holding back news. Her father often told her how his superiors became furious every time they read such an online news bulletin. It was fully understandable the public was eager to consume news as it happens, but crime-related news items were best released by responsible officials only at the right time. It put a major strain on their investigations when everything was happening from multiple angles, with no chance for the police to control the news stream to the public.

Walking on her way to work, she received a call.

"Hello, Lisa-Lotte. This is Josephine Bema from forensics. We have been working all night, and I have big news to share about what happened to your father. I'm still in the office. I know it is short notice, but can we meet at eight a.m.? I would like to have some sleep, so if we can meet now, I would appreciate that."

Lisa-Lotte checked the clock tower time. It showed 7:50 a.m.

She quickly called her colleague Rudy Kotkin and asked him to gather the team.

Just in time, she entered the police station and walked straight toward the situation room. The two walls reserved for evidence and lines of inquiry began filling up.

"Facts and evidence" included the timeline of Luc's death, the Brucker story, Clues One and Two, the chair, and Bernt's mysterious injury. They couldn't yet directly link his accident with Luc's suspicious demise, but there had to be a connection. That was it for the moment; not enough to develop any actionable theories.

The right wall with theories was practically empty. One document listed Gail Starck as having a motive because of Luc's violent behavior. Another one referred to the intense discussion on Luc's Telegram channel, with someone calling himself *CryptoJustice*. The theory was that Luc had been murdered by a victim of the *CryptoSwap* thefts. That was it.

At eight a.m. exactly, she wanted to start the meeting but had to wait. The news about her dad's accident devastated every police officer in Zug. It had galvanized the department. Groups of colleagues were chatting, and she could pick up parts of their conversation. "Can you imagine at such an unfortunate moment, just before his retirement and in the middle of the budding partnership with his Lisa-Lotte?"

When they noticed she was eavesdropping, their conversation stopped.

Finally, they all sat down, and she opened the session.

"Team, allow me to thank you for all the best wishes for my father. He is still in intensive care, and there are still many questions about his recovery. I will go back and see him this morning.

"Also, thanks for being available at short notice. I welcome Miss Bema, our head of forensics. She and her team have been working throughout the night and are eager to update us with their findings."

Josephine Bema, usually called Jos, was surprisingly young to be head of the regional forensics team. With her twenty-eight years, she had made a blitz career at the cantonal police. Her sharp focus, combined with an extremely mature management style, contributed to her success. Jos Bema stood up to address the group.

"Thanks, Lisa-Lotte. Yes, we've had a long night, but it was not in vain."

She had brought a small presentation to illustrate her talk. Lisa-Lotte recognized the picture on the first slide as the box her father had found underneath the chair on the terrace.

"My team has been working around the clock to investigate the modified chair that Detective Berg discovered yesterday. The box he had discovered contained a wireless receiver connected to a valve of a gas container."

Jos Bema pointed to various elements in the photo. The next slide zoomed in on the valve.

"This valve released the contents of a canister into a pipe mounted in the seat cushion. A small heater then vaporized the liquid in the container, causing the gas to be pushed into the seat."

"After many tests, we came to a shocking conclusion. The canister mounted underneath the chair contained an extremely deadly nerve agent called VX. It's an oily amber liquid that evaporates slowly to form a dangerous gas. Even a bit on your skin can kill instantly and is extremely painful."

She looked slowly around the now speechless group. Lisa-Lotte listened with her mouth open.

Then she continued.

"VX gas was created in the 1950s by the United Kingdom for warfare, but since then, the United Nations International Chemical Weapons Convention treaty has banned its use."

Lisa-Lotte put her hand on her mouth. She was shocked. She was no expert on the gas, but suddenly, his paralysis made full sense.

Jos Bema brought it with a sense of drama and paused to let the news sink in. Then she resumed.

"You may have heard that the brother of the North Korean president was assassinated at the Kuala Lumpur airport. That was done using VX gas. We're talking to Bernt's hospital, and based on what they found, we assume he must have been exposed to some residual droplets. One would assume most should have been vaporized, but it could well be that some of the oil leaked out as he turned over the chair."

Jos Bema looked at Lisa-Lotte. "The good news is that knowing your father was exposed to VX gas, the hospital has now started the appropriate treatment. His situation hopefully should improve soon."

As Lisa-Lotte listened to the explanation, her mind was spinning. This ingenious poisoning method opened several new avenues of inquiry. Who created this trap? Who swapped the chairs? If this was remote-controlled, who pressed the button?

Also, as nerve gas was typically a weapon of choice for foreign governmental powers to eliminate opponents, did this imply Luc Starck's murder was driven by political motives? This case could turn out to be way bigger than she'd imagined.

Finally, when Lisa-Lotte realized she'd been sitting on that chair, shivers went down her spine. It was a miracle the liquid had not poisoned her.

"Thanks, Jos, that's great progress. Please pass on my thanks to your full team for the extra hours they put in to come to this shocking conclusion."

"Guys, we need more developments like this. We've all seen the online press is on our backs, and we can't have them continue to beat us with news releases about this high-profile death in Zug. The sooner we solve this, the less embarrassing and disruptive these news breaks become for us. Of course, it's needless to stress that the news we just heard stays within these walls."

"Team, let's conclude this session. I'll see you all for our usual daily at eleven am. I have some urgent things to check and need to visit my dad."

CHAPTER 21
THURSDAY, 24 OCTOBER, 8:12 A.M.

Gail had completely lost track of time, and panic was beginning to set in as she struggled to make sense of her surroundings. The tight, uncomfortable goggles over her eyes cut her off from any sight, and the oppressive silence in the room made her feel like she was trapped in a vacuum. Every breath she took seemed to echo in her chest, and her skin was slick with sweat, her palms clammy against the cold surface she couldn't see.

When she briefly regained consciousness, a wave of anger washed over her. Was she even alive? The thought twisted in her stomach, and she couldn't stop herself from shouting, desperate for any sign that her senses were still functioning. The sound of her own voice startled her, but it was a small relief—proof that she hadn't completely disappeared into the void.

Being in this impossible situation, Gail couldn't help wondering how so many bad things happened in her life and why, over and over again, she'd allowed it to continue.

She'd endured Luc's violence for months and could not make it stop. He didn't deserve her loyalty and care. The unknown worried her the most. She preferred the discomfort of the present to the uncertainty of the future.

When the kidnapper violently grabbed her, her first thought had been, "Shit, not again!" Things had to change. As she had done so often, when Luc was in one of his rages, she activated her survival mode. It was about forcefully changing her mind, and accept she couldn't alter her current situation. The only thing she could control was the way she reacted to it. She had to prove to herself she stood above such cascading misfortune. It was like showing no fear of a dog. She should stop fearing the dog. In an attempt to cheer herself up a bit, she began silently singing, "Row, Row, Row Your boat. Life is but a dream."

While it helped her momentarily to deal with the emotional pain, the physical discomfort remained. There was not a single part of her body that was not annoying or hurting her. Her nose was itching, and however she tried, she could not get her fingers close enough to scratch it. Her wrists felt raw from being shackled to the bed, and her left leg fell asleep from lack of movement. Thirst and hunger dominated her mind; she had not eaten since she had woken up. Maybe good, as so far, she had not had the urge to go to the toilet and had no clue how she would handle that. The self-evident luxury of her villa in Baar was so far away.

She was still blindfolded and still wearing her headset. At least every few hours, they'd lower the volume, allowing her to sleep. During the many hours since she'd recorded the message for Luc, she'd been wondering if she should have told them he was dead.

Several times, she tried to get in touch with her kidnappers, with no luck.

"Hello, anyone there?"

No response. She kept repeating it. At least it gave her something to do.

Thinking about the message, she wondered if they had sent it to Luc's email.

"Hello, I need to tell you something!"

No response.

"Helllooooooo!" She lowered her voice this time, struggling to keep fear out of her voice.

Suddenly, she heard something on her headset. The noise stopped, and the same voice returned.

"Yes?" the man spoke calmly and gently.

"Finally! Where the hell were you? Listen, I need to tell you something." She tried to mask her fear with a voice of authority.

"What would that be?"

A man of few words and barely concealed malice.

"I'm sorry. I assume that the message you asked me to record for my husband did not get answered. Did you receive a response?"

"Why?"

"Well, I should have told you sooner, but my husband, the beloved Mr. Luc Starck, died two days ago. I assume you didn't know he was dead. Maybe you should have done a bit more research before you grabbed me."

Her captor remained silent for a long time. She assumed the voice was discussing what to do with someone else. It took five minutes.

"I hate to tell you this, but you've just wasted twenty-four of your dwindling hours. You should have told us sooner."

"Twenty-four hours? Shall I tell you something, mister mysterious? If you'd given me more information about what you're after, I could have been working with you. I can assure you it's no joy where I am now, so I'd be more helpful if you would let me. What the hell is this about?"

"If you tell us how to access your husband's crypto wallet, you'll be free in a minute. You are playing with fire, Mrs. Starck. I don't think you understand the dangerous position you are in."

"I'm sorry, but there's nothing I could do. I have no access to the private key for his wallet. My husband is dead, and I'm afraid there is little I can do. So, how about you let me go?"

Silence again. She assumed more discussions were taking place. This time, it took longer; she guessed ten minutes, but it felt like hours. Maybe they got confused by her new tactics.

"Hellllooo." Gail was again trying to get a response.

"OK. Listen," the voice finally said. "Let me repeat, your dearest spouse has stolen an enormous sum from us. The bastard ran away with my crypto coins. I don't know if you were aware of what he did and couldn't care less. I'm committed to getting my money back. Your hubby had thirty hours to return my Bitcoins. Because of your stupidity, you have only eight of those hours left. You'd better hurry! If he can no longer respond, who can we contact to get access to his wallet?"

Gail had to think. Of course, she had heard about Luc's *CryptoSwap* and its collapse. She knew Luc had received a lot of bad press and was even interrogated by the police, but she had no details.

She had to buy time.

"Listen, friend, I'm sorry, but I cannot help you with my husband's business, and I told you I have no access to his crypto wallet. Fuck, the bastard caused me enough problems while he was alive, and it gets even worse now that he's dead. I keep dealing with all his shit! Anyway, how do I know you're telling me the truth?"

From the anger in Gail's voice, it was clear she was furious. Luc had gotten her into this disastrous situation, and now she had to clean up his mess.

This time, the response came without delay.

"If you don't want to lose any more time, you'd be wise to believe us. Once our clock reaches zero, I'm afraid your time is also up."

Now Gail got worried. He sounded serious. What to do?

"Well, there's only one person who might know enough. That's my friend Duan Ripa."

While Duan had no access to the key, he was the only person who could help her resolve such a high-tech crisis. "How can we reach him?"

"I'd need my phone to tell you. I don't know his phone number or email address by heart."

Again, silence, more discussions.

"OK, after the beep, leave a message for this Ripa guy. Like the one you left for your husband. Mention you've been taken and are OK, but he only has eight hours to meet our demands. Tell him he can find instructions on *www.cryptojustice.org*. Ready?"

"Okay."

Gail left the message. Next, they asked her for the pin code for her phone. After that, the white noise started again.

She had to talk to them before they disappeared.

"Hey, you! How about a bathroom visit? Or maybe a bit of water or food. You had the indecency to kidnap me. You could at least take care of your guest."

The white noise in her ears stopped.

"Listen, Mrs. Starck, if I were you, I'd keep calm and not talk too much. You're worth nothing to us, and we wouldn't hesitate to silence you forever. Losing your life is nothing compared to the loss we incurred because of your husband. Do you get that? You stupid bitch!"

Instantly, she realized the seriousness of her situation.

"I said, do you get that?" He increased his volume and spoke with an even more intimidating voice.

"Yes, Sir."

CHAPTER 22
THURSDAY, 24 OCTOBER, 8:45 A.M.

After that shocking revelation during the morning briefing, all left the situation room, and Lisa-Lotte was sitting alone at the large meeting table. She got herself a cappuccino and had to process all the news Jos Bema, her colleague, and forensics had presented. She took a sugar cube, floated it on the frothed milk, and saw how it slowly sank into the coffee. Lost in thought, she stirred the milk. She felt like that sugar cube, slowly being sucked into this case. This case was as energizing as it was confusing.

She stood up and moved to the whiteboards. She grabbed a pile of sticky notes and started writing facts on them and stuck them on the left side: VX Gas, Box, Remote Control. Next, she moved to the right side, reserved for theories and questions.

Foreign involvement? The presence of VX gas confused her. That gas was a signature lethal substance of devilish regimes and not something you would find at the local Migros supermarket. If that were the case, this investigation would need higher forces and would be way beyond her pay scale.

Box? Someone should have placed that box under the chair *after* the hotel staff had placed the chairs on the terrace. Investigating that was well within her pay scale.

Standing alone in the empty room, Lisa-Lotte allowed her eyes to wander over the walls lined with boards—each one filled with notes, clues, and threads of the case. A sharp sensation of loneliness swept through her, unexpected and unsettling. Normally, she'd be brimming with self-confidence, certain of her ability to solve any case. But now, as she stood in the quiet room, her hands clenched into fists at her sides. A sinking feeling gripped her stomach. What if she wasn't up to this? What if she couldn't handle it? This was the first time she was facing a murder investigation without her father at her side, and his absence felt heavier than ever. She had always relied on his guidance and experience, but now, it was just her. And for the first time, she wasn't so sure she could do it alone.

She reflected on the importance of this moment. Detective Lisa-Lotte Berg is solving a crime by herself. Her father would be so proud!

There had been other memorable 'first' moments without him taking care of her. The first time that she went cycling, without her father's hand keeping her balanced. Her first time driving his car, with him sitting nervously next to her. The first time that she paid for his dinner, after getting her first salary. All memorable milestones in her memory she would always cherish.

While she was reminiscing, she did not notice how Rudy had quietly stepped in. Without making any noise, he had been observing her, and he slowly approached her, placing a fatherly arm on her shoulder.

"Rudy! I had not heard you!"

"What up Lisa-Lotte? I was looking at you standing there being lost in your thoughts."

"I miss my father and have no clue what to do."

"I fully understand Lisa-Lotte. I'm here to help you. What are your next thoughts about the case?" he prompted her.

"Thanks. I have been thinking, and I'm determined to find out how the chair that had almost killed him was booby-trapped. It would tell us a lot about the criminals behind this scheme."

With a grim smile, she thought of the innocent-looking chair as her 'smoking gun.'

"Someone had carefully placed it in that exact position on the terrace. Overnight, the chairs were removed, then put back the next morning loaded with poison before the breakfast crew arrived at around eight a.m. Did one of them swap it? I have to get this sorted out to get closer to the culprit."

"Go for it, girl. I'm sure you can do this. You owe it to your father!"

Lisa-Lotte went to visit the police surveillance team that had access to the downtown security cameras. They were housed in a small building close to the train station. She explained she was looking for footage from last Tuesday at around eleven a.m. With little effort, the video operator found a clip with the conversation between Luc and Brucker in the red Roger Federer cap and reviewed it frame by frame.

"OK, let's go over it again," she told the technician. Finally, she saw what the man with the RF cap had told them. The video matched his story exactly.

"Now, let's move back. The waiter told us they'd put the chairs back outside at 8 a.m."

The technician dragged the timeline from the video player back to 7:30. They noticed how the terrace was still empty. He fast-forwarded to 8:15 when the waiter began putting chairs around the tables in what appeared to be random order.

"Hmm, nothing yet," she murmured. "Keep going."

At around 9:20 a.m., a van pulled up by the square. Two men unloaded a small podium in pieces. They put everything on a hand trolley and moved it to a spot in front of the aviary.

"Hang on, this may be something." Lisa-Lotte tapped the technician on his shoulder. He slowed down the video.

The guys handling the trolley had stopped to catch one of the podium pieces that was about to drop off the cart. It happened near the table where Luc Starck would die a few hours later.

"Bingo!" Lisa-Lotte shouted excitedly, pointing at the screen.

One man had rushed to catch one podium piece that was threatening to slide off. At that moment, the other worker moved to the opposite side, grabbed a folded chair from under the podium pieces, and swapped it with the chair by the table. The switch took only a couple of seconds. She noted he had a slight limp when walking around the trolley.

They watched the rest of the video, focusing on the event company van. The scheduled event had been a prize ceremony, in which a lottery winner had been announced with a large confetti bomb. A decent group of people attended the event.

Lisa-Lotte typed in the name of the company van on her phone and googled it. *Zug Events* with a warehouse in an industrial park just outside Zug.

Twenty minutes later, Lisa-Lotte entered an industrial park just outside Zug.

She easily found *Zug Events* and pulled up in front of their office. It was a modern warehouse nested in between a local brewery named *Zug Hops* and a wholesale distribution of sex articles, appropriately named *Smooth Operator*.

Through the opened doors of the warehouse, she could see stacks of stage equipment, inflatable castles, lighting, and audio devices. In the warehouse, a burly man was coming out of what appeared to be his office.

She immediately recognized his limping walk. She held out her ID and introduced herself.

"Hello, my name is Detective Lisa-Lotte Berg from the Zuger Cantonal Police. I have a few questions to ask. Are you the owner?"

"Nice to meet you. I'm Heinz Minten. Yes, I'm the proud owner here. Are you planning an event for the police here in Zug? How can I help you?" He acted surprised but friendly.

"Mr. Minten, two days ago, you worked at an event on the *Landsgemeindeplatz*. Do you recall that?"

"Yes, of course, I was there."

Other than by his walk, Lisa-Lotte recognized Minten by his biceps. He obviously spent a lot of time at the gym.

"What was the job, if I may ask?"

"We were contracted to set up the award ceremony for a contest that had been promoted in the *Zuger Zeitung* newspaper. As part of the contract, I had to buy a half-page advertisement in the newspaper every day for a full week. That advertisement contained the rules of the contest. I was really surprised they wanted me to organize such an extensive ceremony because the contest was really very simple. Readers had to mail in their answers, and yesterday, we announced the contest winner with a confetti bomb."

"Who contracted you?"

"That's the weird thing, I never found out. It was an online order that I received three weeks ago, with a generous advance payment in full. We were asked to request a permit for the event from *Stadtverwaltung*, the local commune of Zug, and coordinate with a local magician who was contracted to perform a brief show. We did everything they requested. I was compensated very well."

"How did it go?"

"Perfect. Our instructions were to activate a confetti bomb at 11:03 a.m. exact, and things went like clockwork, if I may say so."

"You seem very pleased with the job," responded Lisa-Lotte, appealing to his ego.

"Yep, all went smoothly until someone on the square suffered a heart attack. It caused quite a disruption, and we finished late."

"Sir, we saw on one of the security videos that a person swapped one chair on the terrace of *Hotel Loewen Am See*. If I'm not mistaken, that person was you."

Minten didn't know how to respond.

After a second's hesitation, she asked him the obvious question.

"Why did you do that?"

Lowering his voice and bending toward her, he said confidentially, "I'm not supposed to tell anyone, but the magician has a so-called 'electric chair.' During the act, someone sitting on a chair jumps up as if he gets a shock, and the magician overreacts as if he is completely surprised. It's hilarious, and I've seen it several times. A special chair is used that, through a remote control, triggers a tiny pin to come out of the seat and makes a surprised audience member jump up. It's great fun. The magician thought it would be a nice touch to use a random chair from the audience and asked us to swap a certain chair among the tables with his prepared chair. That's what we did."

"Did he do the act?"

"No, the guy with the heart attack was sitting on the prepared chair, and when the police and an ambulance arrived, the magician did not dare tell them about that special chair. He was afraid his chair had gone off too early and caused the heart attack."

"Is that man a local magician?"

"Yes, his name is Peter Vogel."

"Mr. Minten, would you mind calling him and requesting him to join us here? I need to ask him some questions."

He grabbed his phone.

While Minten was calling, Lisa-Lotte wandered around the warehouse. She took her time to inspect the soap bubble machines, mist machines, and fake snow generators. It was clear one could call Minten for any type of atmosphere.

While waiting, she deliberated by herself if Minten was telling the truth; was he just being used, or was he the mastermind behind Luc Starck's murder? She was not yet sure, but so far, his story and reactions seemed genuine.

Fifteen minutes later, the magician arrived, looking distraught. She noticed white face paint behind his ears.

Vogel started with an apology.

"Sorry, I had to rush. I just finished a children's show at a local school. I perform magic for anyone aged three to one hundred and three. Just an hour ago, I was Pedro, the magical clown."

That explained the paint.

It wasn't surprising that he seemed so nervous. But he looked too young to be a professional magician with a small straw-colored goatee. He might have been an accountant.

"Mr. Vogel, my name is Lisa-Lotte Berg. I'm with the Zuger police and would like to ask you some questions."

"Go ahead."

"Mr. Minten here explained he contacted you to perform two days ago at the *Landsgemeindeplatz*."

"That's correct."

Lisa-Lotte started to whisper, imitating Minten, "I know about your secret electric chair that you had Mr. Minten swap."

Vogel reacted with an embarrassing smile.

"Can you explain to me how you were contracted for this show?"

"Online through my website. They'd seen my act with the chair and asked if I could do it with a chair from the terrace at *Hotel Loewen Am See*. I was paid upfront and asked to contact Mr. Minten about swapping the chair. They even provided me with a similar chair as on the terrace."

"Mr. Vogel, as you know, someone died on that chair. It seems your chair was used by someone to murder Mr. Starck."

The magician's mouth fell open, and he stammered, "Uh, I'm very sorry to hear that. Believe me, I only did what I was paid to do. My job. I'm hired to entertain people, not to kill them. I've done this act many times without a fatal accident. It cannot be that my trick killed that poor man. Couldn't he have had a heart attack while sitting in my chair?"

Lisa-Lotte ignored his panicky questions.

"Mr. Vogel, where do you store your equipment?"

"In my garage."

"Can anyone but you gain access?"

"No, it's securely locked, and I have a sophisticated alarm installation."

"Do you have video surveillance?"

"Yes, after I had all my equipment stolen twice, I installed a state-of-the-art security system."

"Would you mind checking your video surveillance to see if anyone accessed your garage just before the event?"

"Of course not. I have remote access via my phone and can check the recordings right now." It didn't take him long to discover a surprise in the replay. It was in a video from the day before the show.

"Holy shit. Look at this." He showed his phone to Lisa-Lotte. "The night before, someone had jimmied the door."

It was difficult to identify the intruder since the head and face were covered by a hoodie. He also wore gloves. A brilliant criminal who knew he'd be videotaped.

He had brought something that resembled a folded chair. After a bit of fiddling with the garage door lock, it opened. He stepped into the garage and came out a few minutes later with a chair under his arm. It was clear he had switched the chairs.

Vogel was baffled.

"Holy moly! The alarm should have gone off when he entered the garage. I paid a fortune for that system!"

Lisa-Lotte looked pensively at them.

"Gentlemen, I've seen enough for now. Please remain available in case we have any follow-up questions."

CHAPTER 23
THURSDAY, 24 OCTOBER, 8:55 A.M.

A beeping notification on his phone woke up Duan. Half asleep, he grabbed it and saw he had a new message. When he saw it was from Gail, he sat upright in his bed. Finally, news!

He listened to a similar voice message from Gail that Lisa-Lotte had been played the day before.

"What the fuck!"

Poor Gail. First, she gets beaten up by her husband. Next, he dies, and now *she*'s suffering even more because of him. "Does it never stop for her?" he muttered as he climbed out of bed.

He clicked on the link: *www.CryptoJustice.org.*

2,000 Bitcoins to be sent to
3J98t1WpEZ73CNmQvieavnyiWrnqRhWNLy.

The countdown clock showed:

7 hours, 34 minutes, and 32 seconds remaining.

He'd better keep an eye on this timer.

He debated whether he should call that police girl, Lisa-Lotte Berg, to inform her about the message he'd received. She hadn't impressed him, seemed to have no time, and walked out of the door while he was still talking. Also, he was embarrassed he had lost his temper with her and her colleague. His anger management remained an issue. He knew. Thank God the older inspector returned and helped him out. He wondered how they could let such a young girl handle such an important case.

That police girl was completely wrong to think that Gail just needed time and decided to have a break. The twenty-four hours she suggested he should wait were almost over, so he called her.

She picked up immediately. "Lisa-Lotte Berg." By the sound of it, she appeared to be in her car.

"Miss Berg, Duan Ripa here. You remember we spoke yesterday morning about the disappearance of Gail Starck, and you told me to wait?"

"Yes. Mr. Ripa, my apologies for being that brief to you yesterday. Tell me how I can help you."

"The twenty-four hours you suggested I should wait have passed. On top of that, I just received a voice message from Gail. It mentions she is kidnapped, and they ask for two thousand Bitcoins for her release. I told you! I knew something was wrong! You've lost valuable time trying to find her." This time, he made a serious attempt to manage the anger he felt coming up.

"That's interesting. I'm currently out, but is it okay if I call you later and we meet at the station?"

"Perfect."

While she was nicer, the conversation with that police girl still left him with a nasty taste in his mouth. Again, she showed no sense of urgency. Ridiculous! He could not just wait but had to do something.

Hours were literally ticking away, and he had no idea whom he was dealing with or the best way to find them. If the countdown timer reached zero and something happened to Gail, he'd never forgive himself.

He had to think about his next move and reread the message on his screen that appeared when he clicked on *www.CryptoJustice.org*.

2,000 Bitcoins to be sent…

It was frustrating to realize Luc's crypto wallet contained over 8,000 Bitcoins. More than enough to free Gail. Although she told him emphatically to not care about the private key to Luc's wallet, getting hold of that key seemed to be his only option to free her. He had to find that key—and fast.

What was the last riddle? Having figured out the first one, he felt confident as he refreshed his memory.

De Witch: Train, my name and you're in the game.

Knowing he had only seven hours to find her was added pressure he could have done without. Not a second to lose!

Luc had written, "If anyone can solve this, it's you." Luc had known about Duan's lifelong interest in riddles. His professional pursuits linked to his cryptography interest made riddles and lateral thinking endlessly fascinating. Some people were addicted to crossword puzzles or Sudoku. Duan could spend days mulling over a few simple words, searching for a cleverly hidden solution.

Riddles had always fascinated humanity. It was one of the oldest forms of entertainment. In recent years, they'd begun appearing everywhere. From around 4,000 BC in caves, in the Bible, presented teasingly by the famous Zodiac Killer, J. R. R. Tolkien novels, *Alice in Wonderland* and Shakespeare, all featured riddles.

Duan's first encounter with riddles was when his father introduced him to traditional Chinese word puzzles that the public still finds intriguing today. When he was about five, his father tested him with one that went like this:

Washing makes it more and more dirty; it's cleaner without washing.

His father insisted young Duan find the answer without help. For days, Duan puzzled over that line. Finally, one day, it came to him. The answer was 'Water.' Water got dirty when you washed something in it.

His father was so proud of young Duan.

However, this riddle was different and had much more at stake. He'd need his years of practice and study to unravel this puzzle. It was his ultimate test. He had to pass to save Gail.

Duan relied on a method he'd used frequently to crack complex encryption problems. He filled his bathtub with steaming hot water. Relaxing in a warm bath had several times proved to be an excellent 'brain opener.'

The bath was full. He stepped in and carefully submerged himself until his ears were just under the waterline. Duan, with his eyes closed, was now in his own world.

De Witch: Train, my name and you're in the game.

He free-associated with the sentence and meditated on every word.

The first word, *De?* What could that refer to? He raised himself out of the water, grabbed his phone, and started searching for the meaning of *De.*

One hit came back. *De* is slang and is used by teenagers and those under the age of thirteen. It meant *The*.

Like a submarine, he slowly lowered himself again.

Ok, next one, *Witch*.

The semicolon after *Witch* jumped out at him. Why was that there?

Next, he noticed the capital *T* of *Train*. What was its significance?

My Name must refer to Luc Starck.

You're in the game could hint that the preceding words were important clues.

He further lowered his body until he was fully immersed. His concentration was now total. He was completely in his world, communicating easily with all four rational and visceral minds.

The Witch? He dove into all the witches he knew. Griselda, Cruella de Vil from *101 Dalmatians*, Glinda the Good Witch from *The Wizard of Oz*, Hermione from *Harry Potter*, *The Blair Witch*. No shortage of witches, but the more witch names he found, the more confusing it became. "Okay, let's move on to the next word."

"Train…. Train…," Suddenly, he had no clue why or how, but the word *Train* morphed in his mind into its German translation, Zug.

Hang on, what if the word *Train* was referring to *Zug*? His brain was now working full throttle. Wait, I've got it. *De* isn't *The*. *De* could be *DE*, the international abbreviation for Germany, pointing to *Train* as *Zug*.

Not that it seemed to help him get the private key.

Hmmm. If *Train* was translated into German, what if he also changed *Witch* into German? He sat up again and took his phone into his soapy hands to check the translator.

Although he spoke German, the excitement of the moment made him doubt all his suppositions. He had to be one hundred percent sure. He hurriedly translated *Witch*. His damp fingers flew over the keyboard.

Just as he'd suspected, *Witch* was *Hexe* in German. When he read it, something clicked. Now he was getting somewhere! It felt like he'd been untangling a messed-up ball of wool. Once you start unraveling it, the process suddenly gains serious momentum. *Hexe*….

Hexe could only refer to 'Hex,' short for hexadecimal. Hexadecimal is a coding system used within computer systems but is also used as a notation for private keys. Humans are used to counting in groups of ten, from zero to nine, but computers count in groups of sixteen, from zero to 'F.' After the nine, computers continue A, B, C, D, E till F.

This started to make sense. Private keys comprise sixty-four hexadecimal values: a mix of zeroes till nines and A's till F's.

Fuck! That's it!

Duan jumped out of his bath, still wet, and ran into his office. Standing behind his computer, he clicked the link he'd found on Luc's website, which took him to the screen with the entry field. If his theory was correct, the hex values of the solution of this riddle should make up the private key.

Zug and my name. Zug and Luc Starck.

Duan knew that every letter in the alphabet had a hex value.

Online, he found a table that showed numbers and letters with their corresponding hexadecimal values. He noted that the hex values for upper- and lowercase letters were different and guessed he'd best use the standard notation in which only the first letters of the First and Last names would be in uppercase.

He grabbed a piece of paper and converted *Zug* into hex values. Uppercase *Z* had a value of 5A, lowercase *u* was 75, and *g* translated to 67. To easily read hexadecimal numbers, you group them four by four. He noted 5A75 67. Next, letter by letter, he transcribed *Luc Starck*; 4C75 6353 7461 7263 6B.

He counted the total number of hexadecimal values he had found so far. It only gave him twenty-four hexadecimal values. He needed sixty-four, so he still lacked forty.

He went to the site *www.lucsprivatekey.ch* and typed the hex value for Zug in the input field – 5A7567. He filled the rest with zeros and pressed *Submit*. In less than a second, it showed the result.

0% correct.

"Pfffft."

Of course, the values for *Zug* didn't have to be at the beginning. The excitement slowly seeped out of him. This could take ages. He tried various combinations. *Zug*, all in uppercase, nothing. All in lowercase, also nothing.

"Hang on, let me try something else," he mumbled to himself.

How about if I enter the zip code of Zug, 6300?

He checked the table, translated 6300, entered the hex values into the field, and added the rest with zeros. After he pressed *Submit*, it took longer to get an answer. It felt like ages.

Suddenly, a box popped up.

First 12.5% correct! Well done!

"Bingo!!!!"

He was getting somewhere. Twelve and a half percent made more sense. The hex values for 6300 were eight characters out of the sixty-four he required! He noticed it said the *first* twelve and a half percent were correct, so indeed meant the first four digits were correct. 6300 it was.

"OK, now let's add *Luc Starck* in hex values. Duan cleared the field, entered *6300LucStarck* in hex values, and filled the rest with zeros. He pressed *Submit*.

First 12.5% correct! Well done!

"I'll be damned! Nothing changed. *Not* well done!"

He returned to the riddle. *Train, my name*. He took a seat and kept talking to himself to stimulate his thinking.

"If I translate this character per character, I get *6300, Luc Starck*. What if I include the hex value of the comma and the space after 6300?"

He moved back to the hex table and decoded it.

He entered 3633 3030 2C20 4C75 6320 5374 6172 636B with the rest as zeros. It took ages to show him the results.

First 50% correct! Keep going!

"Dang!"

Duan felt proud, but he was still missing thirty-two hexadecimal numbers.

Suddenly, it felt chilly; he realized he was still sitting damp at his desk, only partially covered by a towel. He stood up to get something to wear when suddenly the website page changed.

A blank page displaying only a single button popped up. It said:

Continue here

Duan felt like he'd been transported into Wonderland.

He was expecting another riddle when he pressed the button on the screen, but what slowly appeared on his computer surprised him so much. The towel slipped down from his lower half and fell on the floor.

CHAPTER 24
THURSDAY, 24 OCTOBER, 10:10 A.M.

After visiting Minten, Lisa-Lotte was in her car when she received a call from the hospital.

"Miss Berg, Raj Vardhan here. I'm the specialist looking after your father. As you may have heard, he has been exposed to VX gas. Since we know that, we have been able to adjust our treatment, and he is doing better. I'm glad to tell you he is recovering."

"What a relief, thank God! Any news about his legs?"

"No, we can only do further testing once he can leave his bed."

"I'm nearby. Is it okay if I give him a quick visit?"

"Of course."

Fifteen minutes later, when she stepped into his room, she was immediately struck by the noticeable improvements since she had left him the night before. Her heart warmed as she saw him manage a faint smile when he noticed her.

She quickly moved to his side, sitting gently on the bed, and pulled him into a soft hug. She held his hand tightly, her voice full of concern as she spoke.

"I'm so glad to see you're doing better," she said, her eyes filled with tenderness.

"Yes," he responded quietly, his voice still weak.

"My blood pressure is back to normal, but the doctor said my long-term prognosis is still uncertain. He said I've been really lucky that the gas had lost most of its potency before I came into contact with it. He seems hopeful that I'm on a slow but steady road to recovery."

She squeezed his hand, her expression softening with worry. "How are your legs? Are you in pain?"

"I still have no sensation whatsoever in them."

Her instinctual reaction was to freak out, but she kept it inside. She did not want her dad to feel any worse than he already was.

"I heard they will do some further tests once you are fully mobile."

Her dad smiled.

"Sorry it took so long to come and visit. I've been running around like crazy."

She told him about the VX gas update by Jos Bema, the discovery of the swapped chair, and her visit to Minten.

Despite his state, Lisa-Lotte could see her father listening closely. When she finished her update, her father was quiet, and she could see him thinking. While his legs might not function, his brain seemed to be in good shape. Suddenly, he started.

"I'd try to find out who controlled that seat. Someone must have pressed a remote control to activate the chair. Find that person, and you may be close to the killer."

"Thanks, Dad." It was amazing to see he kept thinking with her about the case.

"Any news about Gail Starck? Is she still gone?"

She was amazed he remembered her disappearance.

"Yes, Rudy has been looking into this. I'll meet him later this morning."

"Her disappearance is weird. You better keep an eye on it."

"You remember that guy Duan Ripa? He lost his shit when I did not want to drop everything immediately to search for Gail Starck."

Her father nodded.

"I'll talk to him later today. He acted weird. I need to better understand how he fits into all of this."

She hugged her father tightly, the warmth of the embrace comforting her. She missed working alongside him on cases like this. For so long, it had always been Bernt in charge, with her following his lead. But things were different now. She could feel the weight of the spotlight shifting, slowly moving in her direction.

Bernt looked at Lisa-Lotte, his gaze steady but full of quiet pride. He leaned in and whispered, his voice low but reassuring.

"You've got this. This case is already one of a kind, but I know you're the one who can crack it. Make me proud, and show the world what a Berg can do."

Lisa-Lotte's heart swelled with determination. She smiled, her energy returning in full force. With confidence, she practically skipped out of the hospital room, ready to face the challenge ahead.

CHAPTER 25

THURSDAY, 24 OCTOBER, 10:35 A.M.

Standing in front of his desk, with the towel at his feet, Duan pressed *Continue here* on the screen. An image of Luc Starck looking into the camera with a big smile popped up. It was odd to be looking into that emotion-ridden face so soon after his death. Below Luc's face was another cryptic message:

The rest of the key is behind what you see!

Duan tried to remember where he'd seen that photo before. He googled *Luc Starck* and was shown a series of photos spanning several years that traced one man's quick trajectory from promise to failure. In one, Luc was sitting at his desk in a long-forgotten office setting. Some kind of holiday party was going on behind him, but he looked at the camera with an impatient glance. He seemed unhappy about having his work interrupted but might have just put down the glass of amber refreshment by his elbow.

A second was taken at the grand opening of his first business. He was basking in the attention of coworkers and supporters but seemed ill at ease, as if concerned about being found out as a failure.

In the third snapshot, Gail's shoulder and hair could be seen turning away from Luc during what might have been a disagreement during a party. Luc waved a glass at her in a not-entirely friendly gesture.

And finally, there was the picture he'd been staring at a few moments earlier. He clicked on it and landed on the corporate website of BionTic's

About Us page. It identified Luc as co-founder, alongside other leadership team members.

> *Luc Starck is a leading blockchain entrepreneur, boasting a string of successful start-ups. Mr. Starck received his Master's degree in Economics at the Swiss-Italian University (USI) in Lugano. Building on his seed investment,* BionTic *has rapidly grown into a leading supplier of self-controlled DNA registration powered by blockchain technology.*

Duan chuckled when he read the reference to successful start-ups. Indeed, *CryptoSwap* might have started successfully but had quickly become ensnared in politics.

As he stared at Luc's photo, the sentence *The rest of the key is behind what you see* kept echoing in his head. The riddle started with *The rest of the key.* Does it imply this is the last part of the puzzle? This thought energized him, although he had no clue where to start unraveling it.

He double-clicked the photo in the hope the rest of the private key would show up. Nothing happened.

Duan suddenly realized he was still naked and shivered. Time to get dressed!

He checked the timer on his watch: six hours to miss the kidnappers' ultimatum. Six hours to find that private key. He had made solid progress, but there was no guarantee he could keep up his pace and complete the job before the deadline.

While getting dressed, Duan realized he had no idea what to do once he finally had access to Luc's wallet. Should he just transfer the requested 2,000 Bitcoins and wait? How could he send that much money without guarantees that Gail would be released? He had to get in touch with the kidnappers to find out.

As he thought about what to do next, Duan had a promising idea. He grabbed his laptop and began typing an email to Gail's email address.

For Gail Starck's hostage-takers:

Hello, I received your message. We need to talk. I'm ready to pay you the 2,000 Bitcoins, but I require strong guarantees that Gail Starck will be freed. Find my instructions attached.

Duan Ripa

Before sending it, he attached to the email a file named *2000Bitcoins.pdf*.

Tapping into his cybersecurity background, Duan embedded in the file a virus. It would secretly install itself on the device that was used to open the document. He'd used such malware repeatedly with his corporate customers.

He was frequently contracted to organize employee security awareness campaigns to monitor how cautious staff was when opening emails from unknown senders. Hackers hoping to access a target enterprise's computer system could bombard the employees of that company with phishing emails. If even a single employee opened a malicious attachment, hackers could get into the corporate network.

During his last assignment for a company in Zurich, he'd sent out an email purportedly written by the CEO of the company. Its subject line was 'Congratulations!', and its content was an announcement. In the last quarter, business had been so good, the board had decided to offer all staff members a one-month bonus. The attachment contained instructions on how to register for the bonus. Duan had hidden in the attachment the same malware he'd just used. Every staff member, including those in the company's cyber security department, had opened the attachment to register for the bonus. Despite all the news stories warning about hackers, people are so gullible.

Duan's malware would record the device's GPS location, take a photo, and send both to Duan's secure servers. Every time his server received a message from the virus, he'd automatically be alerted.

Duan pressed *Send*. Let the game of cat and mouse begin!

CHAPTER 26
THURSDAY, 24 OCTOBER, 11:00 A.M.

At the Zuger police headquarters' main conference room, Lisa-Lotte's expanding team gathered for its daily stand-up meeting to review the latest news and confirm the day's assignments. Without her father at her side, Lisa-Lotte felt a bit of a loss but was happily surprised at how efficiently she was able to lead the meeting. Her self-confidence was growing by the hour.

"I was just with my father and am pleased to report that he's recovering. He asked me to pass on his best regards and heartfelt thanks for your support."

The group acknowledged her appreciation by tapping on the table. Bernt was a highly appreciated member who was dearly missed. It was a sign of encouragement by all in the room toward Lisa-Lotte.

Near the end of the meeting, she saw Schmidt stepping into the room. He stood in the back and stared at her. His presence made her nervous. He would never normally step in like that. Hastily, she finished the session and stepped to Schmidt. It was clear he came to see her.

"Lisa-Lotte, do you have a minute and join me in my office?"

Walking behind him to his office, she wondered what he had to tell her.

When they stepped into his office, she noticed Rudy already sitting there. Schmidt closed the door.

"Lisa-Lotte, while you have my full support, I worry about the magnitude of this case and your ability to handle its complexity.

"Luc Starck's death has the full attention of Mayor Muller. I see online media are on top of it, and we are under pressure to bring this to resolution.

We cannot afford any mistakes. With your father unavailable for the coming period, we are exposed.

"I thought about it and have asked Rudy Kotkin to be your partner and lead the rest of the investigations. Rudy brings years of experience, knows you well, and is your best man to bring this to a conclusion."

Lisa-Lotte received Schmidt's message with mixed feelings. She was in charge and started to get a good grip on the investigations, and then it was taken away from her. She took this as a sign of mistrust. As a young and ambitious detective, she had hoped this case would offer her the opportunity to prove her skills. At the same time, she indeed felt the pressure was rising, and she could not afford any missteps.

Schmidt saw her inner struggles with his message. "Please do not take this as a bad thing, Lisa-Lotte. This case offers you a unique opportunity. See it as a Master Class in police investigations. Resolve this case and you'll have a bright future ahead."

"But…." Her millennial mindset was still struggling. Struggling with the authority Schmidt displayed and struggling with the empowerment that was ripped away from her. She could not finish her sentence.

"Okay, if you think that's the best, I'll do so." She needed some time to absorb this message.

"Thanks. Now you are here, would you mind updating me on the latest?"

Lisa-Lotte sat back in her chair and looked at Rudy. "Go ahead, you're in charge." The anger in her voice was obvious.

Rudy looked confused but started.

"After the shocking forensics message of this morning, it is clear we are dealing with a crime. We have expanded the team."

"This morning, Lisa-Lotte discovered how the chair that killed Luc Starck got swapped and traced this back to an event company and a magician. Why don't you give Schmidt your report, Lisa-Lotte?"

She was pleased with how Rudy gave her credit and the opportunity to explain her discoveries.

Tell Schmidt listened with full attention.

"Well done, Lisa-Lotte. I love the tenacity you showed to get to the bottom of that chair. I rarely wish to get myself too much involved in ongoing cases, but I think you should put effort into finding out who pressed that remote control."

"Funny you say that. My father said the same."

"You see. Great minds think alike."

"Anything else?" Schmidt looked at both.

Lisa-Lotte responded.

"We investigated Mr. Starck's company *CryptoSwap*. Its bankruptcy got lots of news coverage. The District Attorney interviewed Mr. Starck three times, but no wrongdoing was ever proven. We received at least twenty-three complaints, a few of them threatening. We are tracing each of these complainants to see where they were on the day of Mr. Starck's murder. These complaints point us to the most obvious explanation of Mr. Starck's death."

"OK." Schmidt showed his non-verbal appreciation.

Rudy now took over. They started to act like a couple.

"Oh, and something else. Patrick went to visit BionTic, Luc Starck's company in the Crypto Valley Labs. He met their CEO, Mr. Roberto Giobbi. He said Luc Starck had been very stressed and unusually agitated lately, though Patrick found Giobbi to be very nervous himself."

"Also, we've asked our research team to review BionTic*'s* financials in case they might suggest a motive. As you know, many business relationships can quickly escalate with unexpected and sometimes violent results. I hope to hear more from them later today."

Lisa-Lotte took over again. "To make things even more complex, yesterday we learned that Starck's widow has been kidnapped and is still missing. A confusing message from her kidnappers was sent to Mr. Starck's email, which gave us the impression that the hostage-takers didn't know Mr. Starck was already dead. One theory we are exploring is if Gail Starck could have fled and is faking her kidnapping."

"Somehow, these two cases must be linked."

Rudy took over.

"I have been looking into her disappearance, but so far, there's not much to report. Our efforts focused on geo-locating the phone that was used to send us her messages. It appears it was not connected to the mobile network, but to a Wi-Fi network while using a VPN to hide its local IP address."

Lisa-Lotte added, "We are dealing with smart people her."

Rudy Kotkin raised his coffee mug.

"Oh yes. One more thing. I found out Luc Starck fought a few weeks ago in a downtown bar called *Whiskey-à gogo*."

Schmidt was pleased. It was clear this case had many loose ends.

"Nice find, Rudy. Suggest you and Lisa-Lotte visit that bar. Let me know what you learn."

CHAPTER 27
THURSDAY, 24 OCTOBER, 12:03 P.M.

The Crypto Valley Labs building was behind the Zug railway station. Duan remembered how the first time he visited the building, he'd been so disappointed by its appearance. It was nothing like what he'd expected. He had visualized a futuristic-looking complex. Instead, he found a boring structure that could have been any government office.

Although the exterior was not impressive, inside the Crypto Valley Labs, exciting things were happening. Its coworking space accommodated over 130 of the world's leading blockchain projects. It was the beating heart of the Crypto Valley, which stretched from Zug to Liechtenstein.

He stepped into the reception lobby.

The first thing he noticed was the Bitcoin ATM next to the reception desk. It was one of the few ATMs globally where you could exchange Bitcoins and other crypto coins for cash.

Duan was visiting BionTic following a hunch. When he'd clicked on Luc's photo and was taken to their corporate website, he felt that the puzzle's last solution could be in a picture in the BionTic office. On their website, he'd found contact information for the CEO of the company, Roberto Giobbi, and contacted him to make an appointment. It took little effort to meet him the same day. Mr. Giobbi was keen to see Duan, a friend of the Starck family.

Duan met Giobbi in a meeting room in BionTic's open office.

Giobbi was obviously from the Italian canton of Switzerland, named Ticino. Impeccably dressed, he wouldn't always stand out in a crowd but would always be noticed. The Italians call it *sprezzatura*. The art of well-crafted, apparently effortless nonchalance. It expresses how the always design-conscious Italian man selects his clothes.

Duan, during his study, shared a room with a student lawyer from Lugano who taught him about *sprezzatura*. His roommate pointed out how a Neapolitan-cut suit was subtly different from a Milanese silhouette. The Milanese one would be sober blue or gray, while a Southern jacket made an artistic statement.

Giobbi's bio on BionTic's corporate website mentioned that he'd studied biology at the university in Padua, in the north of Italy, and graduated with distinction. It surprised Duan that Giobbi didn't refer to himself as "Doctor" because an Italian "Dottore" would never miss an opportunity to use his title.

"Thanks for taking the time to see me, Mr. Giobbi. The past few days must have been terrible for you and your team."

"Indeed, too much has happened. First, our founder, Mr. Starck, died under mysterious circumstances, and now his wife, Gail, is gone. I was supposed to see her a few days ago, but she wasn't home. The police haven't been updating us. I hope you can give me an idea of what's happening?"

Duan noticed how nervously restless Giobbi was. His head moved skittishly back and forth. As if he didn't trust Duan and might get attacked at any moment. Giobbi was rather corpulent, and his neck was strapped tightly into the collar of his stylish shirt. The flesh of his neck made a desperate attempt to escape from underneath the collar.

"Sorry, Mr. Giobbi, I know even less than you. My focus right now is to find Gail. We are good friends, and I can't imagine what happened to her. Anything I would say is pure speculation."

Giobbi's nervous tic was getting on Duan's nerves. The man lacked the *gravitas* one expected from a well-educated CEO or a successful entrepreneur. Smart people with bright ideas were not always the best business leaders.

"What exactly is BionTic's business? I read a bit about it on your website but would love to hear it in your words."

Roberto Giobbi started a story he'd obviously told many times. Sharing the story calmed him down. "The idea behind BionTic is enabling individuals to upload their DNA in a blockchain and secure their unique biological identity. We call it DNALink."

Duan had read this on the site, but this was cutting-edge technology that required a more detailed, imaginative description.

"And why would I want to put my DNA on a blockchain?"

"When a client first uploads his DNA onto our site, they're asked to complete a detailed questionnaire. The data describes their social and medical situation, demographic information, etc. Then, they're asked to list the diseases they had, their medical history, and a complete family profile. This anonymized information is only accessible through a private key. Similar to accessing a Bitcoin wallet. I guess you know what I mean?"

Duan chuckled wryly to himself. If only Giobbi knew how neck-deep he was involved with finding Luc's private key. He maintained his polite smile and nodded.

"You have no idea how valuable DNA data is for the medical industry. Genetic research is based on analyzing a large number of DNA samples from a wide variety of individuals. The more relevant data they have access to, the better. They retrieve your medical history and match your DNA to the current medical context. The more detailed your DNA records are in the blockchain, the more interesting your data gets for research institutes and the more you can earn."

"Earn?" Duan reacted surprised.

"Yes, this is all about monetizing your DNA. People do not realize how valuable their body is."

Duan still looked confused.

"Let me give you an example."

"In one medical trial, a client is doing research into thyroid cancer. A very rare form of cancer. Thank God it's often cured, but patients suffering from thyroid cancer can go through terrible pain and suffering. Swallowing gets more and more difficult until they can't eat. For ages, the medical industry has been trying to find what causes cells in the thyroid to mutate and develop cancer cells. Using our DNALink, they found common patterns within groups of patients who suffer from the disease. They discovered that people who've lived or worked for at least ten years in areas with high levels of radioactivity, and that are obese, have a significantly higher risk of getting this cancer."

Duan's thoughts went to the myeloma blood cancer that struck Mina. It is this type of research that would hopefully allow medical science to identify and treat such diseases at an earlier stage.

"The strength of our DNALink system is that you own your DNA and have full control over how it can be used. You can even set the price that companies would have to pay to access your data."

Duan was fascinated by Giobbi's explanation. Giobbi became more relaxed as he spoke about what was obviously his favorite subject. His story made good sense, although Duan wondered how they could guarantee the integrity of the DNA and how they were restricting access to the system.

The cybersecurity expert in him identified enormous risks if this system was not very well protected. It surprised him Luc had never asked for advice on how to secure their data, especially after that *CryptoSwap* crisis. He'd seen so many start-ups ignore the basics and ultimate importance of securing data. Under pressure to monetize their service as quickly as possible, they'd take shortcuts that could become disasters as they scaled up their business.

"How did Luc get involved in this enterprise?"

"We met at our local golf club. I was a better golfer and occasionally gave him tips on his swing. I'd just developed the DNALink concept and was searching for an investor. Luc had earned a major part of his wealth with crypto trading and was looking for the right investment opportunity. He mentioned as we were putting our clubs away that he was looking for something outside crypto trading and saw potential in DNALink. This brought us together and made us the founding partners of BionTic. Our vision is to bring blockchain-based bio and pharma technology to the market as a unique package."

"What is the impact of Luc Starck's death on BionTic?'

"That is something I desperately need to discuss with Gail."

"Thanks for the background. As I told you, my most pressing concern today is to find Gail Starck."

"I understand. But what can I do to help you find her?"

Duan explained the message he'd received from her kidnappers with the ransom demand and how Luc challenged him to solve a set of puzzles that would eventually reveal his private key.

"Part of the solution of freeing Gail is for me to get access to Luc Starck's Bitcoin wallet and get hold of its private key. Do you have any idea where that private key might be?"

"No, I'm sorry. I don't think I can help you. Luc never discussed his crypto affairs with me. He would stop by once a week, leaving company operations up to us."

"Does he have an office here?"

"Yes."

"Can I see it?"

Giobbi walked to the corner and opened an office door.

Duan stepped in and looked around, not knowing what he was looking for.

The first thing he noticed was a framed photo of Gail on the desk. It was touching to see, especially knowing what recently was going on between them.

"Am I allowed to check the papers on his desk?"

"Go ahead. When a police officer was here yesterday, he went through the full pile but, by all means, be my guest."

Duan nosed through the papers, but nothing out of the ordinary was to be found.

He took his phone and showed Giobbi the picture from Luc he'd received earlier that day.

"Do you recognize this photo?"

Giobbi nodded.

"That's from our website. We hired a professional photographer a few months ago to take photos to use for various corporate publications. That was a picture he shot. Luc liked it."

"Do you have another copy of this photo somewhere in the office?"

"Hmm, yes, the one hanging on the wall near the entrance." They walked back. Duan was surprised to have missed that picture on his way in.

"Here you are."

Duan took down Luc's photo from the wall. Ever since he'd read *'The rest of the key is behind what you see,'* he knew he'd have to find such a picture and check the back of the frame.

"May I?" Duan pointed to the photo.

"Go ahead."

Duan removed the picture from its hook, eager to turn it over.

He deeply inspected every part of the back. Nothing.

He opened the frame and took the photo out. Roberto Giobbi looked at what Duan was doing with interest. Luc turned over the photo.

Nothing on the back, either.

"Fuck!"

"What's up?"

"I was convinced that a part of a crypto wallet's private key was on the back of that photo. Is there another copy?"

"No, I'm sorry."

Disappointed, Duan left the BionTic office and the Crypto Valley Labs complex. As he stepped out, he looked at his watch. Five hours remain for Gail. He'd put his hopes on finding the private key on the back of a photo. What a big disappointment! He'd have to start all over again and develop a Plan B. He needed time to think. But with that timer ticking and the deadline getting closer, it was difficult for him to get into the proper thinking mood.

While walking on the street, his phone started vibrating an SOS sequence. Bingo! It meant that the mail he'd sent earlier was opened. His trap had worked!

He clicked the link that took him to the page with the location of the receiver and a snapshot of the camera.

CHAPTER 28
THURSDAY, 24 OCTOBER, 12:27 P.M.

Rudy and Lisa-Lotte were on their way to *Zug Events*. Rudy was driving, which set the tone for their new partnership. Rudy was in charge.

He looked sideways at Lisa-Lotte.

"Lisa-Lotte, I can sense you are still angry about what just happened in Schmidt's room. I want you to know I have the fullest confidence in you."

"Thanks, Rudy." She had calmed down. Thinking about it, she concluded that if anyone had to take over her father's role, Rudy was by far the best choice.

"It's just that I felt I was fully in control and, bit by bit, was bringing all pieces of this puzzle together. But I'm happy you're my partner."

Rudy had worked with her father for many years. The two men had developed a strong friendship, and Rudy had become more than just a fellow police officer to her father. He had been of strong support for her dad when her brother Andi died. Their friendship resulted in Lisa-Lotte having a strong respect for him. Rudy would often join her dad at home for a drink after work. Her father always had a secret stash of absinth.

This alcoholic beverage, from the Swiss canton Neuchatel, for many years was considered a hallucinogenic spirit that led to madness and violence, and at the beginning of the 20th century got banned in Switzerland.

She remembered her father and Rudy sitting in the kitchen and drinking till late in the evening. Her father was playing an accordion, and both were singing traditional Swiss songs. Her mother would look at them with disgust, often leaving the house in anger.

Ten minutes later, they drove up the terrain of Zug events. Lisa-Lotte wanted to go back as she realized she might have overlooked something.

"Hello again, Mr. Minten," Lisa-Lotte said as she stepped into the office.

Minten looked at Rudy. "I see you brought in support troops," he said with a wide smile.

"Yes, this is my colleague, Rudy Kotkin. He only joins for the really tough cases," she said with a sarcastic tone.

Minten's office was a messy place. A miniature model of an inflatable castle was on top of a pile of paper. At the far end of the office, a big safe marked "*Danger*" drew Rudy's attention. Minten saw his interest and, before he was asked anything, explained, "That is where we store our pyro material. Local regulations for the usage and storage of pyrotechnics are very strict. You know I had to follow a training very similar to that of firemen?"

Two of Minten's employees working in the warehouse surreptitiously watched them through the window. This was more exciting than a truckload of event equipment.

"Welcome back, inspector Berg. I did not expect you back that quick."

"How nice of you to remember my name, Mr. Minten."

"How could I forget? Your visit has kept me busy all morning. I could not stop talking about this with my team. That contract was too good to be true, and I knew it," he told them sheepishly. "I should have taken it with a large grain of salt. When I called my wife to tell her about your visit, her answer was, 'I told you so.'"

Lisa-Lotte gave him a sympathetic smile.

"I don't think you could have done anything else."

When he mentioned he had told his wife about her visit, he put his hand in front of his mouth. "Oops, I hope it is okay I told this to my wife, and it's not a secret."

"Well, it's better if you keep our conversation to yourself. This is an ongoing investigation, and if this gets leaked to the press, it will seriously impact our investigations."

"I'm deeply sorry. I'll ensure this conversation stays between us."

"Anyway, is there any problem with what I told you this morning?"

"No, no. All is good. We appreciate your cooperation," Lisa-Lotte said. "We have a few follow-up questions to discuss with you."

"Could you please explain in more detail what you did after installing the stage?"

Heinz Minten looked surprised but explained his installation process step by step.

"After we built the podium, I installed the audio system. That took about half an hour. We hung promotion banners on aluminum stands to attract a larger audience, although the event had also been advertised in the local newspaper."

Minten had to pause and think about what else he'd done.

"Hmm, what next? Ah yes. I loaded the confetti cannons and placed one in every corner. The winners were to be announced with an explosion of streamers. I remember there was extensive discussion about the streamers when I applied for the permit for the event with the local authorities. Because of the Swiss never-ending need for cleanliness, they were extremely concerned about the mess these streamers would make on the square and charged me extra for cleaning up afterward. I went back to the client suggesting we skip the streamers to save money, but they insisted on having streamers and were glad to add extra cleaning costs to the total bill."

"Could you show me a cannon?" Rudy asked. Their interest in his business kept Minten talking.

He walked over to a rigid flight case marked *Cannons*, opened it, and showed them what the device looked like. It was huge, like an industrial pressure washer with a three-foot-long nozzle that the streamers came out of. Lisa-Lotte had often seen streamers being shot in the air during concerts but had never touched the device that produced such spectacular effects. "These are connected to tanks of compressed air. When I press this button, a valve is opened, and the air blows out the streamers with full force."

"How do you fire these four cannons at the same time?"

"They're connected to a remote controller on my control panel. The controller is set up at the back, overlooking the stage, so I have a clear view of everything and can also control the audio."

"Please, tell me, did that man collapse *before*, at the same moment, or *after* you exploded the confetti bombs?"

Minten looked surprised. "Are you implying that I am responsible for the death of that guy?"

Lisa-Lotte looked noncommittal.

"No, absolutely not. I only want to make sure I have the timeline right."

"It happened after the confetti bomb went off. Let me think. Yes, I'm sure it was *after* I fired the bomb."

"How long after?"

"Approximately five minutes."

"Can you show us the remote-control panel? Not just any panel, the one you used this week."

"That's easy. I only have one."

"Here it is. I'm always very careful with it. It not only controls the confetti cannons but also the audio, the lighting, and sometimes Pyro effects we use at various events."

Lisa-Lotte looked it over, inch by inch. "Can you explain to me what I see here?"

"These are faders, and with this, we control the various audio channels and the lights."

"And this pad?" She pointed to an iPad-like screen on the device.

"I can program that with my laptop and control anything. Here are the buttons that allow me to control the cannons." He pointed to a set of buttons on the screen.

"Do you have any other questions?"

"What's this?" Lisa-Lotte pointed to a flap on the bottom.

"Ah, that's a cable holder. If we use stage lights, the light cables feed in there, and that trap keeps the cables securely inside, so they can't come out by accident."

"Can you open it?"

Minten started to get visibly annoyed by her curiosity. She realized he must have felt like being under interrogation.

He unscrewed the flap.

When it was off, Lisa-Lotte inspected the space under the controller.

"What is that part?"

She pointed to a small plastic box inside. A cable from the box disappeared inside the controller. A small antenna was on top of the tiny plastic box.

"No clue. I've… uh… never seen this before," Minten stuttered.

"Mr. Minten, do video cameras monitor your warehouse? I'm interested in some recent footage."

"Yes, of course. Right this way." In his office, he opened his laptop and logged into the surveillance system. He selected the outside camera recording for the entrance. Browsing through the files, he noticed that one night at one a.m., a small, dark figure entered his warehouse. He or she left after ten minutes, carrying something heavy in a bag. Three hours later, the person returned with the same bag and left again in ten minutes.

"I'll be damned." Minten could not believe what he saw. "I thought I'd get a warning if anything moved. I guess that didn't work. Darn it!"

"If you don't mind, Mr. Minten, we'll take this controller for further inspection by our forensic team," Rudy said. She could sense Rudy was impressed with how she handled this investigation.

"Hmmm… well, that wouldn't be possible. Tomorrow, I have another event, and this is the only controller I have." Minten looked quite concerned about the disruption.

"I'm afraid you'll have to find another solution. We need to have this investigated. This box—" Lisa-Lotte pointed at the small plastic box. "—was installed during that nightly intervention."

As Lisa-Lotte pointed to the box, it got loose and dropped out of the space under the controller. It was hanging from the wire that connected it to the controller. As the box was dangling, she noted something printed across the bottom.

'Clue Three'.

CHAPTER 29
THURSDAY, 24 OCTOBER, 12:32 P.M.

Carl Coppen and his team were huddled over his round office table. As with many news websites, they were thriving on so-called *Triple-D Moments*. Death, Drama, and Disaster always attracted the most eyeballs. The average number of daily hits on his blog had grown by seventy-five percent since posting the news of Luc's death. Because their advertisement revenue was directly influenced by the number of site visitors, they peaked the daily advertisement revenue. Carl was determined to keep this story alive.

Yesterday, they posted a speculative story with the headline, *Luc Starck is dead, Gail Starck is gone, Bernt Berg paralyzed. What's going on in Zug?* The story generated a dramatic response with almost 800,000 clicks. That was a record and generated a lot of excitement in the office. Misha and Ilse saw their bonus getting closer.

"Guys, we desperately need an equally compelling follow-up story." They were racking their brains to come up with something fast. In such staff meetings, Carl encouraged everyone to let their imaginations fly in unexpected directions. After a few rounds of crazy ideas, the discussion was going nowhere. Carl stepped in and took the wheel.

"OK, Ilse, you go to the police station and find a good spot to observe. Take an outside seat at the wine bar 'Felsenkeller' opposite the police station and wait. With her father in hospital, I guess Lisa-Lotte Berg is running the team now. Keep a close eye on who goes in and out, and don't come back without a sizzling story."

"Got it, boss. Searching for sizzle."

"Misha, you go visit BionTic and ask for an interview with the boss, Mr. Giobbi. Please do not mention Luc Starck, but just tell them you wish to cover them on our blog. He's a bit high-strung, so give him your calmest bedside manner. Hand him your company card, and he'll welcome you with open arms. Once you're in, ask him some great questions about Mr. Starck. Think of what information you'd include in a human-interest story. Listen carefully and take notes in case he drops any meaty tidbits about the company's finances or future plans. Or, even better, anything that could be linked to Luc Starck."

"Don't worry, Carl, leave it to me. I'm done with cold-calling advertisers; I won't come back till I have a killer front-page article."

"Great guys! I'm proud of you. You rock!"

Carl stayed in the office. He had not felt so excited in ages. Starting this blog was such a well-timed decision. Stopping his high-paid job was not easy, but he learned in his professional career in trading that the difference between an average trader and the exceptional top trader is that top traders know when it is the right moment to walk away from a deal. Over time, he learned how to deal with the paradoxical feeling that when you quit on time, you will feel you quit too early. He once had a boss who always said, *Quitters never Win, and Winners never Quit.* How wrong did he prove him to be?

Carl grabbed his phone and called one of his spies.

CHAPTER 30
THURSDAY, 24 OCTOBER, 1:25 P.M.

Over a late lunch, Lisa-Lotte and her new partner Rudy were discussing the progress of the investigation. Lisa-Lotte had purposefully picked a quiet corner in the canteen.

Rudy could sense she needed to talk. He looked at her, showing concern, and put down his knife and fork.

"How are things going for you, Lisa-Lotte? I can imagine it's not that easy."

"Thanks for asking, Rudy. I'm going through shitty times. Schmidt does not trust me; my father is in hospital and cannot walk. My mother still cannot get over her divorce and avoids talking about my father, even though he is in the hospital. It's one big mess in my head."

She was staring ahead.

"You know Rudy, on one side, I have feelings of love for my mother, but I also have immense respect toward my father, and those torn feelings put me in a challenging situation. I suspect my mother is trying to make me subconsciously choose sides, but the loyalty for my father makes me resist the subtle game she is playing."

Rudy placed his hand on hers.

"And then my father's accident also gives me mixed feelings. As a daughter, it deeply saddens me. I'd never seen my father in a hospital bed. The poor guy."

She continued looking at Rudy, eagerly grabbing every bit of support he offered.

"On the other hand, as a police agent, I know these things are part of the job, and his hospitalization boosts my motivation to figure out who is behind his near-death."

"Yes, Lisa-Lotte, this is not a simple case, but you are doing incredibly well. It's normal for you to have these feelings. I want you to know you can count on me." He gave her a fatherly look.

"Thanks, Rudy." It felt good to express her feelings. It re-energized her.

"We're far from identifying a motive or a suspect, but the good news is that we're another step closer to understanding how Luc Starck died."

"Before lunch, I was with forensics. The remote control in Mr. Minten's control panel activated the mechanism attached to the terrace chair that fatally poisoned Luc Starck. The box had a built-in timer. Five minutes after Minten launched his streamer, the mechanism under Starck's chair got activated. It released the poisonous gas that resulted in his immediate death."

"Finding that remote control was a great catch, Lisa-Lotte," Rudy said while taking a bite of the quinoa salad.

"To be honest, both my father and Tell Schmidt suggested focusing on what had triggered the chair to release the gas."

Rudy continued.

"Whoever is behind this is playing and teasing us. He is inviting us to figure out how things happened. Look at these clues. They are a sign as if he is saying, 'Come on, try to catch me.' It is merely a matter of time."

"It's quite a puzzle, but the pieces are coming together. The man with the cap gets Starck to the terrace. Vogel, the magician, is booked, and through him, the chair is replaced with the lethal one. Next, Minten launches the mechanism; it is a chain reaction of events that, step by step, led to Starck's death."

For a moment, she got quiet and was having a pensive moment for herself. After a few seconds, she said, "You know, I've been thinking, we're trying to solve three clues. What keeps bothering me is, how many are we still missing? It seems like we're almost done now. What do you think?"

"Hmmm, good point," Rudy responded. "What intrigues me is, why would someone leave these clues at all? Something is going on here that we're just not getting. It's one big knotty mystery. I cannot stop thinking about why you would go through so much hassle to kill someone. Why not just hire a contractor to finish the job? Straightforward and with fewer risks for things to go wrong. With this murder, only one action had to fail for the entire plan to collapse."

Lisa-Lotte listened to Rudy, full of attention.

"Rudy, it's time we put focus on finding the mastermind of this. I've thought about it and have developed a profile. At the police academy, I truly enjoyed the lectures about criminal profiling." Although it is heavily debated if profiling had any value in court, it helped her to put herself in the shoes of a suspect.

Lisa-Lotte took a notebook from her pocket.

"I noted what type of person could have done this. First, it's a smart individual. Organizing this is no small feat, and I suspect that the person who has pieced this together knew Starck well. Also, he must be computer literate. Remember Brucker, the man with the cap? He got hacked. That's difficult to do."

Lisa-Lotte spoke deliberately, carefully choosing her words. She could not avoid thinking about her father; when "The Hawk" was biting himself in a case, he rarely was wrong. With each of the moves she made, her dad was on her mind.

Rudy looked at Lisa-Lotte, waiting for what else she had come up with.

"That's it."

"That's it?"

"Yes, that's it."

"Well, a smart, computer-literate person who knows Starck. That reduces it to at least a few hundred thousand people here in the canton of Zug," Rudy responded with a cynical tone.

"OK, let's get into action." Rudy seemed impatient.

"You remember during our meeting when I mentioned Luc Starck fought in a bar called *Whiskey-à-gogo* here in Zug? Why don't you join me in visiting the bar?"

"As long as I do not have to drink absinth with you."

Rudy laughed out loud.

As they stepped out of the police headquarters, they didn't notice Ilse Bamberg, the reporter from *blogchain.ch*, sitting outside on a terrace opposite the exit. When they walked around the corner, Ilse stood up and followed them at a safe distance.

Ten minutes later, Lisa-Lotte and Rudy walked into the bar. It was early; they had just opened. The barman was busy arranging the tables and chairs and filling up the drinks behind the bar.

Stepping into a bar that early always gave Lisa-Lotte an eerie, unhomely feeling. You could smell the alcohol from the night before, and the withered bags under the barman's eyes revealed he had just stepped out of bed. It did not help that Lisa-Lotte drank little alcohol and detested bars.

Lisa-Lotte walked to the barman and introduced herself.

"Hello, I'm detective Lisa-Lotte Berg from the Zuger police, and this is my colleague, Rudy Kotkin. I understand three weeks ago, you reported a fight here in your bar?"

"That's correct. Two of your colleagues came to make a report."

"I'm here to ask about the men who were fighting. When you called to report the skirmish, and my colleagues arrived, the men had gone?"

"Yes, I told them that one of them was Luc Starck. He was a regular here in the bar. The other guy I've seen before, but I don't know who he is. I don't think he's from Zug."

The barman described him but couldn't remember the details. He was rather short and had dark hair. That was what he could recall.

Lisa-Lotte looked at him, hoping he had more to tell. He did not.

The barman asked, "I know Starck died earlier this week. Do you think the fight has anything to do with his death?"

"As you did not file any charges, and none of the guys did either, we left the case. Now Mr. Starck is dead, so we want to have a closer look at it."

As she finished her sentence, Lisa-Lotte pointed to the video camera hanging in the corner.

"Do you have a recording of the fight?"

"I guess so, come."

They walked into a small storage behind the bar with a desk with a computer, locked in between two piles of crates of beers. The barman logged in and searched.

"Hmm, it was on a Wednesday three weeks ago. It was early. I guess around four or five p.m."

After a few mouse clicks, he smiled, proud to have found the video so fast.

"There you go."

Lisa-Lotte studied the clip intensively. Rudy was watching over her shoulder on the screen. It was surprising to her how poor-quality surveillance videos often had. The video showed two men talking. She recognized Luc Starck as he was facing the camera, but the other guy was only visible from the back. Suddenly, they stood up, and the other guy threw Starck with a swift judo move on the floor and walked away. Before leaving the bar, he turned his head to look at Starck. He looked straight into the lens.

Lisa-Lotte reacted instantly.

"Holy Fuck, I know that face."

She grabbed her notebook and went several pages back.

"There you go. It is Mr. Duan Ripa. He is a friend of the Starck family and came to report Mrs. Starck's disappearance. When I did not react promptly to his request to find Gail Starck, he got very aggressive. He seems assaultive. Here we see him again unable to maintain his poise."

She turned to the barman.

"Sir, may I take a screenshot of the frame where we see this guy's face? One of my colleagues will return tomorrow with a formal request for you to hand over this video as evidence."

Lisa-Lotte and Rudy returned to their table.

"It's weird, huh? Again, that Ripa guy. Let me Google him. Duan Ripa is not a common name."

Lisa-Lotte typed his name and found only a few hits. LinkedIn showed one Duan Ripa living in this region. He was from Zurich. With great interest, she read his profile on the website.

"Wow, we may be on to something, Rudy. Let me read you his profile."

> *Mr. Ripa is a seasoned cybersecurity expert running a security consultancy and specializes in various encryption and hacking techniques. No cyber-criminal is safe when Mr. Ripa is chasing him.*

"Allow me to reread this and now compare it with my profile.

"First, I said, the person we are looking for is a smart guy. Mr. Ripa is an encryption expert. Check!

"Next, he must be a computer expert. Mr. Ripa is a cyber expert. Check!

"Finally, number three is the motive. We just saw Mr. Ripa fighting with Luc Starck.

"A close match to my profile, if I may say so." Lisa-Lotte was pleased with her analytical skills. The Hawk would be proud of her!

"Let's go visit Mr. Ripa. Hang on."

She grabbed her phone, took a selfie of herself and Rudy, and sent it to her father. *Me and my new partner,* she added as a message.

From a table in the back, Ilse Bamberg watched the scene inside with interest. She'd been able to follow most of the discussion between the police officers and the barman. Through the open door, she could see the screen of the security video, although part of the conversation between Lisa-Lotte Berg and her colleague was hard to follow. She ordered an early Aperol spritz and started writing her article while her memories were still fresh.

CHAPTER 31
THURSDAY, 24 OCTOBER, 2:22 P.M.

When Bernt woke up that morning, his first thoughts went to the ongoing investigation. While he had the fullest confidence in his daughter, being bedridden and not at her side frustrated him immensely. He felt utterly helpless.

Thank God he felt his legs regaining sensation from the top downwards. There's a bit more in his left than his right leg. Still, it was obvious that walking would still be too much.

He couldn't remain passive in this case; he had to do something. As he looked around, he noticed next to his bed the privacy screens used by hospital staff when performing procedures. With extreme efforts, half hanging out of his bed, he managed to reach out and, with his fingertips, pulled the screens and set them up around his bed. At the head of his bed, he found a clipboard with blank sheets of paper. Fortunately, a drawer next to his bed contained a pen and a roll of paper surgical tape.

Bit by bit, he frantically started replicating the whiteboards from the situation room at the police office. On the left, he scrawled the names of every individual involved, each name a potential thread in the tangled web he was trying to unravel. In the center, a chaotic brainstorming board was filled with hastily jotted scenarios, each more complex and twisted than the last. On the right, an action list began to take shape—a catalog of tasks and unresolved loose ends.

Within 30 minutes, all three sides of the space next to his bed were smothered with papers covered in scribbles. He moved them frenetically from screen to screen, shifting and reshuffling as if trying to conjure some form of truth from the chaos. A few times, he grabbed his mobile phone and messaged some colleagues at the office. His muttering grew louder and more urgent, punctuated by sharp, anxious breaths.

Suddenly, the heavy breathing halted. His eyes darted over the tangled mess of notes and scribbles, and for a moment, the room seemed to close in around him. Then, as if a storm had suddenly cleared, a wide smile formed on his face.

In the midst of this, he heard familiar voices in the corridor. As he moved the left screen aside, he saw Lisa-Lotte and Rudy stepping in. He immediately noticed that Lisa-Lotte was carrying a paper box from Bakery Bachmann, known for its Zuger Kirsch Torte—a local specialty pie filled with Kirsch liquor.

"Delivery for the Hawk!" they cheerfully said as she stepped towards his bed. She placed the box on the cupboard next to his bed. "I hear alcohol speeds up recovery, so enjoy!"

Her dad laughed and greeted them with a joke.

"Do you know how an Egyptian likes his pie?"

Lisa-Lotte shrugged, knowing a daddy joke was being launched in her direction.

"Any way mummy makes it!" Bernt's belly laugh gave the joke too much credit.

"I see you're healing well. Even your stupid jokes are returning." Rudy said.

"Rudy, great to see you, my friend. Thanks for taking care of this young lady."

Lisa-Lotte kissed him. "You look much better, Dad. How do you feel?"

"Yes, definitely much better."

"And your legs?"

"I can feel them improving. Later today, they'll take me for some exercises. Although I do not think this year I will be able to qualify for the Olympics."

A good-looking nurse stepped into the room with a trolley, serving coffee and tea.

"Ah, I now see why you are not rushing to return," Rudy said with a wink.

"What the heck is happening here?" Rudy pointed to the screens around his bed.

"Guys, you can't expect me to just lie here passively. I've developed a solid theory about what might have happened. I still have some questions, but I'd like you to start looking into this."

Lisa-Lotte stared at him.

"Please take your time to recover, Dad. But…." She hesitated, choosing her words carefully. "But…we do welcome your help. We're making some progress, but we're not sure what to do next. Schmidt is making it clear he expects this case to be resolved quickly. That guy stresses me out. I don't know how you manage to work with him."

"Okay, let me share my thoughts."

He scanned the screens around his bed for a moment.

"First of all, I'm convinced the murder of Luc Starck and the disappearance of his wife are unrelated. These are two separate cases."

"Why, Dad?" Rudy and Lisa-Lotte were completely focused on him.

"Well, why would someone kill Luc and then kidnap his wife? It doesn't make sense to me. No, these are two distinct cases."

He continued, "Gail is an obvious suspect. She has a strong motive, given the many violent outbursts she endured. However, acquiring VX gas is way beyond her capability. If she was done with Luc, a divorce would have been a much easier route. Although I admit, it's easier said than done. No, it's not Gail."

He pointed to a paper labeled "Gail" pinned in the section marked "Unlikely Suspects."

"Next, I considered it to be one of the victims of the *CryptoSwap* bankruptcy. Some of them could have a criminal background. They're into Bitcoins, might have access to VX gas, and wouldn't hesitate to kill the person who caused them to lose a lot of money."

Lisa-Lotte and Rudy both nodded in agreement.

"But there's one issue. Why would someone kill Luc if they suspected him of stealing their coins? With Luc dead, they wouldn't get their money back, and if they did it, they would have tortured him in an attempt to get access to his crypto wallet."

He pointed to a paper labeled "Crypto Victims" pinned just below Gail.

"No, I have two prime suspects for you to focus on: Roberto Giobbi, the CEO, and Duan Ripa, the hot-tempered guy we met at the police station. I have some ideas about these two, but I don't want to influence your investigation. Review this with the team and let me know what you find."

Bernt was cautious not to appear as though he was trying to take control of the investigation, leaving room for Lisa-Lotte and Rudy to handle the case.

"Thanks for your analysis, Dad. That Duan guy is indeed on our radar. We just learned he had a fight with Luc Starck a few weeks before his death."

Bernt glanced at Rudy with an *I-told-you-so look*.

"Dad, listen. I wrote up an analysis of the suspect. What do you think?" After reading him the profile enthusiastically, she noticed his unimpressed expression.

"I see you're as unenthusiastic about this analysis as Rudy. You guys are such a great encouragement," she said with a wry smile.

"No, it's a good start, but there's more. Whoever acquired the VX gas had access to a black-market resource. Is there a VX online store?"

He couldn't resist making a small joke, which made his daughter roll her eyes.

"Nope. What kind of person would have access to such a black market?"

"Hmm, criminals, for sure."

Lisa-Lotte looked up. "You know, you can find almost anything on the internet these days. I once heard about something called the Dark Web. It's like an Amazon store for cybercriminals."

Bernt was surprised by his daughter's technological knowledge. Could she have picked this up from casual internet browsing?

She looked at him. "You know what? A Cyber Security Expert without doubt would know how to access and use the Dark Web."

"Is that supposed to be something I understand?" Her dad looked confused.

"Never mind, Dad. I think you might have just helped us a lot."

"I urgently need to look into something. I'll be back tomorrow. Keep getting better, OK?"

Her father looked surprised by her sudden departure.

"Oh, before I forget. You'll never guess who messaged me."

"The pope? Bill Gates?" Lisa-Lotte couldn't resist returning a silly joke.

"Your mother! In a sudden wave of sympathy, she must have wondered how I was doing. Or she was just making sure her alimony was secure."

"Come on, Dad, she isn't that bad."

He smiled at her. "OK, you're right. It was a wonderful gesture. She is the best wife I ever had." He agreed with a sarcastic smile.

"See you tomorrow, smartass."

As they walked toward the hallway, her father gave her one of his usual parting shots. "You know what the Jedi told his ex-wife?"

"No, but I have a feeling I'm about to find out."

"May di-vorce be with you!"

His laughter was still echoing down the hallway as they stepped into the elevator. As they walked out of the hospital, Lisa-Lotte's phone beeped. It was from *blogchain.ch.*

> *Has Luc Starck been killed by a mysterious Judo fighter?*
>
> *Blogchain.ch learned that a few weeks before his death, Luc Starck fought with a stranger in a bar called Whiskey-à-gogo here in town. Did this stranger take revenge this week? Was he behind Luc Starck's murder?*

The rest of the story was a rehash of previous facts already published in past articles. "Look at that." She showed her phone to Rudy.

"How the hell do they know that? Did that barman leak the story? It was only an hour ago we were in that bar."

"It is clear we need to be very careful and act fast. This will not put Schmidt in a better mood. It is better to act proactively; I will talk to him. Do not worry."

She now realized how good it was to have Rudy at her side.

CHAPTER 32

THURSDAY, 24 OCTOBER, 2:24 P.M.

Duan was walking outside the Crypto Valley Labs, looking at his phone at the SOS alert he just received. He felt proud his trick had worked.

He connected to his server, and his screen displayed two icons, one with a map and one with a camera. Selecting the camera icon brought him face-to-face with an unfriendly-looking Asian man. For a moment, he was worried that it was Gail who would have opened the email, but he was relieved to understand she wasn't working at cross-purposes with him.

He studied the photo of the Asian man. Based on the man's build and expression, he suspected this was the Asian who had threatened Luc. 'Oddjob' indeed. So, did this guy both kill Luc and kidnap Gail? That would not make sense, would it? Next, he clicked on the location icon. A map opened. A flashing blue spot was blinking in the middle.

He zoomed in. The dot was over a remote area below the Zugerberg, an Alpine hill that rose six hundred meters above the city. It offered perfect views of the city, the lake, and surrounding areas.

He enlarged the map and switched to satellite mode. Next to the dot, a building could be seen from above. From overhead, it looked like one of these private holiday chalets, popular for weekend getaway rentals. A dirt path, a few hundred meters long, connected the building to the main road.

A nice quiet spot to hide someone. Remote without neighbors. It definitely fits the bill.

Instinctively, he checked the timer on his watch. Just under three hours to go. What to do? Call the police? That police girl had promised to call him back but again took it very easy. Should he leave the house and visit that chalet? Or was it better to keep trying to find the private key? Neither option was guaranteed to succeed, and the clock was ticking.

What would he do at the chalet? Ring the bell and ask to speak to Gail? That might be funny in a Hollywood movie, but not in real life. What if nobody answered the door? Break-in? None of these were attractive scenarios. Something had to be done, and fast.

Gail meant a lot to him, much more than he'd realized.

Every time he thought of Gail, a flash of Mina popped up. Both showed that same naughty look… they both enjoyed drinking a Cosmopolitan… and binge-watching *Sex and the City*.

As the days passed since Mina's death, the two women fused in Duan's mind. Sometimes, he'd forget which of them had done or said something. The more important it was to him, the less certain he'd be sure of who he was remembering.

So, saving Gail wasn't just about Duan helping a friend. It was about keeping the last woman he'd loved real for as long as possible.

The idea of Gail being held against her will generated a tsunami of anger inside Duan. He had to go to the Zugerberg. If only to walk around that chalet. He knew he'd sense Gail's presence and save her if she was indeed inside.

As he was leaving his house for the drive to Zugerberg, his phone rang.

"Good afternoon, Mr. Ripa. This is Detective Lisa-Lotte Berg from the Zuger police. Apologies it took me some time, but when you called me this morning, I promised to call you back."

"Ah, yes. I hope you have some good news?"

"I can't tell you. However, I think you wanted to talk to me about the disappearance of Gail Starck. We also have several questions for you. Can you please come to the same police station where we spoke earlier? If it isn't too much to ask, we'd like to see you immediately."

"Of course not." How could he refuse? It was all or nothing with that girl. One moment, she had no interest in talking to him. The next moment, she wanted to see him without any delay.

Eager to learn what they'd found out and if any of it could help him solve those clues, he drove to Zug. What was so important they wanted to talk to him right away? Why was she so mysterious?

Thirty minutes later, Duan walked into the police building at picturesque *Kolinplatz* square, next to the historic Altstadt, the old town of Zug. He guessed the building dated from the sixteenth century and asked himself if it had always been a police station. Inside, it had been tastefully decorated. Compared to his visit yesterday, things felt different. Somehow, there was a change in the atmosphere, a darker mood hanging inside. Then he noticed some agents whispering together. He had read about the police agent who was injured yesterday and wondered if that was the reason.

Lisa-Lotte picked him up at the reception and led him to an interview room.

"Mr. Ripa, thanks for coming so promptly. Please meet my colleague inspector Rudy Kotkin. Have you heard from Mrs. Starck since you reported her missing?"

Oops, straight away, a question that forced him to be careful. Should he tell them he knew her location? The last time he'd met this policewoman, she hadn't impressed him. He decided to keep quiet and see what direction this conversation would take.

"No, unfortunately not. I had hoped that you had good news for me, and that's why you asked me to come. I hope nothing serious has happened?"

Lisa-Lotte ignored his question.

"I'm interested in your relationship with Luc Starck. How well did you know him?"

"His wife Gail and my wife Mina were very close. Almost sisters. That's how I met Luc."

"Were you close with him?"

"Well, we met regularly, but I can't say Luc and I were buddies. Luc was a loner, not someone who would easily open up. No, we definitely were not friends."

"Did you have any issues, arguments, or whatever?"

"Hmm, not that I'm aware."

Lisa-Lotte searched in her papers.

"As per the information here, you called Luc Starck last Tuesday at 10:55 a.m., a few minutes before his death. Why was that?"

Oops, he had to think.

"Ah yes, I finally decided to buy crypto coins and wanted to ask his advice. He was on his way to an appointment and had no time to talk, so I hung up. I do not think the call lasted even a minute."

The girl stared at him and kept silent. Just long enough to make him feel uneasy. Again, she flipped through the pile of papers in front of her.

"Mr. Ripa, what can you tell us about this photograph?"

Lisa-Lotte removed a photo from a folder on the table and pushed it across to him.

Duan picked it up and recognized it right away. The picture showed him leaving *Whiskey-à-gogo*. He was looking straight into the camera. Caught dead to rights.

"What do you see in this picture, Mr. Ripa?"

"Myself."

"Do you remember when and where this was taken, Mr. Ripa?"

"That was in the bar *Whiskey-à-gogo*. Several weeks ago, Luc invited me to meet him because he needed my help. He said an Asian-looking individual had physically threatened him."

"What help did he need from you?"

"Nothing special. He told me about the threats he had received and wanted me to be aware in case something happened to him. I told you about these threats when we met last time, but you seemed to have ignored them."

"We had several drinks, and Luc started making derogatory remarks about Asians. I had a Chinese father and got offended. I wanted to leave, but Luc kept ranting. I remember that when I looked at his reflection in the red lights of the bar's front window, he looked demonic. Like a raging bull with his nostrils growing with every inhale."

"It may have been the alcohol, but before I realized, I instinctively took him in a Seoi-Nage, a judo shoulder throw I'd practiced many times in my youth."

Lisa-Lotte took another photo from her folder and moved it across.

"Like this?"

"Yes, I did a lot of judo in my younger years."

"Did you two ever fight before, Mr. Ripa?"

"No. Not at all."

"Did you bear any ill will against Mr. Starck?"

"As I said, we were never good friends. The bastard has been doing dreadful things to his wife, and the poor girl has bruises all over her body."

"How do you know she has bruises all over her body, Mr. Ripa?"

Duan suddenly realized it sounded like he'd seen Gail naked. Too late.

"She lifted her shirt and showed me. She mentioned Luc's extreme violence and showed me some bruises. I felt so sorry for her."

"Were you aware of the violence against Mrs. Starck before Mr. Starck was murdered?"

"My wife may have mentioned it to me, but only when Gail showed them to me the day Luc got murdered did I realize how severe it was. The poor girl."

"How would you describe your relationship with Gail Starck?"

A chill went down his spine, and it all clicked at once when he realized he was now being interrogated in a murder investigation.

"Hang on, are you suspecting me of something?"

"We have some important questions for you, Mr. Ripa. Luc Starck's murder and Gail Starck's disappearance are still active investigations. We will interview anyone who knew both of them."

"So, you need to know all about my relationship with Gail?"

Lisa-Lotte nodded.

"As I just mentioned, I knew Gail through my wife, Mina. They were friends for many years. I didn't tell you, but my wife, Mina, died six weeks ago from an aggressive form of cancer."

Duan intentionally avoided giving any details about Mina's death.

"I'm sorry for your loss, Mr. Ripa."

"Thank you. Gail selflessly supported me after Mina's death. She's been very good to me."

"Mr. Ripa, I'm sorry to ask, but when you talk about Gail Starck, it's with so much love and tenderness in your eyes. Do you have any romantic feelings for her?"

That simple question blindsided Duan. He realized he loved Gail, but nobody had ever asked him that directly. Gail and Mina were so alike, and his love for Mina was still there. His feelings for Gail had grown far beyond that of a close friendship. Thinking about it, he realized that, yes, he loved her. *What to answer?*

"Weird, you ask. I can't deny I am close to Gail. Both of us are grieving the loss of our partners. Yes, I do love Gail. She is great, and I just can't imagine what she must be going through now."

"How serious is your relationship with her?"

"For God's sake, what do you mean? I've made myself very clear. I love her. Are you asking if I fucked her? No! Gail is suffering as we speak. Instead of running around in circles with these prurient personal questions, you should be out looking for her. Go do your fucking job!"

As he said these words, he closed his right hand into a fist and smashed it loudly on the table. He looked at the girl detective for any reaction. There was none from her or that bump on a log, Rudy, who hadn't said a single word.

"Yes, you too, dumbass! Get into action and find Gail! Hop-hop." He clapped his hands.

Lisa-Lotte remained silent, staring evenly at Duan.

Duan had said what he'd wanted to say but found the silence unnerving. Rudy stayed as quiet and observant as he had been the whole time.

Without saying a word, the three of them were holding down the table.

The silence continued for twenty seconds, which felt like as many minutes. The clock tower across the square chimed once. Far away, a phone was ringing, and people were talking. Duan was determined not to break the silence first.

He felt like he'd been thrown into a Sergio Leone spaghetti western, with suspicious stares and deathly silences replacing the dialog.

After what felt like an endless pregnant pause, Lisa-Lotte gave him a last stare and asked melodramatically, "One last question. Where were you on Tuesday at eleven a.m.?"

"At home in Zurich, working."

"That will be all for now. Please remain available for further questioning, Mr. Ripa. My colleague will accompany you to the exit."

At the door, Duan shook Rudy's hand and said sarcastically, "It was a joy chatting with you."

While Rudy was showing Duan Ripa out, Lisa-Lotte was by herself. She was reflecting on the outburst by Duan Ripa she just witnessed. They now had met twice, and twice he had an emotional outbreak.

It was clear Ripa was someone who had challenges with anger management. Could he have killed Luc Starck in such a moment of rage?

When Rudy returned, Lisa-Lotte summed up her impressions of the interview.

"Our friend, Mr. Ripa, is a hot-tempered guy. First, he floors Luc Stack in a bar, and now lost his temper when we asked him a few very simple questions. We learned he loves Gail Starck. He is a computer expert, and he has no alibi for the time of the murder. No, Mr. Duan Ripa is ticking more and more boxes. Let's have him followed."

Rudy looked at her and paused for a moment. "Well, remember, with what we know now, the person who is behind all of this started this murder well before Tuesday eleven a.m., so Mr. Ripa's whereabouts do not really matter."

"Hmm, yes, well observed Mr. Kotkin. There you have a point. The fact is that I do not trust him, and we better keep a close eye on him. Do you agree?" While formally Rudy was in charge, Lisa-Lotte kept running the show.

Within fifteen minutes Rudy had authorization to trace Duan's phone and for a team to follow him. He was their only genuine lead at this moment, so they couldn't afford to lose him.

Duan Ripa knew more than he'd told them.

Lisa-Lotte was sharpening her Hawk-like intuition and felt that following Duan Ripa was their only option to get Schmidt off her back.

The game was on!

CHAPTER 33
THURSDAY, 24 OCTOBER, 2:53 P.M.

Gail was beyond exhausted—she was drained, desperate. For hours, she hadn't heard a word from her kidnappers, and with each passing minute, the hope she'd clung to seemed to slip further out of reach.

How long had it been since she sent Duan that message?

Five hours? Ten? Who could keep track anymore? Time had become a blur. Her entire body screamed, each ache more insistent than the last. Her leg had locked in a cramp that she couldn't shake, her back twisted in ways that made her want to scream, and her arms—her poor, raw arms—itched constantly, a maddening reminder of her captivity. It felt like laying in an MRI: blindfolded, unable to move, and itching…it always found the weirdest, most unreachable places.

Sleep was a distant memory, but the tears? They came without warning. She hadn't stopped crying for the last hour, a steady stream of frustration and pain she couldn't hold back. The emotional pressure felt like it might crush her if the physical pain didn't do it first.

What could have happened to the messages she recorded? She was struggling to stay positive. It was just a matter of time before someone found her. Or was it? Who would miss her first? Duan? Roberto Giobbi from BionTic? Or one of her study friends at the university? What if nobody missed her? Or her messages to Luc and Duan were not received?

She'd placed all her hopes on Duan. The way he supported her when she'd told him about Luc's death helped a lot. After those dark months of the past, Duan brought her back into the light. His worries about her were sincere because he cared about her. Like she took care of him for many weeks after Mina's passing.

Her thoughts wandered back to Luc and what happened to him. Every time she thought of him, she got angry. Angry at what he'd done to her and the mess he'd made of his life and, as a result, of hers. She did not pity him.

She tried mindfulness exercises that Mina taught her to help her deal with the physical pains. The body trip. Mina had explained how the power of the exercise wasn't in the body's journey itself. Her thoughts would drift, so she had to refocus back on her body. That process of the wandering mind and refocusing had to become a natural reflex, as it is for experienced meditators.

Okay, she tried again, focusing on her breathing this time. Slowly inhaling through the nose, keeping it in and slowly out through the mouth. After repeating this three times, she couldn't get her mind off Mina. First, about all the times they went out for seafood. They adored sea platters; if either of them ate oysters, they'd send the other a picture of the meal.

These evenings out were truly memorable, with endless flirtations, excellent wine, and non-stop giggling. She suddenly thought about one evening out with Mina fifteen years ago. An older guy at the next table, sitting by himself, got attracted to Mina and joined them until they'd emptied the wine bottle. The American enjoyed their company so much that he ordered another bottle and then another one. They were teasing and flirting with him and gave him the time of his life. He fancied Mina and couldn't resist showing off. He was ostentatiously rich and showed them pictures of his mansion and his penthouse in New York. At the end of that fun evening, he insisted Mina return with him to the United States. Despite the appeal of a luxury lifestyle and the effects of so much alcohol, she politely declined. They exchanged numbers and names and remained in touch.

At home, the girls looked him up on the internet. To their big surprise, he turned out to be the ex-husband of Kim Cattral, the famous American actress featured in their favorite series, *Sex and the City*. They couldn't stop giggling.

"Can you imagine me in New York having sex with my own Mr. Big? It could become an episode of *Sex and the City*."

It was non-stop laughing and, typically, unexpected developments.

Oops, her memories drifted again. Back to my breathing! It was so difficult to focus.

However hard she tried, it was impossible to keep her focus for even ten seconds. Perhaps because of the discomfort, her thoughts kept taking weird turns and getting lost among many diverting memories. Her head was one big labyrinth of confusing thoughts.

While trying to control her thoughts, she thought she heard a noise. *He was there.* She forced herself to be strong.

"Hello? Are you back?"

She'd changed tactics this time and became more aggressive.

"Can you, for God's sake, tell me what the hell is going on? This game has been ongoing long enough, and it is about time you let me go. Nobody is home. My husband is dead. Neither Duan Ripa nor the police cares about my fate. The show is over. Nada. It's time to leave. Adios."

She stopped talking to see if her tirade triggered a reaction. Nothing. No noise.

"Hola, could you prepare me a hot bath and a glass of Ruinart champagne, please?"

Silence.

"Coucou, do you know you are fucking annoying? You should have been more careful with your bloody Bitcoins. That would have saved both of us a lot of misery. Hellllooooooo!"

"Are you done?"

Same accent, same guy.

Suddenly, her arm was stretched at a ninety-degree angle away from her body. It got strapped against an ice-cold piece of metal that was attached to the bed.

The sudden feeling of freezing steel shocked her.

"What the hell!" she shouted.

He whispered in her ear, "Remain quiet. It will be over soon."

When her left arm was grabbed, she realized her kidnapper was wearing cold rubber gloves, and it scared her. *What the hell was happening?*

He grabbed her left pinky finger, and she suddenly lost all sensation in it. She heard a noise as if someone was spraying it.

Initially, she had a sensation of something burning hitting her. However, that feeling disappeared soon, to be followed by an intense feeling of numbness. To test, she squeezed her thumb and first finger but could not feel the fingers coming together.

The spraying continued for almost a minute.

* * *

"No more Mr. Nice Guy!" he muttered to himself in Chinese.

He regretted he was forced to hurt Mrs. Starck.

The fact his polite messages had triggered no reaction from Luc Starck or that Duan guy kept him busy. The disrespect toward him annoyed him big time. They didn't seem to realize he'd traveled halfway around the world to Zug to get his crypto coins back, determined not to fail.

He came fully prepared to take brutal action if necessary. As a gentleman, he felt sorry about what he was going to do to Gail, but he was left with no choice.

Whatever happened, he wouldn't leave Zug until every Bitcoin was safely back in his wallet.

Yong Chi took a mini video camera and, mounted it on a tripod set up near her feet and raised it to its highest position. Now, he had a perfectly framed shot of her upper body. A click of the button started the recording.

He stood behind Gail and lifted the taped-up goggles from her head. Long enough so her face became visible for the camera, and for her to realize what was happening. Before she could get adjusted to the bright lights in the room and see her attacker, he put the goggles back on, and she was blind again.

He bent forward and whispered into her right ear, "Please say out loud that you are Gail Starck and that unless they pay two thousand Bitcoins as per the instructions found on *www.CryptoJustice.org*, even worse things will happen to you."

When he said the words, *Even worse,* he could see she started to shake.

She followed his directions and recorded the message. It was audible in her voice that she was afraid and completely spent.

When he was done, he took a container from the duffel bag and poured liquid ice from the container over her left hand. He placed the container on the small table beside her bed.

By now, she should have lost all sensation in her full left hand and a part of her lower arm.

Yong Chi reached again into the duffel bag and pulled a heavy bolt cutter used to cut steel fences out of it. With a swift movement, he placed Gail's pinky finger in between the cutter and squeezed the cutter blades together.

Gail's left pinky finger dropped almost silently from her hand into the container.

With her left finger almost frozen, Gail Starck should have barely felt anything, just a tug. When she finally figured out what happened, she shrieked like a banshee.

"You fucking bastard!" she yelled, followed by a long, high-pitched scream. Then she swooned.

He had to use this tactic several times as a young criminal in China, and it had always worked. One almost humorous incident involved a Japanese *yakuza* whose gang was trying to muscle in on Yong's territory. When they drugged the burly thug and prepared to amputate his pinky as a message to his boss, they discovered that half of one pinky was already gone!

Luckily, they had a finger on the other hand they could work with.

Yong let the girl scream and put on a fresh pair of gloves. He took the little finger from its container and placed it on the palm of her left hand. With his phone, he took a picture of her hand holding her pinky. He checked the photo and placed the finger back in its container.

From his medical case, Yong took a bottle of disinfecting alcohol and cotton balls and started cleaning the top of the stub of her left pinky. He taped off the top and covered it with a rubber-protecting tip. When he was done, he took a step backward and looked at his work with pride. Good job!

"Open your mouth. I will give you a heavy painkiller. You'll need it."

It was clear the girl was still in shock and couldn't say anything. She opened her mouth and put out her tongue.

He placed a pill on it.

"Don't swallow yet. I'll get you some water."

He carefully poured water into her mouth.

"I'll leave three more pills on the table, just above your head. You'll need them. Don't take a second one unless the pain's getting worse, or you'll run out. I gave you some extra movement with your right hand so you can reach them."

Yong left the room. In the kitchen, he took her finger from the container and placed it on a cooling element. He wrapped a pink ribbon around the pinky and tied a neat bow. Next, he put a letter he'd prepared in a matching pink envelope. Finally, he took the memory card from his camera and inserted it into a small video player. He took all the items and placed them carefully in a gift-wrapped box.

As a last action, he took his phone, selected the photo of the amputated finger, and sent it to an online news outlet. Nothing would stop him from getting justice.

With a sense of accomplishment, he brewed himself green tea.

CHAPTER 34
THURSDAY, 24 OCTOBER, 3:12 P.M.

A determined Yong drove his rental car into downtown Zug from the chalet.

He parked near Coop City, a local department store. After a short walk, he reached *The Door*, a standalone door like the one on *The Truman Show*, built on the edge of the lake to attract tourists. When opened, *The Door* only contained a stairway, leading visitors down a flight of steps to an underwater observatory where they could see… murky lake water and a few fish.

Yong stepped carefully down the wet stairs. He'd picked this location carefully. It was symbolic of how this trip was going, with its beautiful setting leading to nothing. Yet.

At the foot of the stairs was a metal grille to sluice out rainwater that had dripped from underneath the doorway. He lifted the heavy grille and carefully positioned a medium-sized waterproof box in the space underneath the iron grid, just inside the sewer entry. After making sure the box was stable and out of sight, he replaced the grid.

He climbed up the stairs and sat on a lakeside promenade bench. It gave him a perfect view of *The Door*. Armed with the relaxing espresso he'd bought from the little kiosk behind him, he took his time for a much-needed bit of rest.

He meditated peacefully for two minutes on the lake, the Alps, and the tranquil Zug skyline. He deeply inhaled the fresh Alpine air, so different from what he'd grown up with in Shenyang.

Sitting alongside Lake Zug sipping his coffee, it was easy to forget he was in town on very serious business.

He grabbed a phone from his bag and dialed a saved number.

"Hello?" a high-pitched man's voice answered.

"Is this Mr. Roberto Giobbi from BionTic?"

"Yes, it is."

"Are you at this moment at the Crypto Valley Labs?"

"Yes, I am."

"Listen carefully, I will only say this once. If you wish to get Gail Starck back alive, go now to *The Door* at the border of Zuger Lake. There's a metal grille at the bottom of the stairs. Lift that grille and take out the wrapped gift box. Follow the instructions inside. Oh, and…. no police, you are being watched. Please hurry." He hung up and imagined Giobbi looking down at his phone, wondering what the hell had just happened. This week had just been one surprise after the other for poor Mr. Giobbi.

While waiting for Giobbi to arrive, Yong stood up, took the sim out of his phone, and broke it. He casually walked over to the lake, checked to make sure the coast was clear, kneeled, and acted as if he had to tie his shoelace. Before standing, he tossed the phone into the lake.

Armed with another espresso, he walked back to his chair to wait for things to get interesting.

Ten minutes later, he noticed a pudgy, smart-looking businessman plodding nervously toward *The Door*. When the man got closer, Yong could see large damp spots under his arms. Poor Mr. Giobbi had been running. He recognized his face from BionTic*'s* corporate website. Giobbi went into *The Door*. Yong visualized Giobbi opening the box at the bottom of the stairs. He thought he heard a scream. Soon after, visibly shocked, Giobbi exited *The Door*, grabbed his mobile phone, and made a call. Within a few minutes, Yong saw two police officers arriving by bike from the old town side of the city.

From across the street, Yong watched Roberto Giobbi explaining to the police agents, with many expressive hand gestures, how he'd collected his 'present.' With his mission accomplished, Yong drove back to the chalet. It was rented for two weeks and was the perfect hideout. Remote, a nice soundproof bunker, and close to Zug. Exactly what he needed.

CHAPTER 35
THURSDAY, 24 OCTOBER, 3:33 P.M.

Duan drove his car through beautiful rolling hills, connected with lush green meadows, with snow-capped mountains as a backdrop. Following the blue spot on his phone's map was easy. The well-maintained road curled itself along the Zugerberg. With every hairpin turn, the stunning views of the surrounding mountains, Zuger Lake, and the forest changed. It was like driving in a Swiss postcard. After all these years, that landscape never failed to please him.

Without any trouble, he found the dirt path entrance that should take him to the chalet. Half-hidden behind the trees was the building, set against a slope. The chalet was like many vacation homes in this area, rented by hiking lovers attracted by the region's scenic walking routes. During the winter, hikers changed their gear and became cross-country skiers.

Duan parked his car along the main road a hundred meters past the end of the dirt path. As he rushed up to the chalet, he ignored the gorgeous view of Zuger Lake. The sweet aroma of pine trees energized him to be ready for whatever he'd encounter in that chalet.

Keeping a safe distance, he gave the chalet a quick reconnaissance. If anyone asked what he was doing, he could always pretend to be a lost hiker.

There was no car parked in front or movement inside. All safe.

The chalet's main entrance was on the first floor, on the left side. He first gently tried the basement door. It was closed. Duan tried to open the main door. Also closed. *Fuck!* He checked for a key under the doormat or planter but couldn't find any.

He'd noticed that at the back of the chalet, a small window had been left open, about two meters above the ground. Using the many wood logs around here, it only took a minute to stack enough of them to reach that window. With a small jump, he reached the window ledge, and then he squeezed himself inside through the small opening.

Duan stood still for a moment in case his arrival had alerted anyone inside the house. All was quiet. The room he had dropped into looked unused. Suddenly, he remembered to switch off his mobile phone. He always had to chuckle when, in a movie, someone was hiding, and his phone would start beeping and reveal his hiding place. *Amateurs!* That wouldn't happen to him!

He explored the house. The bedroom on the left looked occupied, with men's clothes hanging over a chair. He took his time to search for any form of identification. No luggage tag, no passport, no wallet, no other pieces of paper. There had to be something. He checked under the mattress, all the drawers, and on top of the closet. Nothing. Time to move on.

He examined the other two rooms on this floor. They seemed unoccupied.

He heard voices coming from the floor downstairs. What to do? He had no means of defending himself. Leaving now was not an option. Should he call the police and ask for help? He decided to at least have a look.

Carefully, he crept downstairs to the ground floor, trying to avoid any creaking wooden steps. Like stepping on a frozen lake, his right foot first came down on the outside edge of the step. Then, he gently moved his weight on that right foot before moving with his left. As soon as he could peek into the living room, he ventured a look. Nobody.

The voices seemed to come from the kitchen.

He tried to peek in but saw no one.

When he stepped in, he found it was the radio he was hearing. He relaxed. It was your typical Swiss chalet kitchen, with a wooden bench and a kitchen table covered by a white tablecloth with red decoration. The kitchen was empty. Nobody was in this house.

Finally, he moved down to the basement more quickly because these steps were solid concrete. It had a small hall area with two doors and one heavy concrete door. That must be the nuclear bunker.

Since the 1960s, Swiss municipalities have made it mandatory for large homes and residential buildings to have nuclear bunkers. Duan always found it a weird law for a country that prides itself on its neutrality; its last war was in 1798 when Napoleon invaded the country.

He managed to move the door handle upwards and pull the heavy door open. In this bucolic place, with no urban noise, the only sound came from birds and trees moving in the wind. The squeaking bunker door broke the serene silence, like the climactic scene in a horror movie. Even the bunker's chilly air was creepy as he tiptoed his way into the bunker. It was completely dark.

The silence was eerie, and the air felt heavy. Duan immediately sensed something was off. He whispered Gail's name but did not get any response. His hands were exploring the wall in the darkness, searching for a light switch.

When he found it and switched on the light, he saw Gail lying on a foldable massage table. For a moment, his breathing stopped. *Was she dead?* In a matter of seconds, a wide range of emotions, jumping from shock, disbelief, sadness, and anger, shot through his body.

She wasn't moving. He softly called her name, no reaction. He held the back of his hand up to her nose and felt her heavy breathing. *Thank God she's alive.* How could he get her out of this position?

"Gail, wake up! It's Duan." Whatever he tried, he could not get any reaction. She was well tied against that bed, and he would have to carry her out.

Just as he noticed the bandage on her left hand, he heard a car pulling up across the gravel.

"Oh my God, what now?" he squealed, looking in panic around the room.

He just had time to leave the bunker. Quickly switched off the light and closed the concrete door. There was one other door in the hallway. He jerked that door open. It was the door to the heating area, nice and large, with plenty of places where he could hide.

In a dark corner behind a large boiler, he found a place to wait until the coast was clear. He glanced nervously at his watch. Just one hour to go. He'd better not be stuck down here for long.

CHAPTER 36
THURSDAY, 24 OCTOBER, 3:54 P.M.

When Roberto Giobbi emerged from *The Door's* staircase, he was still unsteady and sweating. Underneath the grille, he'd found a small, wrapped box. When he unwrapped and opened it, there was an amputated finger tied up with a pink ribbon, rolling up against a cheap video player.

Visibly in shock, he screamed and almost dropped the box and its grisly contents onto the slip-proof stairs.

He sat down on the driest stair he could find, read the letter, and played the video, which showed Gail lying on a massage table. When he saw Gail's finger being amputated, he gagged.

Barely recovered from the shock, he put everything back in the box, replaced the grill, ran up the stairs, and frantically called the police.

When they arrived, he was still trembling and stuttering.

"Here, look!" he shouted at the bicycle policemen. "There's a fucking finger in that fucking box." He had completely lost it. "It is Gail Starck's. Here's a video that shows it being cut off!" He jabbed his finger at the video player's button. "That's Gail…Gail Starck, you know, the widow of Luc Starck, who got killed earlier this week! Who the hell would do something like this?" Giobbi spoke in garbled, panicky sentences.

"Sir, please put the box down carefully on this bench," the senior officer instructed. "Don't touch it again. We'll take it to the police station for fingerprints."

The officer placed the box in a plastic evidence bag that he pulled from his bike bag.

At the police station, Giobbi was taken downstairs to an interview room. He explained more calmly to a detective on Lisa-Lotte's team what had happened.

"About one hour ago, I received a phone call from someone who told me threateningly that if I wanted to see Gail Starck alive again, I had to go to *The Door*. He told me that at the bottom of *The Door* staircase, underneath the grille, I would find a wrapped box."

Giobbi continued shaking and stammering. His shirt was dripping wet. A desk sergeant brought him some water so he could relax. Once he'd calmed down, he retold his story.

"I found what looked like a woman's finger in that box, wrapped with a pink ribbon. Along with it was a miniature video player, in which a video showed Gail having her pinky amputated! What kind of twisted mind would do something like this? I hope you can grab that bastard fast."

"Did you find anything else?" the Lieutenant asked.

"There was a letter demanding money they claim was stolen from them. They said they only took her finger this time, but if we want to see the rest of Gail alive, we'd better pay them two thousand Bitcoins."

A forensic investigator joined them. First, she took Giobbi's fingerprint. She then put on rubber gloves, opened the box, and inspected its contents one item at a time. Each item went into an evidence bag.

It was as Giobbi had described. The contents of the box were still freezing cold, and the note inside read:

> *It's about time you take us seriously. If you want to get the rest*
> *of Gail Starck back alive, send 2,000 Bitcoins to our wallet*
> *3J98t1WpEZ73CNmQvieavnyiWrnqRhWNLy.*
> *Visit www.CryptoJustice.org for full details.*

The agents checked the link. It displayed a large countdown clock that showed:

> *0 hours, 35 minutes, and 23 seconds.*

Giobbi's written statement was taken, and he returned to his office at the Crypto Valley Labs. None of the officers would have bet on him getting anything done for the rest of the day.

Lisa-Lotte arrived at the station shortly after Giobbi had left. When she heard Roberto Giobbi's story from the detective who had interviewed him, she rushed to the forensics officer to go over the box's contents herself.

Lisa-Lotte read the note and whispered, "We received a similar message two days ago. We have no clue yet who's behind this, but I wouldn't be surprised if whoever did this also is responsible for the injury of my father."

One of her colleagues walked in and showed her his mobile phone. His browser was displaying *blogchain.ch*.

Gail Starck kidnapped!

Blogchain.ch just received a shocking photo of Gail Starck, confirming she has been kidnapped. The picture shows her undergoing severe torture and is too shocking to be shared. Gail Starck is the widow of Luc Starck, who was murdered earlier this week.

The silence of the Zuger police is shocking. Despite our repeated requests, the police are not making any statements about Luc Starck's death. They mentioned Starck died a natural death, but this picture confirms the Starck family is under serious threat.

Zug and the full blockchain community deserve full clarity!

She had barely finished reading the article when she noticed Captain Tell Schmidt walking in her direction through the long corridor. He had his eyes focused on her and as he got closer, she could see the anger on his face and noticed him breathing heavily through his nose.

He stopped straight in front of her and stayed quiet for a second. His nostrils were widening as he breathed. "Lisa-Lotte, come to my office. Now!"

She followed him as he walked back down that long corridor.

When she entered his office, he immediately closed the door behind her. Without hesitation, he pointed to the *blogchain.ch* article that was visible on his computer screen and said, "This is getting completely out of hand. You cannot imagine how much damage these fucking articles do to us. I just had

Mayor Muller on the phone, and he demanded this entire case be resolved within the next twenty-four hours."

As he spoke, his voice got louder and louder.

"I'll give you and Rudy one more day to bring me results, find Gail Starck, and tell me how her husband died. If by tomorrow this time you still have nothing, I will have to intervene and take action. This cannot continue!"

Schmidt's face was red from anger.

Lisa-Lotte remained silent. Schmidt's expectations were completely unreasonable, but this was not the moment to argue. The only right thing to say was, "Yes, sir."

She turned around and walked out of his office.

CHAPTER 37
THURSDAY, 24 OCTOBER, 4:12 P.M.

Duan was still squatting behind the hot water heater in the dark boiler room. He had growing cramps in his calves but resisted the overwhelming urge to stretch. Barely daring to breathe, Duan realized this could take forever. The oily smell, combined with the dust in the air, irritated his lungs, and it took all his effort to not start coughing.

He desperately tried to follow what was happening outside his hiding place. When the arriving car stopped, he heard only one door opening and closing, so only one person was there. Also, the footsteps on the gravel of the dirt path appeared to be from one person. Good!

The outer door opened, almost immediately followed by the squeaking bunker door. How hard he tried. It was impossible to grasp what was happening in that bunker.

What to do? He had no clue who was out there. He had only seen the photo of that Asian individual and if that was the Oddjob whom Luc had described, it would be a challenging task to surprise him with his rusty judo skills. *What to do?*

Suddenly, he had an idea. He switched on his phone and sent a message to Gail's email account and an SMS to her mobile. Hopefully, whoever was in the chalet with him would read it. It said:

I've got the Bitcoins. We need to talk.

After ten minutes, he received a reply.

Just transfer them to the mentioned wallet address and we'll talk.

He should have expected that response. Somehow, he had to get that person away from the house.

This time, he tried a bit more direct.

Meet me in the old town on the south terrace of the casino. I'm in a rush. Don't keep me waiting.

Five minutes later, he smiled at the sound of a car driving away down the gravel driveway. His impulsive plan had worked! After ten more minutes, he tiptoed out of the dark, musty room. The silence was deafening. Every sound seemed to be absorbed by the forest and the nearby mountains. The only noise was his steps creaking across the floor. *What if a second person was there?*

He checked his timer: less than twenty minutes to go. *He'd have to move fast!*

Apparently alone, he hurried to the bunker door and entered to check on Gail. He looked more closely at the very bulky bandage and wondered what could have happened.

He whispered her name twice, but she did not react. Gently, he touched her face and got the same result. Next, he slapped her a bit more forcefully. Gail was completely unconscious. To get her out, he'd have to drive right up to the house, carry her to his car, and get her to a hospital as soon as possible. Not a moment to lose.

He had no clue what would happen when that timer reached zero.

* * *

From the moment Yong returned to the house, he had known someone else had been there. Just before leaving, as a precaution, he'd hung a nearly invisible piece of woolen thread between the bunker door and door frame after closing it. When he returned, that thread was on the floor. Someone had entered the bunker. The big question was if that person was still in the house. He had to be extremely careful. After all the unexpected developments of the past days, he would not have this messed up. *No way!*

He had configured a rule to have all of Gail's mail forwarded to his email address. When he received Duan's messages, he immediately realized they were trying to get him away from the house. He played along, left, and drove fifty meters up along the road. He parked his car and returned straight to the house, dodging between trees so he couldn't be seen.

Carefully, he slipped in through the side door on the main floor and peeked down the stairs into the basement. The light from the open bunker shone into the hall downstairs. He had been right; someone was in the house. He waited by the bunker door, waiting for the person to come out.

Just as the man stepped out of the bunker, Yong's strong, muscular arm grabbed the guy from behind and squeezed around his neck. He pulled the smaller man back into his barrel chest. With his deep voice, he whispered in the guy's ear. "Don't even think about trying anything."

The two of them stood like that for almost a minute. Sweat pearls from Duan's front head dropped on the fire dragon tattoo on Yong's biceps. Yong's plan was to keep him in this deadlock and just see what happened.

* * *

Duan told himself to remain calm and come up with an unexpected attack. He was going to let the guy keep this grip as long as he could sustain it. At a certain moment, he was going to lose his concentration, and at that moment, Duan had to make a move. After almost two minutes, he felt the iron grip loosen a bit. This was the moment to act. Reaching over his head, Duan grabbed the inside of his assailant's right arm. With his left hand, he reached high onto Yong's left shoulder and grabbed his coat. Next, Duan lowered his body and leaned forward, grabbing Yong with him. Leveraging his entire body weight, he pulled Yong over his back and threw him onto the hallway floor.

The guy's heavily muscled torso thudded to the floor with a breathy exhalation. Then he bounced nimbly back to his feet. Lowering his head, he ran full speed into Duan's chest, trapping him against the wall and pushing all the air out of his lungs. Duan realized this guy was tough and that this fight wouldn't be easy. Asian, muscular, and possibly a martial arts master.

With the guy's head still pressing his body into the wall, Duan jammed his right knee upward into his face, crushing his nose. Blood sprayed across the floor.

The Asian man lost consciousness for an instant and then was back again. He took a brief moment, obviously considering his next move. Still squatting, he took a step backward and pivoted on his left foot. With his extended right foot, he hit Duan straight into the back of his calves. This knocked Duan off his feet and down onto an elbow. While he was down, he kneed Duan in the stomach and punched him in the side of the head. Duan shook his head to stay conscious. The intensity of the fight and the strength of his opponent were taking their toll.

From the side of his now blurring eye, Duan noticed an ax leaning against the wall behind the man. He shuffled to his right, hoping the guy would then circle to his left, allowing him to grab the ax and give his opponent a fatal blow.

But he saw where Duan was looking, turned, and spotted the ax. He took a few steps backward, grabbed and lifted the ax above his head, paused for a moment to take aim, and lunged with the ax toward Duan's head. At the last split-second, Duan turned his body away. The side of the ax bounced off Duan's twisting shoulder and bounced off the floor right next to Duan's head. He felt sparks jump into his ear as the iron hit the concrete.

Duan, still gasping for breath, saw the ax rising slowly again and stopping just above his head. The guy glared down at him with a satanic smile, ready to start his ultimate swing.

* * *

The love of ultimate power and control that had always fueled Yong's life in crime overwhelmed him. He wasn't thinking about money or anything except his god-like potential to destroy another human being. Duan's nose was pouring blood across his face. It was flowing into his eyes and blinding him. The ax lifted again and was aimed at Duan's head like a pile waiting to be driven deeply into the ground.

Just as Yong began the fatal final blow, the door smashed open.

"Police! Raise your hands and step aside. Now!"

CHAPTER 38
THURSDAY, 24 OCTOBER, 3:18 P.M.

70 minutes earlier

Rudy Kotkin was driving one of the two surveillance cars following Duan Ripa at a safe distance. He had his eyes fixed on a small screen mounted on the dashboard, indicating Duan's location with a blinking dot. They were still in the city, and he saw Duan driving toward the southern part of the lake.

"Hmm, Ripa lives in Zurich and drives in the opposite direction. What is he up to?" he mumbled to himself.

Suddenly, the dot moved away from the lake.

"He just took a left at the Casino. I think he goes direction Zugerberg." Rudy briefed the surveillance car driving behind him.

"Guys, we will have to slow down as the road gets very windy. We cannot mess this up. Please take over." The other surveillance car passed him, just in case Ripa remembered the car behind him. The road continued for a few kilometers. Suddenly, he saw the dot slow down and stop.

"Did you see he stopped about 500 meters from here?" He checked with the other team.

"Yep, we've just passed Ripa and confirmed he stopped his car along the road. We parked our car a few hundred meters up from his car."

Rudy saw the dot move away from the road onto a small path on his map. After a while, the dot disappeared.

"He is gone. He must have switched off his phone."

He contacted the others, and they agreed to meet at Ripa's car. After they united, they went ahead to the location of his last signal and promptly found the chalet. From behind heavy bushes around the chalet, they observed the unfolding scene.

Rudy moved toward a colleague and whispered in his ear.

"I don't trust this. Why would Ripa go to this remote location? This is a perfect place to hide something or someone. Do you think what I think?"

They looked at each other and nodded.

"I sense we are up to something here. I'm going to call for help and ask for an intervention team to join us. We can no longer wait!"

Fifteen minutes later, the intervention team arrived. Lisa-Lotte joined at the same time. Rudy had texted her about the developing situation. The intervention squad positioned themselves in their tactical gear behind the chalet in between the trees. One member was equipped with a long-range directional microphone but could not pick up any sound from the house. The big wait on what would happen had started.

Shortly after, an Asian-looking man returned from his mission to town and entered the main house. They were surprised to see him leave only a short while later. When he returned after a few minutes, Rudy moved toward Lisa-Lotte. "What the heck is he up to? You think Ripa is working with an accomplice?"

"No clue, but I did not trust Ripa from the moment I met him. You see, my profile was not that far off." She gave him a smirky smile.

Suddenly Rudy saw his colleague with the headset and microphone move to the commander of the team, who was next to Lisa-Lotte. Although he whispered, they could follow the conversation.

"Things are getting rough inside, and we think the two men are getting into a heavy fight. I suggest we get ready to enter the house."

The commander looked at Rudy. In the end, he was in charge.

Rudy did not hesitate. "OK, go ahead."

Three men from the intervention team positioned themselves outside the door.

When they heard metal hitting the concrete floor, it was clear the fight had grown deadly, and they knocked down the door and entered with their guns drawn. Rudy and Lisa-Lotte followed at a safe distance.

One member shouted, "Two heavily injured men, medics required!"

Rudy observed the scene and saw they had captured two men, each with a heavily bloodied face. Behind him, he heard someone shouting into a mobile radio for urgent medical help.

One member had stepped into the bunker and shouted, "There's a lady here tied to a bed!" Rudy, followed by Lisa-Lotte, stepped through the open bunker door and found Gail Starck on her bed. She was unconscious but alive. *Thank God!*

In no time, policemen, paramedics, and technicians had occupied the area, and the once bucolic landscape had become a parking lot.

They separated Yong and Duan at gunpoint. The situation was not clear. Why were these men fighting? Who was who? Had they both kidnapped that lady?

The Asian guy, who'd only suffered a bloody nose, was taken to the police station in Zug. Gail, still unconscious, went by ambulance to the cantonal hospital in Baar. Finally, two paramedics checked Duan Ripa's injuries. His face was covered in blood, and he still felt groggy from Yong's punches. His first comment to the police officer who'd cleaned off the blood was, "How is Gail?"

"You mean the lady? She's gone to the clinic for observation and treatment."

When the medics reported Duan had no life-threatening injuries and had been treated for his wounds, he was also taken to the police station.

CHAPTER 39
THURSDAY, 24TH OCTOBER, 5:37 P.M.

Lisa-Lotte and Rudy interviewed Duan in the same room where they'd met a few hours earlier. It was getting dark outside. One light in the ceiling was broken, which caused the room to be poorly lit and gave it a shadowy, oppressive atmosphere. Rudy suggested that Lisa-Lotte lead the interview.

It felt to Lisa-Lotte like she was grasping at straws and wished for the tenth time that day her father could be there.

The Hawk had a real gift for observing and analyzing whatever was going on in front of him. What could he make of a bizarre case like this, in which everything seemed to occur outside their field of vision?

Intuition, she knew, wasn't some mystical form of perception. It grew out of little details and insights accumulated over years of experience. It seemed to be her most valuable but poorly developed asset in this case.

As an officer, you can't be indecisive. You don't always have the luxury of sitting around and making a list of pros and cons. Not every decision can be based on complete information and clarity. But listening to your gut and developing a strong intuitive sense of what's happening and what to do about it made all the difference.

She recognized that she simply didn't yet have enough years on the job to tap into such a pool of knowledge.

And this case was extraordinarily complicated and dynamic. By any measure, the most complex one she'd ever handled. She was glad to have Rudy at her side.

Now, she had to stop daydreaming and start the recorder.

Ripa's face was cleaned up, but he still looked like a car wreck.

"Mr. Ripa, my colleague Rudy and I weren't expecting to see you again so soon." She gave him a sardonic smile.

"The pleasure is all mine." He returned her expression in kind.

"Please note we are here to interrogate you about the kidnapping of Mrs. Gail Starck."

Rudy informed Duan of his rights.

Duan looked shocked.

"Hang on, are you considering me as a suspect? In that case, I think I wish to wait for a lawyer."

"Well, my colleague Rudy just told you that you may get one. Is there a lawyer we can call?"

"Well, my preference is to get outta here as soon as possible. Let's see what you have to ask me. This is obviously all one big misunderstanding. OK. How can I help you?"

"What happened in that chalet at the Zugerberg?"

"It's a long but exciting story. As I mentioned to you the last time, I only had one goal: to find Gail. I got a message from her kidnapper with his demand for two thousand Bitcoins. I pinpointed his location by inserting a piece of tracking code into the emails we exchanged. That led me to the chalet where Gail was kept. I went to search for her, and that Asian guy showed up and attacked me."

"You seem to be brilliant with computers."

"It's a job requirement. I work as a security consultant."

Lisa-Lotte showed Duan she was impressed.

"Mr. Ripa, we only spoke a few hours ago, and you did not talk about your contact with the kidnapper."

"You clearly had no interest in locating Gail and considered me a suspect. I went to see you twice, and both times, you simply ignored me. So, I decided it was best not to tell you everything. Did you not just say I have the right to remain silent?"

"Mr. Ripa, to avoid any further surprises, I suggest you share everything you know. We've wasted enough time with you. What else did you decide not to tell us?"

She could see Duan having a pensive moment. *What else was there to tell?*

"I honestly don't have that much more to add. My goal has always been to find Gail, and that's what I've been focused on. I really cannot tell you more about Luc Starck's death. It's about time you share what you've discovered about the murder with Gail Starck. After three days of investigation, the poor girl is still in the dark. Gail deserves answers and closure from you."

Lisa-Lotte wasn't used to having people under investigation telling her what to do. She breezed past his complaints and returned to important unanswered questions.

"Mr. Ripa, do you see any link between Gail Starck's disappearance and her late husband's death?"

"I guess that's for you to tell me. This is your case." He could not resist being cynical and self-righteous again.

Lisa-Lotte looked Duan straight in the face.

"This investigation is not a chess game, Mr. Ripa. We're trying to identify the link that ties these things together."

She paused, the only sound in the room the tick of the large wall clock.

"Well, let me help you," she continued. "There is one common factor in Gail Starck's disappearance and her husband's death, and that is *you*." She pointed a finger at him menacingly.

Duan looked genuinely surprised.

"Me? In what sense?"

"First, we learned that you and Luc Starck fought in a local bar. Then you admitted having romantic feelings toward his wife and not having a very high opinion of him. So, I imagine you aren't too distraught about Mr. Starck's demise. His death gave you *carte blanche* to pursue Gail Starck. That gives you a motive."

"Your call to Luc Starck just before his death. Are you sure it was to ask for his advice, or was it maybe a check to ensure he was on his way to a meeting you had planned?"

"Also, the last two times we met, you demonstrated to have a serious anger problem. Next, we just found you at the chalet where Gail Starck was being held, once again involved in a fight. This story has Duan Ripa written all over. What's your explanation, Mr. Ripa?"

Making a suspect feel uneasy and pressured was a common police interrogation technique that Lisa-Lotte had practiced. She made Duan confused about how to explain.

"I understand this looks weird, but I am not involved in Luc Starck's murder. Why don't you wait until Gail is awake? She'll confirm my side of the story. I also hope you're going to talk to that Chinese wanker. He has a lot more to explain." He pointed to his damaged face.

Duan felt angry and victimized, but this time could handle it more maturely.

"Thank you, Mr. Ripa. We plan to see him next and will visit Gail Starck later today in the hospital. Until we complete those interviews, please remain here in case we have any further questions. Let us know if you need anything while you're waiting."

Duan looked frustrated and tired; he knew Gail would clear it all up.

Lisa-Lotte and Rudy left him and held a quick conference in the hallway.

Rudy told her, "He's right, you know. We need to see Gail Starck first and get her side of the story. When will she be ready for questioning?"

"The doctor said they hope she'll be conscious and able to talk in a few hours."

"Ripa's story just sounds too good to be true. He is hiding something very relevant to our investigation."

"One thing we need to keep in mind."

"What's that?" Lisa-Lotte asked.

"Despite all this drama, we're no closer to solving Luc Starck's murder."

* * *

Yong was waiting in an interview room three doors down the corridor in the basement of the police station. The waiting took ages. Finally, a policeman and woman stepped in.

"Do you require an interpreter?" they asked.

Yong shook his head. "No." His English was perfect, and he cooperated as much as he could. He'd told them where to find his passport in a briefcase hidden in the chalet, that he was thirty-two and came from mainland China.

He noticed the police officers seemed to have rarely encountered a suspect so self-contained and polite. Their initial cold and forceful attitude gradually became milder. He'd been brought up to respect authority but wasn't in awe of anyone, especially *Gweilo,* Cantonese slang for Westerners. As a lifetime criminal from 'The Middle Kingdom,' he'd been brought up with a low opinion of other races. His priorities were what mattered, and he felt no need to coordinate with anyone else. People were with him or against him, period.

These policemen were just complicating his long, expensive journey to recover his missing money, and he had no doubt which side they were on. They were just minor obstacles in his righteous path.

The man who fought him in the chalet's basement had surprised him with a good move or two but, of course, in the end, had been vanquished. Without police intervention, that nuisance would have been taken care of and someone else would be cleaning brains from the concrete floor.

He would soon prevail, and these people would go back to being useless. No hurry or discomfort.

He folded his hands on the table, leaned forward, and patiently waited to take the next step toward regaining his wealth.

The girl turned on the recorder and mentioned the time and date and the names of all in the room.

"Mr. Chi, my name is Detective Lisa-Lotte Berg, and this is my colleague, Rudy Kotkin. We are here to discuss the kidnapping and serious injury of Gail Starck. This interview starts preliminary legal proceedings against you. You may remain silent and are not obliged to answer our questions. You may also appoint a defense lawyer or request a public defender. Finally, you can ask for an interpreter. Do you understand?"

He nodded.

"For the record, Mr. Chi just nodded to confirm he understands his rights," she said.

"We have several questions for you. I understand you are a resident of China. What are you doing in Switzerland?"

Yong's decision to cooperate was because he considered Switzerland as a civilized country with a centuries-old legal tradition, slightly like his own country. His thinking was if he could explain how Luc Starck had stolen his crypto coins, it should become clear why he'd traveled halfway around the world to regain what was rightfully his.

Of course, kidnapping the woman had backfired. Instead of speeding up the return of his assets, it had landed him in this uncomfortable position. It had been a calculated risk. He assumed that a fair-minded judge would consider his difficult situation and make reasonable allowances. Despite certain similarities, this was not China.

Yong told them his full story, from his initial Bitcoin mining period, the need to transfer his coins abroad, his selection of *CryptoSwap*, and the disappearance of his crypto coins.

"I can prove Mr. Luc Starck stole my coins. It may be too technical for you, but if you allow me to speak with your cybercrime unit, I will show them the evidence and convince them I'm fully within my rights."

"Let me repeat my question, Mr. Chi. Why did you come to Switzerland?"

"After it became clear Luc Starck would not return my coins, I tried to resolve my dispute reasonably with the help of some fellow Chinese here in Zurich, but that didn't work. I had no other choice than to travel to Zug myself and sort things out face to face."

He looked at the agents, hoping they would look at him with comprehension, but that was not the case. They kept their neutral, cold poker face.

"When I arrived earlier this week and tried to contact Mr. Starck, I couldn't reach him. He ignored my messages. I learned he lived in Baar and visited his house. When I couldn't talk to him at home, I changed plans and took his wife. Her kidnapping had always been part of my plans in case I had to increase pressure on him. I had come fully prepared."

"When was the last time you were in contact with Mr. Starck?" the young female police girl asked.

"A week ago on the Telegram channel, posting under the name *CryptoJustice*. After he resisted the pressure from my friends in Zurich, I made it clear to him that he better cooperate or he'd put his wife in danger. I'm pretty sure you must have seen these conversations and know I speak the truth."

"So, you didn't speak or meet Mr. Starck while you were in Switzerland?"

"I did not."

"When did you arrive?"

"Two days ago. In my briefcase, you'll find my boarding pass and my passport with a customs stamp, which should show the date of entry. Also, I should have somewhere a train ticket from Zurich to Zug. I'm not sure when Luc Starck got killed, but you will find I was not yet in the area."

"Thank you, Mr. Chi. We formally arrest you for the kidnapping of Mrs. Gail Starck and will hold you here while we continue our investigations."

He accepted his unfortunate fate and calmly accompanied two officers to the detention area.

* * *

As Rudy and Lisa-Lotte stepped out, Rudy looked at her and said, "It is clear Mr. Chi kidnapped Gail Starck, and our friend Mr. Ripa was not involved."

"Indeed, but it is also clear Chi did not kill Luc Starck, and my friend Duan Ripa still has lots of explaining to do."

CHAPTER 40
THURSDAY, 24 OCTOBER, 6:59 P.M.

Gail, still groggy, half opened her eyes. She was confused about where she was. She remembered being held in the concrete bunker, but this looked nothing like that. *What was happening?* Flashes of vague memories came back to her. About Luc. About Luc being drunk and hitting her. About her crying in bed. It took her efforts to process these thoughts and push them into the background. Every time a memory got clearer, she fell asleep again and lost it all again. Like an old radio trying to tune into a station but losing reception.

When she opened her eyes, she saw the contours of a person in front of her.

"Hello, Mrs. Starck, hello?"

"Huh," was all she could get out.

"Mrs. Starck, you are in the cantonal hospital of Baar. My name is Stanis. I'm your nurse."

She had difficulties processing all. "Hospital? Why am I here?"

"Let's not worry about that now. You better first recover, and then we can have that conversation."

Gail thought she said something but did not really get it and fell asleep again. That process repeated itself a few times.

When she woke up again, she didn't know if she had slept for two minutes or two hours. Whatever had happened to her, it certainly knocked her down. She slowly reopened her eyes and saw that nurse again.

She now noticed the bandage on her left hand.

"What's that?" She raised her hand.

"You had a minor accident, but it is all okay. We will talk about it later."

She looked through the window and could see leafy branches swaying outside her window and sunshine. They'd never looked so comforting before. Gosh, she had missed that during the past few days.

She fell away again and, after a moment, opened her eyes. She thought she was seeing that nurse again, but when the person started speaking, she noticed her voice had changed.

"Hello, Gail. This is Lisa-Lotte Berg. I'm from the police in Zug. I'm here with my colleague Mr. Rudy Kotkin." The woman offered her a cup of water. She raised her upper body, accepted the cup, and sipped a bit from it.

Yes, it felt as if she was slowly recovering and more aware of what was happening around her.

She looked at the woman sitting on her bed. Vaguely, she recognized her.

"Hello, yes, I think we met a few days ago."

It took much effort, but she now recognized that lady from a visit to her house.

"Yes, I came over to inform you about the death of your husband."

Only now Luc's death came back to her. It seemed like an eternity had passed. So many things had happened to her.

"I'm not sure if you fully remember what has happened over the past days, but I have a few questions, and it's important that you tell me what you know so we can proceed with our investigations."

The nurse stepped into the room to check if all was OK. Gail looked at her and smiled back at her. All was good. The nurse left again.

She looked at the policewoman.

"Gail, can you tell me what you remember from the past days?"

She had to go deep, but bit by bit, things came back. She told her about being taken at her house, waking up in a bunker, the endless waiting, the headset, the messages she had to send, and the confusion. Suddenly, she remembered the guy cutting off her little finger. She looked at her hand and the bandage.

Rudy saw her looking at her hand.

"Well, you have been lucky. After your kidnapper cut off your pinky, he kept it on ice. When we received it, we stored it in a freezer, and here a surgeon reattached it. He cannot guarantee flexibility or full sensation would return, but with a pinky, that is less important. To manage the pain, the doctor has given you some powerful painkillers. That's why you are still feeling so groggy."

"Gail, did you ever see your abductor's face?" Lisa-Lotte asked.

"No, not really. He took off my goggles for a few seconds, and I saw that he was small and muscular. There was no time to study his face more fully. He looked Asian, but I could be wrong. It all went by so fast. Oh yes, I remember his voice was electronically changed while he was talking to me."

"Gail, when we found you, there were two men in the chalet where you were held. They were in a heavy fight. One is named Yong Chi, and the other Duan Ripa. Do these names mean anything to you?"

"Well, Chong Yi, or whatever, no. But Duan Ripa, yes, he is a close friend of mine."

"Could Mr. Ripa have been your kidnapper?"

"Oh my God, no! How could you even think this? The kidnapper took off my goggles, and I know Duan very well and definitely would have recognized him." Despite the painkillers, she was suddenly passionately coherent.

Lisa-Lotte looked at her. "I hear what you are saying, Gail, but we have witnessed a side of Mr. Ripa you may never have seen. If I were you, I would be very careful with jumping to conclusions and be extremely cautious with him."

"Absolutely not. Duan has been such a help to me since Luc's death. He has nothing to do with my disappearance. What do you know about the other person?"

"He claims to be a victim of your husband's *CryptoSwap* company and blames him for having stolen his crypto coins."

Gail sighed, wondering when this whole *CryptoSwap* saga would end.

By now, she was fully conscious again, and it had all come back to her. She asked for another cup of water and finished it in one go.

Lisa-Lotte moved her chair closer to Gail. Her knees gently touched the bed.

"Gail, since we saw you last, so much has happened. Allow me to update you on the progress of our investigations."

Gail wondered what other surprises she was about to hear. With everything she'd gone through lately, she was prepared for anything. She steeled herself with a deep breath.

"Mrs. Starck, I'm sorry to tell you, but your husband was murdered."

Gail showed the same neutral reaction as when she was informed of Luc's death.

"Do you know who killed him?"

"Not really. We're looking into several theories, but nothing is certain."

Gail could sense the policewoman knew more than she'd told her.

"Since we spoke, has anything new related to your husband's death occurred to you?"

Gail thought about her last tumultuous evening with Luc.

"Well, there is one odd thing he said that last evening."

"What was that, Mrs. Starck?"

"Luc was unusually depressed. He rambled on about problems with his company, BionTic, and that he was receiving threats from *CryptoSwap* customers. These threats upset him the most because some were now threatening to hurt me. He saw himself as a colossal failure, was miserable, and drank a lot that evening. I could see he was spiraling. He even said he considered suicide as the only way to end his misery. I became so frightened; I kept my distance so he couldn't touch me.

"It was the first time he'd ever threatened suicide. He said, 'My death will be a huge surprise.'"

"Could you see your husband committing suicide?"

"Oh no, he was too big a coward to do that."

Lisa-Lotte hoped Gail would continue talking. When she remained silent, she had another question.

"Did your husband tell you specifically what kind of problems he was facing at BionTic?"

"No. He just mumbled, 'That bastard Giobbi is driving BionTic into the ground.' When Luc was in one of his moods, everything and everyone sucked!"

Gail had been staring off into space. She finally looked up at Lisa-Lotte as if seeking confirmation.

"He was a coward, but isn't it a coincidence that twenty-four hours after I heard him considering suicide, he was dead?"

Lisa-Lotte put her hand on Gail's arm reassuringly.

"Based on what we've learned, Mrs. Starck, your husband has definitely been murdered. Without any doubt."

"You can only say that for sure if you know who killed him. Do you?"

"Well, let me say this, we are exploring a few options. I have a few more questions about Mr. Ripa."

"You are not going to tell me Duan killed Luc, are you?"

"Well, we can't rule out anything. We have seen a side of Mr. Ripa you may never have encountered before."

Gail raised her eyebrows. "What do you mean?"

"We learned several things about him. First, a few weeks before the death of your husband, they have been seen fighting in a bar here in town."

"Fighting? About what?"

"He claimed it was about nothing, but still serious enough to grab your husband with a judo move and throw him over his head on the floor. But there is more."

Gail eagerly awaited what else there was to be said about Duan.

"We also know that the murderer of your husband was a computer expert, and Mr. Ripa definitely is one."

"He is not the only computer expert in this area. But why would he have wanted to kill Luc?"

"We have not yet ruled out it to be a crime of passion. Mr. Ripa admitted to having romantic feelings for you, and not having Mr. Starck around suits him very well."

"I think you are crazy and one hundred percent wrong."

CHAPTER 41
THURSDAY, 24 OCTOBER, 7:28 P.M.

Lisa-Lotte and Rudy walked out of Gail Starck's room with mixed feelings. They were happy to see she'd recovered but felt sorry for all she had to go through over the past few days. Lisa-Lotte decided it was best not to tell her everything and buy some time before sharing any details. While they now knew *How* Luc had been murdered, they still lacked the *Who*, and Gail still had a strong motive for it.

It was time to visit their other patient. Lisa-Lotte had never been in a hospital as often as she had over the past few days.

They took the elevator down two floors. In the elevator, she looked at herself in the mirror.

"Wow, I look so tired. Look at these bags under my eyes."

"Come on, you're gorgeous, don't be that depressive." Rudy tried to cheer her up.

"I guess it's the stress after I met with Schmidt. He really gets on my nerves." She looked forward to talking to her father.

Earlier that day, Bernt had been released from the intensive care unit, which was a good sign. When they walked into her father's room, he cheerfully said, "Look what the cat dragged in! I thought you'd forgotten me, and you haven't answered my messages. I was getting worried."

"No need, Dad." She was happy to see him smile. He looked much better.

"No pie today?"

She kissed him. "Sorry, Dad, we are way too busy solving crimes. You chose the wrong time to relax in the hospital like this. Speaking of relaxing, what are you reading?"

Bernt closed his book. "It's about anti-gravity."

Lisa-Lotte was surprised by her father's newfound interest in science.

"Yes, it's impossible to put down."

Bernt laughed louder than ever.

Lisa-Lotte still had to get used to his stupid jokes but looked forward to them at times like these.

Rudy updated him on their meeting with Duan, Gail's ribboned amputated pinky delivered in a wrapped box, the rescuing of Gail at the Zugerberg, and the fight between Duan and Yong Chi.

"Wow, all that in just eight hours? So much while I was just lying around!"

"We need your help, Dad."

"Again?"

"We're happy we found Gail Starck but can't find any new leads in the death of her husband."

She told him about the heated speech they received from Tell Schmidt and the ultimatum he had given her. "I'm desperate to resolve this case. Please help us." She grabbed his hand tightly.

Bernt looked at her and was silent for a while.

"Something has been bothering me. All the contacts with that Federer Cap guy, the magician, and Minten went via email, right?"

"Yep."

"Has our cybercrime unit tracked down the email accounts?"

"I'm still waiting to hear from them. I also asked them to trace the payments made to Minten and the magician Vogel."

Bernt smiled. "You see? You're doing fine without me! If I were you, I would take a deep breath and list all the surprise scenarios hovering out there in left field. People without a motive or whom we've never discussed. There might be a piece in this gigantic jigsaw puzzle we can't quite put our finger on. Creative and lateral thinking can sometimes crack open a case that seems to have reached a dead end."

Lisa-Lotte jotted down a couple of sentences on her pad.

Rudy stepped out of the room. "Bernt, I'll leave you two alone. All the best, my friend."

"Bye, Rudy, and thanks again for taking care of her."

When they were together, Lisa came and sat on the side of his bed.

"I completely forgot to ask how you're doing. You certainly look much better."

"Yes, I feel fine. I have some sensation back in my legs. I was even hoping they would release me today, but it's late now, so hopefully, that happens tomorrow."

"Great news!" She hugged him. "Any messages from Mom?"

"Nothing. I guess she's glad these days not to be running into me in town so she can enjoy life again. You know, your mother always accused me of having zero empathy."

"Did she?"

"I just don't understand why she felt that way."

Bernt started laughing until Lisa-Lotte finally got his joke.

She bent over the bed, grabbed her father, and held him tight.

"I miss you. We were such a team, and having this case is getting too much for me." She kept him in her arms and could not resist crying. The stress of the past days had to get out.

"It's okay, darling. You're doing well. I feel sorry I'm not there with you, but I know and feel you can do this."

She looked at him with her watery eyes and saw he struggled to keep his emotions. Emotions he usually hid behind his jokes.

"I feel so useless, darling. I'm stuck here while you're working your ass off on this case. It would have been so nice for us to solve this one at the end of my career."

"I know." She cleaned her tears with a tissue while handing him the box.

"OK, enough. I'm outta here. We've got a murder to solve. Love ya!"

CHAPTER 42
FRIDAY, 25 OCTOBER, 9:28 A.M.

The next morning, Gail was released from the hospital. The morning's blood test had been normal, and she showed no apparent negative effects from her torture at the chalet.

It felt odd to be at home alone. The villa was lonely and empty. Filled with echoes. Her espresso cup was still in the coffee machine from when she was kidnapped. Luc's shoes were waiting neatly in the hall, and his laptop was on the table. Time had stood still in this place. She realized it would take a while for life to return to normal. The house that had given her so many sweet memories that were pushed away by recent events. For the past months, it had been her house of hell.

Would she stay here or sell it?

Her thoughts kept drifting back to Duan. Where was he? Had the police let him go after her statement yesterday? The words from that policewoman haunted her through the night:

"We've seen a side of Mr. Ripa you may never have encountered."

She couldn't shake it. Could Duan—her Duan—have killed Luc? The idea of it sent a cold tremor through her body. Duan had always been gentle and thoughtful. In her darkest nightmares, she couldn't picture him murdering her husband. And yet, the police must have had their reasons to say something so devastating. She felt lost, her heart heavy with uncertainty. What should she do? Should she call him? What would she even say?

She sat frozen in her kitchen for what felt like forever, drowning in confusion, her hands trembling as she reached for yet another cup of coffee. Time blurred, with each moment a battle between fear and the need for answers. Several times, she picked up her phone, her fingers hovering over his number, but she couldn't bring herself to dial. The thought of hearing his voice, knowing he might have killed Luc, twisted her insides. How could she speak to the man who could be responsible for her husband's death?

But deep down, she knew. She couldn't stay in this state of confusion forever. The only way to know the truth was to call him.

His phone only rang once before he picked up.

"Hello, is this Mr. Ripa?" she said jokingly in an attempt to hide her nerves.

"I just woke up and was about to call you."

"Thanks, Duan. You've been on my mind the entire night! I guess we have a lot to catch up on, don't you think?"

"Yes, I was released late yesterday. I've tried to call you so many times." He sounded relieved to hear her.

"I hope the police didn't cause you too much trouble. I'm so sorry you got dragged into all this."

"They finally realized I had nothing to do with your kidnapping and let me go. If you are home now, I could come right over."

"Of course. Can't wait to see you."

When she hung up, she stared ahead of herself. *Was she doing right by inviting the potential murderer of her husband into her home?*

Twenty minutes later, Gail opened the door and welcomed Duan. She wrapped her arms around him, hugging him and crying at the same time.

His head was covered with bandages, his nose had a large plaster, and the only part of his face that was visible was badly bruised. "I am so happy to see you, Duan."

"Even in this condition?" He laughed, although just smiling was already painful.

"Yes, of course. What do you think of my new accessory?" She held up her left hand, still heavily bandaged.

Gail placed two cups of espresso on the counter.

She started telling him everything about what had happened to her. The confusing messages she was forced to record, the amputation of her pinky, and the endless solitary waiting in discomfort. She couldn't hold back the tears any longer. The past days had been so brutal; she felt like she was going through every terrible moment again.

"Cry, Gail, just let it all out." Duan folded her in his arms. The bags under her eyes revealed she had slept little, and this was not her first cry. "I can't imagine facing an ordeal as horrible as yours. You are so resilient!"

"Well, it looks like you didn't have it so easy, either," she said, wiping away her tears.

"You're so much like Mina. My well-being was always her priority."

Duan led Gail into the living room and to the sofa. They stayed close and sat hip to hip, arm to shoulder, as Duan related the complete story from his perspective.

Duan shared how he'd discovered her location, the violent struggle in the basement, and the relentless interrogations and accusations by the police.

Gail raptly listened as he described how he'd hidden tracking software in his message and how her kidnapper had been tricked into leaving the chalet.

"My priority was to move you out of that place, so I went to get my car, but suddenly he'd returned. We had such a tough fight, Gail. Lying on that concrete floor and seeing that ax and his satanic smile, I thought I was a dead man."

Gail covered her mouth in despair when Duan described his fierce struggle with Yong Chi.

"Oh, Duan, I feel so sorry for you." It was her turn to hug him, her left hand raised in the air.

"Ow, that hurts!" he shouted when she put her arm around his neck.

"It's still sensitive." Duan gave her a caring smile. "How is your hand?"

She shrugged and gave him a mock salute with the bandage.

After a moment of basking in each other's warm presence, Duan slapped both knees in frustration.

"I still can't get my head around what happened to you, Gail. It's all so unfair. When I saw you in that bunker, I felt devastated and furious. Thank God this is finished. The real shocker was when that policewoman suspected me of your kidnapping, and I was involved in Luc's death. Can you imagine? Bunch of morons!"

For a moment, the conversation stopped with both lost in their thoughts, processing the events of the past days.

Duan finally broke the silence.

"Did the police give you any more details about Luc's death?"

"Oh yes, absolutely. They explained to me Luc has been murdered."

Duan looked surprised, "Murdered? Did they say by who and how?"

Oops, what to say?

It would be odd to tell him about their crime of passion theory. The past minutes together had been so natural and so normal. Gail absolutely could not imagine Duan had a hand in killing Luc.

"No, but I'm sure they know more than what they told me."

"Remember, I told you that Luc had threatened to commit suicide?"

"Yes. On that last evening together, wasn't it?"

"Indeed. They now claim a suicide has been ruled out."

As Gail spoke, Duan caressed her right shoulder. He got her another espresso, still working to help her relax and find a little peace.

"Was it that young blond police girl that mentioned Luc was murdered?"

Gail nodded.

"She is utterly useless." Duan kept silent and looked at Gail.

Lisa-Lotte's last words came back to her.

We have seen a side of Mr. Ripa you may never have encountered.

She kept wondering what she meant with these words. Was there indeed a side of Duan she did not know? Did Duan have anything to do with Luc's death? It confused her. Just as she had these thoughts, Duan looked at her with a serious look.

"What's wrong, Duan?"

"I need to tell you something important."

"Tell me."

"I need to confess something."

She did not know where to look. She felt her hands getting sweaty.

She started to shiver. What was he going to confess?

Duan swallowed. It was clear he was struggling with something.

Suddenly, her thoughts went to that afternoon after Luc's death, when Duan came to Baar to comfort her. She recalled that odd remark from him that went something like, "You may look back to Luc's death as the best thing that ever could have happened to you."

Did Duan kill Luc, and was he going to confess it to her?

He spoke with a trembling voice. "That Lisa-Lotte girl suspected me of killing Luc. Their theory was that I killed Luc to be with you. She even asked if I loved you."

Gail did not know how to react. She was scared.

"And?"

"And what? If I killed Luc or if I loved you?"

"Did you kill Luc?" The question came out before she realized it.

"Are you serious?" He looked at her with a surprised face. "Of course, I did not kill Luc. Why should I? Do you really think I could have done that?"

He gave her again that odd, cold facial expression.

She did not know how to react. She observed Duan closely as he spoke these words and thought, *OK, let's test that crime of passion theory.*

"What did you say when she asked if you loved me?"

Anticipating his answer, she was reflecting on her feelings for him. The recent events had brought them close, and she had seen a part of Duan she had never seen before. However, it was different from how the police used these words. The Duan in front of her took the initiative, did not wait, spoke up, and, if required, would not shy away from a fight. That new masculine side of Duan made her realize she had feelings for him she had never felt before. She fancied him being close to her. His presence had a calming effect on her. *Did she start to love him?*

Duan looked her in the eyes. "Her question took me by surprise. I had to stop and think, but it did not take me much to realize I do love you. We've gone through so much in recent weeks. Gail, I've never felt this close to someone other than to Mina." He kept staring into her eyes. The look in his eyes changed as he confessed his feelings to her. By the time he stopped talking, she saw that unique look of someone in love.

Such a sweetheart. No way he could have killed Luc!

He raised his cup, paused for an instant, and gently kissed her on the lips. "I love you."

Even though that kiss was hanging in the air, it still took her by surprise, and she did not know how to react. *What to say?* To reciprocate his actions, she kindly took her right hand, placed it on his neck, and slowly started rubbing him. Carefully trying not to hurt him.

Before they knew it, dusk started sliding over Baar; the afternoon was turning into evening.

"What do you want to do for dinner? Shall I order us a couple of sushi platters?"

"Great idea." Gail didn't hesitate. She loved sushi.

"Duan, I hope you can stay here with me tonight. It would be wonderful to have you close to me after so much loneliness."

"Of course. And I'll need someone to help me replace these bandages." He gave her a naughty smile.

There were several good sushi restaurants in Zug. Duan had done some contract work with one of the most popular, Negishi Sushi Bar on *Baarerstrasse*, and the proprietor owed him a favor. So, he ordered a super combination platter with a small bottle of *Otokoyama Tokubetsu Junmai* sake. Nothing but the best for such a special occasion.

While enjoying their delightful meal, Duan changed the topic. "Are you sure you still do not want to have anything to do with Luc's crypto coins?"

"Yes, absolutely. That hasn't changed," Gail grimly responded while patiently trying to lift a sashimi slice with her chopsticks.

"After what just happened to me, anything having to do with Luc will forever be bad news. You know what? It all started with that bloody Mr. Sashimi Nakamoto."

Duan laughed and almost dropped his seared tuna nigiri sushi in his bowl of soya sauce.

"What's so funny?"

"You meant Mr. *Satoshi* Nakamoto, but said, *Sashimi* Nakamoto!"

They couldn't stop laughing. The sense of relief this unintentional joke brought was magical.

"Anyway, whoever. If that Japanese guy had never come up with his crypto shit, I might have lived a quiet life, and Luc would still be with me."

They had just enough room to finish the delicious seaweed salad.

"Sorry. You wanted to say something, Duan. What was it?"

"When your kidnapper asked for Bitcoins in return for your freedom, my only option was to search for the private key of Luc's wallet. And I came close to finding it."

Duan told Gail about his conversation with Luc a few weeks before the murder, the emails he received after his death, the series of riddles, and how he'd cracked most of them.

Gail listened, hardly able to believe what she heard. Finally, she said, "I hope you understand why I did not want to have anything to do with his coins, but I appreciate the effort you put into it, Duan."

"You know, I thought a lot of the book *The Da Vinci Code* while working my way through these riddles. I even wondered if I was being filmed with a hidden camera. It was all so unreal."

"Cheers to my modern Professor Robert Langdon." She raised her glass.

As they laughed together, sitting ever closer on the sofa, Gail wanted to run her fingers through Duan's hair. She had to settle for gently patting his bandages.

"Speaking of puzzles and riddles, do you think that's what Luc meant when he said, 'My death will be a big surprise?'"

"May well be. The more I now know about Luc, the more I realize he liked his puzzles and riddles."

"I'm just stuck on my last riddle. At least, I hope it's the last one. It says, *The rest of the key is behind what you see!* Do you have any clue what that could mean?"

"Not really. If you take it literally, it could mean that this part of the key is *behind* something."

"Exactly, that's what I thought. I even visited the BionTic offices and found an official photo of Luc. I checked the back, but it was empty. Do you have any other photos of Luc here?"

"Hmm, yes, plenty of digital ones, but printed, not many. Hang on, there's our wedding picture." Gail went to the bedroom and came back with a framed wedding picture. Duan opened it. There was nothing.

"I'm so disappointed in myself that I cannot resolve this last one. Maybe we are right, and we just need to continue looking for the proper photo with something behind it. But I'm afraid I missed something. I remember when Luc told me about this, he said, *If there is one person who will figure it out, it's you.* I wonder if he overrated me."

"Leave it for now, Duan. It's not that important to me. Sometimes, by setting aside a puzzle like this for a while, a solution spontaneously dawns upon you."

"I see we finished the sake. How about we change to wine?" Gail didn't wait for him to answer. She opened a new bottle and refilled his glass. A delicious *Chasselas* from the Swiss Lavaux region. "Cheers."

They went back to the living room, enjoyed their wine, and chitchatted. It was so relaxing to have a normal evening after the past few very stressful days. It was like friends catching up. Duan talking about his work, Gail dreaming about vacation destinations, and together cherishing the fun memories they'd shared with Mina.

"Remember that time we went biking near Lugano and passed an elderly guy cycling up a mountain?" Gail asked. "Mina and I laughed at him; he was struggling so much to get his bike moving at the bottom of the climb. We were so sure he would collapse before reaching the top. Guess what? Just before we reached the peak, the old guy casually waved as he passed us. We got a serious case of giggles. Luc scolded us for behaving like a couple of teenagers."

Duan laughed. Sipping his wine, he said, "I'm glad you asked me to stay. I'm not sure I could have driven home. Are you sure I can use the guestroom?"

"Guestroom? What kind of damsel in distress would banish her knight in shining armor to the castle's guest room? I need someone by my side. Very close to me." She looked at him with that same soft liquid gaze as Mina put up after she'd drunk too much wine and was in seduction mode.

Duan playfully looked over his shoulder like there was another man behind him, then pointed innocently at himself.

"Moi? How can I refuse?" Duan raised his glass, and they toasted a last time. He half stood to give her a longer, more sensual kiss. When he stopped and drew his head away, she eased her hand to the back of his neck, gently pulled him closer, and turned up the heat. Then she started kissing him passionately. The salty soya taste bonded them into one.

All the mounting stress was released through the shared expression of long-suppressed love. The alcohol relieved their pain and inhibitions. Kissing each other gently across their shoulders and necks. His hands slowly crawled up underneath her shirt and warmly cupped her breasts.

They walked softly toward the bedroom, holding each other steady. The passion continued while they undressed, continuously holding eye contact. They desperately needed this closeness and feeling of safety. Although this moment had been a promise hanging between them for so many months, it still blindsided them.

Duan was the first one in bed, wearing only his shirt. Gail joined him after a minute in the bathroom. It felt so odd to share a bed with a woman, while it was also so natural. Was it because they'd known each other for so many years? Had they always been in love? Was she sharing the bed with the murderer of her husband? She was still so confused.

Gail moved her body closer to him. Her legs touched his foot. Duan wiggled his toes, and Gail's leg moved back in a teasing stroke. Neither spoke a word. He smelled the light perfume she had applied while preparing herself in the bathroom.

"Hmm, that smells nice," he whispered.

"You recognize it? It's *Miel d'Amour*. My favorite brand."

"*Miel d'Amour*? Honey of Love? You are not seducing me by any chance, Mrs. Starck?"

"I already did. You don't mind, Mr. Ripa, do you?"

When he turned his head, he looked straight into her wide, inviting smile.

Then they kissed again. Their bodies intertwined. The tension of their simmering passion didn't release – it only grew more and more intense.

Yet, this was not the moment to take it all the way. They slowed down, cuddled, and wished each other goodnight. Duan rested his right arm across her toned belly. Just before sleeping, Gail grabbed his hand and moved it to cover her full breast. They fell asleep.

CHAPTER 43
MONDAY, 12 AUGUST, 1:14 P.M.

Ten weeks earlier

Fritz's mind worked overtime as he meticulously prepared this complex murder. The first step was securing the necessary funds. Purchasing VX gas wouldn't be cheap, and various accomplices needed to be paid. According to his project spreadsheet, he would need at least 180,000 Swiss Francs. To be safe, he rounded it up to 250,000 Swiss Francs. But where could he find such a large sum?

Recently, Fritz listened to a podcast about a popular scam known as the "CEO fraud," introduced in France by an Israeli scammer named Gilbert Chikli. Fritz was amazed at how easily Chikli convinced corporate leaders and celebrities to hand over huge sums of money. The podcast detailed how one large bank had lost several hundred thousand Euros to the scam. The key to the fraud was knowing personal details about the bank's senior finance manager, which helped the scammer gain the victim's trust.

Desperate to secure funding, Fritz decided to try the scam himself.

He had identified five major banks in mid-sized Swiss towns, each with a female head of Treasury. Fritz theorized that if he called with authority, these women might be more likely to follow his charming orders. He gathered personal information from their social media profiles and then tracked down their mothers' phone numbers.

He made his first call.

"Hello, is this Frau Rozenbaum?"

"Yes, who is this?"

"My name is Paul Brouwer. I work with your daughter at the bank. We're colleagues," Fritz said, deliberately withholding his real name.

"Alright, how can I help you?" The mother sounded surprised.

"We're preparing for our annual Employee of the Year award ceremony, and I'm pleased to tell you that your daughter has been nominated. However, this is all very confidential, so please don't mention it to her."

"Oh, okay?"

"Your daughter is incredibly skilled and a joy to work with. I'm sure she has a bright future at the bank." Fritz added, laying on the flattery.

"I can imagine," the mother said, sounding slightly embarrassed and unsure how to respond.

"We're planning a surprise celebration, similar to the TV show *This Is Your Life*, where we'll invite to the party people who have been important in her life."

"Oh, how nice!"

After that warm introduction, Fritz was able to easily gather key personal details like her daughter's primary school, her best friend, pets, favorite actors, songs, and more. Before ending the call, he again emphasized the need for absolute secrecy to maintain the surprise.

It worked! Fritz repeated it with another two mothers.

With this treasure trove of information, Fritz was ready to move to the next phase: calling the heads of Treasury at the bank to see who would fall for the scam. All he needed was to gain their confidence, stress the importance of secrecy, and make them feel they were part of an exciting, secretive operation.

Fritz rehearsed his script meticulously before making the first call.

"Hello, this is Agnes Rozenbaum."

"Hello, Agnes. My name is Eugene Burger," Fritz said, adopting a deeper, more authoritative voice.

"I'm the head of internal affairs at the bank. I'm currently investigating some suspicious cash losses at your branch."

"Okay…" Agnes replied, clearly caught off guard.

"I've been working on this case for several months and have evidence that your boss is involved. We need your help to finalize the investigation. This is highly confidential, which is why I'm calling you personally. You are not to mention this to anyone, especially not your boss, your husband or even your mother. This has to stay between us. Is that clear?"

"Yes," Agnes said, her voice trembling.

"Please move to a private location where you can't be overheard."

Fritz walked her through the script, and Agnes seemed to fall into the trap. But when Fritz called back the next day, Agnes had developed second thoughts and refused to continue.

For the next bank, Fritz used a new burner phone and SIM card. This time, the woman named Lidy, on the other end of the line, sounded older and more easily intimidated by Fritz's authority. Toward the end of the conversation, Fritz lightened the mood by referencing information gleaned from her mother.

"Thank you so much. I know this won't be easy, but I'm here to help. Once this is all over, let's meet to celebrate. Michael Bublé will be performing in town soon. The bank sponsors his concerts, and my team plans to attend. Would you like to join us?"

"Oh my God! I love Michael Bublé! I'd love to!" the woman exclaimed.

"Gotcha," Fritz muttered after hanging up.

After several days of regular contact, this second mark was eating out of Fritz's hand.

The next call would be crucial.

"Hello, Lidy, this is Mr. Burger," Fritz said, maintaining an air of formality.

"Hello, Mr. Burger."

"Listen carefully. Do you have something to take notes near you?"

"Yes, sir."

"Tomorrow is D-day. At exactly noon, you will meet me at Restaurant *Bahnhof*, just outside the Olten train station. Bring 250,000 Swiss Francs in 200 Franc notes in a Migros plastic bag. Sit at the table by the window."

"At 12:05, walk to the last stall in the men's bathroom. Knock and whisper. *'Brennerpass.'* When you hear as reply someone whispering, *'Mont Blanc,'* slide the bag under the door. Then return to your seat."

"We'll mark the money, and within thirty minutes, someone will enter the restaurant and place the bag back next to your table. When you return to the bank, put the money back from where you took it. That's all you have to do. We will take care of the rest."

"Understood?

"Yes, sir."

"Remember—no one can know about this!"

The next day, Fritz watched from a distance as Lidy walked into the restaurant and took her seat by the window. Everything went exactly as planned. When the bag slid under the stall door, Fritz's heart pounded in his chest. He grabbed it and left immediately.

Before leaving, Fritz glanced back through the café window and saw Lidy still sitting there. He called her briefly to praise her for handling the secret operation so well. Then, with a quick stride, Fritz headed for the train station just in time to catch the next train to Zurich.

How easy it had been to get a bank official to hand over 250,000 Swiss Francs! He was ready to move forward with his meticulous plan.

CHAPTER 44
FRIDAY, 25 OCTOBER, 10:00 A.M.

Rudy and Lisa-Lotte were about to start the team's daily stand-up. Awaiting all to get seated, they looked out the window with each a warm cappuccino in their hand. For the first time this season, the Alps were full of snow on the peaks. Lisa-Lotte needed this Zen moment, as she was not looking forward to today's session. She felt things were not progressing! Numerous times, she had replayed yesterday's conversation with Schmidt in her mind. The pressure was getting too much for her. The twenty-four hours he had given them would expire today by four p.m. By then, they were expected to have resolved the case. Worried, she checked her watch.

"I see you are stressed, Lisa-Lotte. Don't worry, I will manage Schmidt. I've known him for so many years. He's always the same."

"I barely slept. I can't wait for this case to be over."

"You want me to start the meeting?"

"No, I'll do it." She did not want her uncertainties to be visible to the wider team.

When she turned around, she saw the full team sitting, all eyes on her. Time to get started.

"Folks, welcome to day four of this investigation. The good news is, we freed Gail Starck thanks to the carefully coordinated efforts of our crack team."

Everyone clapped in appreciation. The youngest team member let out a discreet whistle.

"But we aren't ready to cheer yet. We still need to solve the murder of Luc Starck and are running out of time. We desperately need to wrap this up.

It's Friday, so let's close this before the weekend. The payments for Minten and the magician Vogel. Do we have anything new on this?"

Suzanne, a female detective from Financial Investigations, spoke up.

"Yes, both were paid with gift cards. As you know, such cards are popular among criminals as an anonymous form of payment. Minten and Vogel said they had been really surprised to be paid like that."

Lisa-Lotte looked curious. "Any clue why they did not mention it when we spoke to them? They could not have forgotten something essential like that."

"They explained business had been slow these days, and their services weren't as unusual and entertaining as they were before. They were thrilled to get such generous windfalls and decided not to look their gift horses in the mouth."

"How much did they get?" Lisa-Lotte asked, trying to sound not too curious.

"Mr. Vogel was paid 2,500 Swiss Francs and Mr. Minten 15,000 Swiss Francs. Not bad for a day's work. Apparently, they were paid in gift cards of a value of five hundred CHF each."

"Too bad! Unfortunately, that's a dead end."

Lisa-Lotte turned to another detective.

"Freddie, anything interesting with the email addresses that were used?"

"I went over them carefully with our cyber investigations unit and learned a lot. We traced the emails sent to Brucker, Vogel, and Minten and contacted their internet providers to retrieve the IP address of the sender. It turned out they used a temporary email service, like *www.burnermail.io*. This generates a one-time, therefore untraceable, email address. People often register for these services to sign up for internet services, so they don't have to use their private email and disclose their identity and personal data."

Lisa-Lotte looked depressed. One lead after the other led to nothing.

She looked around the room, searching faces for anything encouraging. Unfortunately, everyone was either going through their notes for the umpteenth time, studying their folded hands, or desperately avoiding eye contact with her. It was the worst stand-up this week. She already visualized Schmidt shouting at her.

Officer Patrick raised his hand.

"I may have something. Yesterday I mentioned our financial investigation unit found that BionTic, Luc Starck's company, is possibly suffering from cash-flow problems. They went to visit the company's house bank with a warrant to review their account for any suspicious transactions. They concluded the current account has been draining money, and with the current burn rate would run out of cash next week."

"Good one, Patrick. Finally, a spark of hope." She even showed a slim smile.

"Anyone else with good news?" she tried in a desperate tone.

"I have an update." Oli, a junior officer from the cybercrime unit, raised his hand, hoping to keep things moving, including his career.

"Lisa-Lotte, I've been looking into accusations by Yong Chi that it was Luc Starck who had emptied the crypto wallets. I met with Mr. Chi. He's an incredibly skilled hacker. I've never seen anything like it. He logged in to the server on his home computer and proved to us that his *notepad* application had indeed been hacked. Every day, Yong saves five backups of his computer files for exactly this kind of situation. It showed the application had been changed right after he'd registered his account with *CryptoSwap*. It could not be a coincidence."

Oli stood up and placed a hardboard poster with a world map on one of the whiteboards in front of the meeting table. "The following story is quite complex, so I brought a printout so you all can better follow it."

He looked around the room with a pleased smile, clearly happy with his proactive approach.

"Go ahead, Oli, you make us curious," Lisa-Lotte encouraged him.

"I spent several hours with Mr. Chi. He jumped quickly from one server to the next. Too bad he's chosen a life of crime. His talents would be worth a lot to many companies. Because of the traceability of Bitcoin transactions, he proved how his coins had been moved from one wallet to another wallet. A few minutes later, that wallet was used to distribute the coins over various crypto exchanges around the world."

He pointed to the poster, which started with a box named *CryptoSwap* placed in Switzerland. Various arrows connected boxes that were placed across the globe, each with different cryptocurrency signs.

"At these exchanges, the Bitcoins were swapped into other crypto coins, like Ethereum and Solana. This was repeated several times. It's impossible to follow it on the fly, but with his commitment to documentation, Mr. Chi had it all sorted out."

The team was listening to him, some with their mouths wide open. Oli continued.

"The way Chi figured out it was Luc Starck who was behind this theft was impressive."

He pointed to the last arrow that pointed back to Switzerland.

"At SEBA bank, a local crypto bank here in Zug, the crypto coins were exchanged for Swiss Francs and transferred to a regular UBS bank account. Now he had an account number and could link it to a name. He asked a Swiss contact with a UBS account to do an internal test-transfer to the account where his crypto coins were transferred to."

"So how did that prove that the account belonged to Luc Starck?" Lisa-Lotte looked curious.

Oli continued, "Any transfer in Switzerland must be made with a valid name of the receiver. His contact first did a test transaction with a random name. That one was declined. But when he used that account number with Luc Starck as the recipient, it transferred successfully. That was the proof he had been looking for. It confirmed his coins finally ended in Luc Starck's account."

Oli looked at the group with satisfaction as if he had figured it out and not Yong Chi.

"After hours at his laptop, I was convinced that Luc Starck had robbed his customers at *CryptoSwap*."

Lisa-Lotte responded. "I think I understand most of it, but you lost me with Ethereum and Sultana."

"Solana," he corrected her. "Those are other crypto coins, similar to Bitcoin. As of today, there are nearly twenty thousand different cryptocurrencies active in the world."

He enjoyed giving his colleagues an introduction to the world of crypto fraud.

"Imagine I stole a hundred U.S. dollars from your bank account, transferred them to my account, then transferred fifty U.S. dollars to another account, exchanged it into Euros, and moved thirty of these euros to yet another account. Etcetera. That's how it was done. If you repeat this ten times, it becomes impossible to track the funds, but that's exactly what Yong Chi did. He showed me one large flowchart which documented the various movements of his coins. Luc Starck stole Chi's money, as well as the coins of other *CryptoSwap* clients. There's no longer any doubt."

Lisa-Lotte listened intently. Oli had done an excellent job of explaining one part of the complex world of crypto.

"OK, let's say he stole from his customers. How much closer does this get us to solving the murder? Yong Chi had an alibi for the time Luc Starck was murdered. If he had killed him, what would he gain by kidnapping Mrs. Starck? It makes no sense. We definitely can remove Yong Chi from our list of suspects."

As she said these words, she realized they were further from solving this murder than ever. The negative feelings she had before this session turned out to be so right.

Rudy observed Lisa-Lotte and noticed how she could not hide her disappointment. He realized she needed help, stood up, and put his hand on her shoulder as a sign of encouragement.

He started, "Lisa-Lotte, while this may not appear to be our most productive stand-up session, it shows tremendous progress. Your father always says that eliminating suspects, leads, and options is as important as finding new ones. By the way, talking about progress. I texted your father, and he just told me he will be released today."

Lisa-Lotte was pleased Rudy had taken over from her. He felt the moment and stepped in right when she needed it most. He looked at her and continued.

"So, what's next? We have three major leads. First, based on what we just heard, we should put our energy into compiling a list of ex-customers from *CryptoSwap* who filed a complaint. Check each one of them for opportunity and alibi. Where were they this week? Talk to them about *CryptoSwap* and notice how they react to your questions."

"Second, we must continue chasing the main player. Someone has been pulling the strings from behind the curtain. We keep saying that but made little progress in identifying him."

He pointed to the list of questions on the board. "If we know who that is, we'll be very close to solving this murder."

Somehow, Rudy managed to cheer her up again.

"Lisa-Lotte, why don't we visit BionTic and see if Mr. Giobbi has recovered from the shock of finding Gail Starck's pinky and see if he can tell us about their financial challenges? He has some major explaining to do."

CHAPTER 45

FRIDAY, 25 OCTOBER, 11:30 A.M.

Was Luc Starck killed by his business partner?

Blogchain.ch learned that the day before his death, Luc Starck was having a loud argument with Roberto Giobbi, the CEO of his company BionTic. Was there a business dispute, or were it financial troubles, that got out of hand with fatal results?

That morning, Misha Weitz had been hanging out in the Crypto Valley Labs coffee shop. He had been trying to get an appointment with the BionTic CEO, but Mr. Giobbi was not available for interviews. Desperate for a story, he went to their office to see what he could pick up.

At a certain moment, he noticed a girl entering with a BionTic badge hanging around her neck. Using his natural charms, Misha started talking to her, mentioning the loss of their seed founder, Luc Starck. It was a good opening hook; the girl was desperate to talk and obviously liked Misha. Fishing for news, Misha asked her how things went with BionTic.

"Very good. The company is growing extremely fast. They make me work crazy hours. But they haven't paid me since last month. I'm such an idiot to stay here."

"I can imagine that sucks, Bea."

The girl looked surprised when he mentioned her name. When he noticed her look, he pointed to the badge around her neck, showing her name.

"Luc Starck must be dearly missed," he tried.

"He was a nice guy, although we didn't see him often. In a way, that's good, as he and our CEO seem to have a tense relationship."

Before she realized it, she'd told him about the fight the partners had the day before Luc Starck died. Everyone in the office had witnessed it; they couldn't hear most of what was said, but it was a furious, extended, and loud discussion.

Gotcha! Misha thought. He had his news story for the day. Carl would be pleased.

Misha had barely left when Lisa-Lotte and Rudy arrived at the Crypto Valley Labs building.

The receptionist went to his office and announced their arrival. Giobbi invited them to join him in a meeting room decorated with DNA-related photos, showcasing the various global projects that had adopted BionTic's DNALink technology.

"Mr. Giobbi, I hope you've recovered from yesterday's traumatic experience."

"It's going to take some time. Last night, I even dreamed of opening the box and that finger poked me in my eye. It was the most shocking thing I've ever seen."

Lisa-Lotte looked suitably sympathetic. She'd share this melodrama with her dad. He found stories like this hilarious.

Giobbi continued.

"I can't tell you how pleased I am that you could locate and free Gail. I haven't spoken to her yet, but I will call her this evening. The poor woman. I hope she's out of the hospital?"

"Yes, she's back home and feeling better."

Rudy took over, "Mr. Giobbi, how would you describe your relationship with Luc Starck?"

By the looks of his reaction, it was clear Rudy's question took him by surprise.

Giobbi took a long moment to think about his answer.

"Let's start at the beginning. I have known Luc for several years. We met at the golf club across Zuger Lake in Rotkreuz. Waiting to putt during one of our games, I pitched him the BionTic concept, and he was immediately enthusiastic. He provided start-up capital, and I was named CEO."

"Not sure you answered my question, Mr. Giobbi. On a scale of one to ten. How would you rate your relationship with Mr. Starck?" Rudy, on purpose, put more aggression in the way he asked the question.

It had its effect on Giobbi as he nervously touched his face.

"Definitely an eight. We've known each other for years, and Luc fully relied on me to run the business. Maybe even a nine. Why do you ask?"

"How are things business-wise with BionTic?"

"Perfect," Giobbi replied. "We have a growing number of users, and every week sign up new beta customers. Things are going very well."

Lisa-Lotte continued, "Have you recently had any major disagreements with Luc Starck, Mr. Giobbi?"

He glanced at the ceiling and answered, "Me and Luc? Disagreement? God, no! We were like this." He put his two index fingers side by side as his Italian grandmother would do in Ticino.

"Thanks. If things between you were so good, why, on the evening before his murder, was Luc Starck extremely depressed and spoke about you," she began reading from her notebook. "Saying 'that bastard Roberto Giobbi is driving BionTic into the ground.' Do you have any idea what he meant by that?"

She wasn't surprised to see him turn a lighter shade of pale.

Bernt had prepared her well to become a good interrogator. Upon graduation from the Academy, he'd treated her to a vacation in Lago Maggiore and Milan on the condition they would use the travel time in the car to practice interrogations. He grilled her on how to shock possible criminals into dropping their masks in the interview room. This had paid off well.

"Was it because of your financial issues?" She added that as a lucky shot.

Giobbi looked around nervously, and sweat pearls broke out across his forehead. He pushed two fingers from his right hand at the inside of his collar to give his sweaty, meaty neck some air.

She noticed his reaction and, to add to his discomfort, said, "You'll save yourself a lot of time and me a lot of hassle if you simply tell the full story." She glared menacingly.

"OK then, things were actually not as good as I suggested, although the issues we were facing occurred because business got too good."

Lisa-Lotte lost him. "So, things are going bad because they're going so well? You'll have to explain that."

"Recently, we signed up beta customers for a DNALink trial. Before we knew it, we'd added fifteen test clients, ten more than we could realistically handle. Every new beta-user requires new capital investments to finance their requirements, and because of this sudden influx of customers, we were soon running out of cash. We urgently needed new funding to keep up with our growth. Does that make sense?"

"Yes, Mr. Giobbi, I may be a blonde policewoman, but I follow you. Please continue."

"Last week we had a closing meeting for a due diligence exercise conducted by a US-based venture capitalist company named *Kaps Capital* that was thinking of investing in BionTic. I got raked over the coals by one of their analysts, Erna Casper, a real bitch. I messed up that session big time when she grilled me on our financials. Their conclusion, after that dramatic meeting, was not to invest in BionTic. Afterward, Luc got upset and shouted at me for ten minutes about the lousy job I'd done. He said *my* incompetence was driving *his* company into the ground. He screamed I should resign, effective immediately, and let him take over as CEO. It happened right here in my office, and everyone heard it. What upset me the most was that he spoke about *his* company while the idea behind DNALink had always been completely *mine*."

"And how did you respond to his accusation, Mr. Giobbi?" Rudy asked.

"I spent the evening mulling it over and decided I would resign the following day. Our contract stipulates that DNALink is my Intellectual Property, so my plan was to find a new investor. I never got that far because of Luc's death. His death was a tremendous blow; despite his anger management issues, Luc was a great guy. I will miss him."

Lisa-Lotte observed his body language. Giobbi appeared to be honest and started removing a welling tear from his right eye.

Was it real or an Italian drama?

"So, remind me, where were you last Tuesday at eleven a.m.?"

"Here at the office. Many people here can confirm that."

It matched what he'd told her colleague Patrick during his earlier visit.

"Thank you very much, Mr. Giobbi. So, what are your plans now with BionTic?"

"That is exactly what I intended to discuss with Gail the day she disappeared. Today, I'll ask her to invest in the company and offer her to accept a board position. We urgently need support."

Giobbi looked desperate and ready to fight for the survival of his business.

"Nothing will stop me from realizing my dream."

"OK, thanks. Hopefully, that conversation will go your way."

As they walked toward the elevator, Rudy suddenly stopped and looked at Giobbi. "One more quick question. Did you invest any personal crypto coins in *CryptoSwap*?"

"Yes," he answered, surprised.

"You must have heard several *CryptoSwap* customers lost Bitcoins with them. Did you lose any?"

Giobbi stuttered. "Uh, yes. It was terrible. I had given them a hundred Bitcoins in custody and lost all of them. Luc told me I was a victim of a cybercrime."

"Did you believe him?"

"Of course I did. Why wouldn't I?" As he answered, he avoided eye contact and shrugged his shoulders, both a clear sign of lying.

"It's okay then." They stepped into the elevator.

As they were getting into the car, Lisa-Lotte looked at Rudy and said, "Hmm, another one with a reason to kill Starck. No shortage of suspects. This story keeps getting more and more curious."

Rudy added, "If it continues like this, you and I are the only ones without a motive." He smiled at her.

Her mobile phone started buzzing several times.

The first one was a notification from *blogchain.ch* about the loud dispute between Giobbi and Starck.

The second one was more surprising. It was a message from Hans at headquarters. "Lisa-Lotte, Rudy, please come to the office. We just received an email. Its subject says, 'Clue Four.' Please come back right away. Hans."

The last message was from Schmidt. "Hope you did not forget our conversation from yesterday. I need to see Rudy and you by 4 p.m. today at the latest."

"Shit!" Full of stress she drove away at full speed, with Rudy looking in bewilderment at her.

CHAPTER 46
MONDAY, 19 AUGUST, 10:27 AM

Nine weeks earlier

The preparations for the murder were progressing meticulously, just as Fritz had envisioned in his carefully constructed project plan. Every step had been thought out in advance, every detail scrutinized. His method would be efficient, silent, and—above all—untraceable. After extensive research, weighing the pros and cons of various lethal methods, Fritz decided that nerve gas would be the most effective weapon. Its deadly potency and the element of control it offered made it the perfect choice. However, finding and purchasing the ideal nerve gas would be anything but simple.

Fritz was no stranger to the dark web, that shadowy underworld of the internet where legality and morality dissolved into the abyss. The dark web was an encrypted network, completely hidden from the standard internet. Accessing it required specialized software, such as the TOR browser, which allowed anonymous browsing, leaving no trace behind. It was like stepping into a clandestine supermarket where almost anything imaginable was for sale—drugs, weapons, hacking tools, counterfeit documents, and even contract killers. Fritz had used it many times before for professional purposes, though never for anything of this magnitude.

This time, however, he needed to navigate deeper into a part of the dark web that he rarely ventured into, *illegal warfare utilities*. This was a world where biological and chemical weapons, military-grade equipment, and cutting-edge technologies developed in secret government labs were traded between shadowy figures. The stakes were higher here. The people involved in these transactions were dangerous, and the slightest misstep could lead to a fatal outcome.

After days of browsing through various forums and marketplaces, he finally found what he was looking for—a seller based in Russia offering canisters of VX nerve gas. VX was one of the most lethal nerve agents ever created. Odorless and tasteless, just a few drops could kill in minutes by disrupting the nervous system, causing the victim to suffocate as their muscles ceased to function. Russia is one of the few countries that still actively develops nerve gas. They produced VX at the notorious *Signal Institute* in Moscow, a facility under the control of the Russian Federal Secret Service. While the institute operated in secrecy, corruption within its ranks made it possible for certain employees to smuggle out small quantities of the nerve agent and sell them to buyers with deep enough pockets.

The seller's listing featured a few grainy photos of the nerve gas canisters, which resembled ordinary CO2 cylinders used to carbonate water. The innocuous appearance of the canisters only added to their appeal. They could be easily transported without raising suspicion. Fritz knew he had found exactly what he needed, but the price was steep. Two canisters would cost him 75,000 Swiss Francs—roughly $75,000. Still, money was no object in this case. He transferred the funds through a series of anonymous cryptocurrency accounts, ensuring that the transaction couldn't be traced back to him.

Arranging for the canisters to be smuggled into Switzerland was another challenge, but Fritz had connections. Over the years, he had cultivated a network of intermediaries skilled in getting contraband across borders. After a week of tense waiting, the canisters finally arrived. He was instructed to pick them up at a dingy, low-lit bar in Zurich, the kind of place where deals like this happened without anyone asking questions. The air inside the bar was thick with cigarette smoke and stale beer. As Fritz walked in, his pulse quickened, but outwardly, he remained calm and composed.

The exchange was swift and discreet. The canisters were handed over in a non-descript black duffel bag, just as promised. As Fritz walked out of the bar and into the cool night air, a sense of accomplishment washed over him. He had what he needed. The plan, so long in the making, was well on track. He was now on the home stretch.

But as he carried the canisters back to his rented apartment, a strange thought crossed his mind. For all his meticulous planning, for all the steps he had taken to ensure success, there was still something thrillingly unpredictable about what came next. Nerve gas was not just a tool of murder; it was a weapon of mass destruction. Handling it was akin to holding death itself in his hands and, with it, the power to control fate.

This was the part Fritz both relished and feared. The moment when everything would come together—or fall apart.

CHAPTER 47
FRIDAY, 25 OCTOBER, 12:53 A.M.

The moment they stepped into the police station, Hans was waiting for them at the entrance and showed them the message they'd just received.

Sender: luc_is-dead@mymail.com
Subject: Last and final Clue. 'Clue Four'.

Hello,
I hope you are making solid progress in the investigations into the death of Luc Starck. If not, you may wish to talk with Mr. Fred Bongers from Zug.

Ask him about Jeannette.

All the best!

"Wow. This case could not get any stranger. Clues keep knocking on our door! Do you guys think the Luc who sent this is Luc Starck? Weird! He died three days ago. More and more, I get the impression someone is playing with us." She looked at Hans and Rudy, who both looked puzzled and confused.

Rudy added, "This whole clue thing is so odd. Why kill a person and then offer help to solve the case? We're dealing with a very devious criminal mind."

Lisa-Lotte scratched her head. Their adversary's cleverly presented clues kept opening new mouse holes without them getting any closer to a solution.

"Let's try to stay positive. A cryptic clue is better than no clue. And at least this appears to be the last one. Let's track down Fred Bongers."

Lisa-Lotte typed the name on her phone's search engine. There was only one Fred Bongers in Zug.

"Fred Bongers, according to his LinkedIn profile, is a 'seasoned project manager with recognized coordination capabilities and the unique ability to make the impossible a reality.'"

"Just what we needed, another magician!" Rudy exclaimed with a smile.

The image of a nondescript but friendly-looking middle-aged gentleman was looking at them from his LinkedIn profile.

"Hmm, the ability to get impossible things done. Let's invite Mr. Bongers to join us for a cup of tea and a few questions."

A few hours later, Fred Bongers was waiting at the intake desk when Lisa-Lotte went to introduce herself. They moved to the interview room, where Rudy was sitting at the far end of the mirror.

"Mr. Bongers, thanks for coming in on short notice. My name is Detective Lisa-Lotte Berg, and this is my colleague, Rudy Kotkin. We have a few questions for you."

Bongers didn't look particularly nervous. He looked more intrigued by the situation and curiously looked around to see where he found himself. As he was straightening his tie, Lisa-Lotte saw him stare intensely at the large wall that was half covered by a traditional interrogation room mirror. He kept maintaining a charming smile. Bongers was a 'tip-top' gentleman.

"Yes, I look forward to learning exactly why I'm here. I must admit it's my first time inside a police station. I hope I did nothing wrong." Straight, confident, and logical. He not only looked like a project manager, but he also acted like one.

"Mr. Bongers, not sure how to put this, but has anything remarkable happened in your life recently?"

"My life? Oh no, it's boring and not worth mentioning. Let's cut to the chase. What is the real reason for your intriguing invitation?"

Bongers was a man of action, everything straight to the point.

"Mr. Bongers, are you sure there isn't anything you'd like to tell us?"

"Of course not." His full face remained, showing that patient, charming smile.

"Who is Jeannette in that case?"

For an instant, Bongers' face changed and took on a frowning look.

"Why don't you explain everything behind this story?"

Lisa-Lotte had no clue what was going on, but the name Jeannette visibly triggered a response. She waited impassively, hoping he'd started talking. Then he did.

"Jeannette? I have no clue who you are talking about." Bongers' worried face turned back to neutral, and he looked sincere in his answers.

His reaction disappointed her. *Was he calling her bluff?* She gave it another try.

"Mr. Bongers, we did not invite you to come here to play games. We know everything, and you would save yourself lots of trouble if you told us everything about yourself and Jeannette."

Bongers remained quiet.

"You want us to call her?" Another lucky shot.

"Oh, no. Please keep her outside of this. She does not deserve that." Bongers' rosy complexion turned pale. He bent forward over the table and buried his head in his hands. An instant and total transformation.

"Who the hell told you about that? Do you also have the pictures?"

The calm and collected Bongers continued to collapse like an office building being demolished. Lisa-Lotte gave him another moment to pull himself together. She poured him a glass of water. After a nip, he started.

"A few months ago, a man came to my apartment in Zug. He did not introduce himself, and I didn't recognize him. He said, *This is a message for you* and gave me a large manilla envelope. Then he turned around and walked away."

"What was in the envelope?"

"A dozen photos of Jeannette and myself."

"Who is Jeannette?"

"I work as a Project Manager at *Zug Machines*. We produce industrial kitchens. I've been working there for over twenty-three years. We are a small, privately owned company by Mr. Roland King. Jeannette King is his wife. A couple of months ago, I met Jeannette while walking in the forest during my lunch break. I recognized her from our annual Christmas Party. She's a charming and attractive lady. We ran into each other more often, and what had started as innocent encounters gradually became a secret love affair. At least I thought it had been a secret until I received that envelope. It contained many photos, photos of me kissing Jeannette passionately and of us sneaking into a hotel. They were taken with a telephoto lens. I was so embarrassed. I immediately told her, and we didn't dare see each other anymore. Knowing we'll be together at our Christmas Party in a couple of months already makes me sick."

"Mr. Bongers, was there anything else in the envelope?"

"A letter. I suspected this meeting could be related, so I brought it with me." He took it out of his briefcase and handed it to her. She read it and passed it to Rudy.

Halfway through reading it, Rudy stopped breathing, and his eyebrows went up.

"Wow, and you did all of that?"

"Yes, everything as you read. They explicitly mentioned that if I didn't follow their instructions to the letter, these pictures would be sent to my boss and my wife. Next year, I will be married for twenty-five years, and I've worked at *Zug Machine* for twenty-three years. If these photos become public, it will be the end of my career and my marriage. What could I do? What they asked me to do were unusual tasks, but nothing illegal as far as I know."

She noticed how he looked at her, hoping she would agree with him. "Mr. Bongers, I can't be sure. We'll need to study this with legal experts."

Bongers looked relieved. "You have no clue how happy I am. I can finally talk about this. For weeks, I've been living in confusion and hoped that you could reassure me today. Do you have any idea what I was asked to do?"

"We have a suspicion. I do not wish to scare you, Mr. Bongers, but it seems you've been an unwitting accomplice to a murder."

"A *murder*? What I was doing had nothing to do with any murder! Am I now suspected of killing someone? That's unbelievable!" Bongers stood from the chair, then sat again, his well-manicured hands fluttering in front of him like birds.

Lisa-Lotte studied his body language. He looked sincerely shocked and incredulous. The project manager, used to having everything under control, suddenly saw his world being turned upside down.

"Who's been killed?"

"You may have read about it. Last Tuesday, a murder took place on the *Landsgemeindeplatz* on the terrace of *Hotel Loewen Am See*."

"No, I was traveling most of the week. Who died?"

"Someone called Luc Starck. Does that name ring a bell?"

He sped through his mental database. "No, not really."

Lisa-Lotte searched in a folder and removed a picture of Luc Starck. She pushed the photo in Bongers' direction over the table.

Bongers got red and flustered. His hand shook.

"You know this man, Mr. Bongers?"

"No, I do not know him, but I recognize him. You won't believe it. This is the guy who brought me the envelope with the pictures and instructions!"

CHAPTER 48
FRIDAY, 25 OCTOBER, 3:30 P.M.

Back at Zuger police station, Lisa-Lotte had called the full team together for an urgent meeting. Everyone gathered in the investigation room. Lisa-Lotte spoke over the diminishing hubbub.

"Guys, this may well be the breakthrough we were hoping for. Earlier today, we got another email. This one was marked 'Clue Four'. The clue was to investigate a certain Mr. Fred Bongers, a project manager here in Zug.

"We invited Mr. Bongers to visit us and just finished talking to him. What he told us was so extraordinary, we've called this special meeting to make heads or tails of it."

Lisa-Lotte described Bongers and the embarrassing story of his trysts with Jeannette, his boss's attractive wife. The team snickered quietly about his awkward situation.

"The most surprising part was the list of instructions he received." Lisa-Lotte held up a copy of the letter from Bongers. "Bongers received detailed orders, similar to the instructions Brucker received from the man with the red cap."

She projected the instructions onto the wall behind her.

The to-do list that will save you:

With the attached receipt, you'll be able to open a storage locker at Zurich's main train station. In that locker, you'll find a box containing two smaller boxes.

Send the following emails, as per below.

Mailing One.

- *Login to mymail.com with the following credentials: user = yourmaster@mymail.com, password = I@mYourControl*

- *Once logged in, you'll find several emails saved in the Drafts folder*

- *Next week on Monday send the draft mail marked Magician Vogel Reminder, to vogel@swissmagic.ch, and the draft marked Minten Reminder to info@zugevents.ch*

Mailing Two.

- *Use email account: user = yournightmare@mymail.com password = I@mYourPain.*

- *Look in the Drafts folder. Next Wednesday, send the email to BruckerBoy@mailbox.com. Wait for confirmation via email.*

- *In case you receive no confirmation mail within five days, send the draft mail to Nouninou@supermail.com.*

- *Wait for a reply with the text Done and send the mail with subject Surprise is Deleted to the same address: BruckerBoy@mailbox.com (or Nouninou@supermail.com).*

- *From the box you found in the storage locker, take the box marked #1 and post it next Friday. It is already addressed, and the postage is paid.*

- *Wait for an email from user BruckerBoy@mailbox.com, with the contents Received. In case you do not receive this within ten days, take the box marked #2 and post it. Wait for confirmation from Nouninou@supermail.com.*

As Lisa-Lotte addressed the team, she saw her father entering at the rear of the room. She spoke a bit more loudly for his benefit and continued her briefing. She quickly winked at him in greeting.

"Mr. Bongers unwittingly became the master coordinator of Luc Starck's murder. Bongers, a professional project manager, was the perfect choice to implement the killer's project with no slip-ups. Bongers is the missing link we've been looking for. But nothing like what we've been expecting."

The team looked stunned. They did not know about this case's expanding scope and complexity.

"And that's not all. As we might have expected, the big surprise ending came when Mr. Bongers identified a photo of the man who'd brought him the envelope with instructions."

Lisa-Lotte built up the tension. "You won't believe who it was."

She waited two seconds.

"It was the victim, Mr. Luc Starck himself."

No one moved, clearly stunned. Members looked at each other, wondering if they had heard her correctly.

"Remember how Mr. Starck had been talking about suicide to his wife the evening before he died? Knowing what we know now, Mr. Starck most likely organized his own murder!"

One team member in the back raised his hand.

"If this is true, who emailed 'Clue Four'? We received that email *after* Luc Starck's death, and Bongers would never have sent a message that could incriminate him."

"I've been thinking about that. Remember Mrs. Starck said her husband mentioned his death would be one big surprise? Well, this certainly was that. Can you imagine how much time he must have spent organizing and executing this plan?

"Well, this is how I think he did it."

Standing in the doorway, Bernt proudly watched his daughter in action. She was fully in charge, the same way he or any other senior officer would have wrapped up a major investigation. The Berg police tradition was in excellent hands.

"Luc Starck's first dealings with the global crypto world had been a disaster. He saw how easily others had walked away with his hard-earned crypto wealth and could do nothing to prevent it.

We can't be sure this traumatic experience led Starck to start *CryptoSwap*, but it's now clear he repeated this theft on his customers, orchestrating a cyber-attack to empty his customers' wallets. He couldn't be sure he could cover his losses, but it evidently gave him the sense of satisfaction he needed."

Lisa-Lotte took a sip of water. She had a lot to explain.

"Starck underestimated the reaction from some of his more sophisticated customers on this crime, as well as their determination—he was threatened with death. He tried to ignore it, but their threats continued; on top of his ongoing business setbacks, it finally became too much to bear. Yong Chi proved Luc had stolen the coins. As a professional criminal, he wasn't about to stop hounding him. This must have made Luc feel helpless and triggered a deep depression."

She checked the room for questions, but they were so concentrated on listening to her that she decided to continue.

"He started BionTic – an anagram for Bitcoin – to move away from the world of crypto and thought he'd found in Roberto Giobbi a trustworthy ally. But financial pressure and disappointment finally pushed him over the edge and led him to engineer his own murder. Having orchestrated the cybercrime at *CryptoSwap*, organizing his murder wouldn't have been too great a challenge. Of course, he could have committed suicide as he'd threatened to do, but that would forever have marked him as the loser who'd stolen from his customers and started a business that collapsed."

"No, being murdered would allow him to end his misery and save face by becoming a victim. Despite our earlier conclusion, we're now certain that Luc Starck planned and carried out his own murder."

The team listened to Lisa-Lotte holding their breaths, amazed at how cleverly she'd figured this out.

Lisa-Lotte now turned to the detective colleague who'd asked about 'Clue Four.'

"Luc Starck prepared the Clue Four message ahead of time to be delivered after his death. He sent us that message because he wanted to be sure we realized he'd killed himself to show how clever he'd been. Organizing his murder was his ultimate success, a masterpiece. And boy, did he pull the wool over our eyes!"

The same detective raised his hand again.

"And how about contracting that magician and event organizer? The break-ins at their place?"

"I suppose Starck organized that himself beforehand or even did it himself. Remember how these break-ins were done just before his death? He had it all figured out. I think you all agree. It's a work of true genius."

Lisa-Lotte paused to acknowledge her father's 'return to the fold.' Most team members had been so focused on Lisa-Lotte's report that they didn't notice him walk in.

"Team, let's warmly welcome back my father, Bernt Berg." She gestured toward him, and he feigned a self-effacing show of humility, along with a sincerely grateful smile.

Bernt accepted the spontaneous applause and modestly thanked them. He gestured back toward his daughter to continue. This was her meeting, after all.

Rudy wrapped up.

"Before you all go, let's update our operational timeline on the board to be sure we haven't missed or forgotten anything. In a few hours, we'll validate our working assumptions, then present our conclusions to Gail Starck first thing in the morning."

They took a step back, and both hugged Bernt. "So happy you're here!"

"Good timing, I see." He smiled at them.

Today, he was a proud father, holding his precious daughter at arm's length and watching her familiar face glow and blossom with professional confidence and grace.

Just as Lisa-Lotte wanted to leave the room, she noticed Schmidt walking toward them.

She looked at her father and Rudy and whispered to them, "Oh my God. We completely forgot to see him. The events of the past hours kept us so busy. What does he want?" Mentally, she was preparing herself for a thunder speech. She tried to read his mood as he came closer.

"Lisa-Lotte," he said in a loud, authoritative voice.

"Yes, sir." At these moments, it was always best to show respect.

"I heard about the latest developments from Rudy and wish to congratulate you on the tenacity and focus you showed to bring this case to resolution. Well done."

An immediate sense of relief and calmness descended upon her, and she sighed in relief.

CHAPTER 49
SATURDAY, 26 OCTOBER, 8:38 A.M.

Duan woke up early and gazed for a moment at Gail, who was beginning to stir, still in a light sleep. It had been several weeks since that last morning with Mina when he'd awakened next to a woman. He just hadn't felt the urge. Yet, being close and intimate with Gail felt very normal and familiar. He moved closer, enjoying the warmth of her body. He kissed her lips softly, waking her up. When she saw Duan, she enclosed him in a sinuous embrace and held him tight. The passionate kisses of the night before picked up again as if they'd never stopped.

"Don't leave me," she whispered.

"Who said anything about leaving?" Duan murmured with a smile.

"You'd better not!" She gave him a naughty smirk.

Then Gail's phone rang.

Duan realized Gail was talking to his 'friend' Lisa-Lotte from the police. She signed off by saying, "I'll see you in an hour."

Gail looked at her new beau. "The police have a breakthrough in Luc's murder and asked if they could come here to update me."

"Exciting! You think it's okay for me to be there?" Duan asked.

"Of course!"

"In that case, I'd better shower and get presentable. Why don't you tell them you've asked me to come and meet you here? No need for them to know I slept here."

"Sure."

Duan walked to the bathroom door.

"Hey, where are you off to?"

Duan looked surprised. "I told you, I'm going to shower."

"Already? We still have an hour." She reached out languidly and pulled him back to bed. "This recuperating girl needs more attention, love, and endless kisses. Doctor's orders."

As soon as Lisa-Lotte rang the intercom, Gail opened the gate for her and Rudy.

"Hello, Inspector Berg, isn't it?"

"You have an excellent memory. How is your hand?"

"Thanks for asking. It's still quite sore, but the zinc supplements seem to speed up the healing process."

"Very glad to hear that. Let me introduce you to my partner, inspector Rudy Kotkin."

"Why not join me in the kitchen, and we can chat there? By the way, I've asked my friend Duan Ripa to join us, if that's all right. I understand you already had the pleasure of meeting each other."

Duan, sitting at the kitchen table, was enjoying a freshly brewed espresso macchiato.

"Hello, Mr. Ripa. Hope you're also feeling better today." She pointed at his bandages.

"Pleasure to see you again, Detective Berg and Inspector Kotkin. Yes, thank you. I went to bed early and have been lying low today. Rest is the best medicine." He glanced in Gail's direction as if to share a private joke but thought better of it.

"Gail told me you have a major development in Luc's case. I can't wait to hear what you've found out." He gave them a polite smile as if their earlier acrimonious exchanges had been forgotten.

"Yes, indeed, yesterday we made the breakthrough we'd been hoping for. To make a long story short, we're now convinced your husband wasn't murdered but committed suicide."

Lisa-Lotte waited a moment to check their response.

Duan could not resist reacting.

"You have no clue what you are doing, do you? Just yesterday you told Gail that Luc was murdered and now suddenly he committed suicide! Just like when I came to report Gail's disappearance, and you did not want to listen, or when you suspected me of murdering Luc! What is this? A professional police investigation? Or a multiple-choice test?"

Gail placed a hand on Duan's arm to calm him and took over. "Indeed, when we met at the hospital yesterday, you had ruled out suicide and were convinced he was murdered. What changed?"

Lisa-Lotte sighed. "This is where it gets complicated. Your husband concocted the most complex way to commit suicide. Didn't he tell you his death would be 'a big surprise'?"

"He did indeed."

"We learned he delivered a set of instructions to someone he had blackmailed into orchestrating his murder, but this man didn't know he was doing anything illegal."

Gail and Duan looked confused and studied each other's faces as if looking for clarification.

"Hang on," said Gail. "Luc forced someone else to kill him?"

"Not kill him directly, but he coordinated a series of events with several other people. Each of them was asked to perform a relatively innocent task, but the combination of these ultimately led to his death."

She was confused but let them continue talking, hoping she would eventually catch up.

"We discovered four clues during our extensive investigation over the past few days."

Lisa-Lotte told them the story about the first three clues and the incredible sequence of events they triggered. The way she told the story made it clear she had been reciting that story many times the past day. She spoke for five minutes and concluded.

"I must admit we still do not comprehend the level of complexity and planning your husband had gone through to orchestrate his death. Even my most senior colleagues at the police station had never seen something like this. It is unique."

"Typical Luc, always coming up with something different. What a hassle to kill yourself." Gail sighted.

She noticed Lisa-Lotte swallow. "And, unfortunately, almost killed my father."

Gail looked shocked. "Ah yes, you came here with your father to report Luc's death. What happened to him?"

"Let's skip that part for now. It was a regrettable accident, but thankfully, he has fully recovered."

Lisa-Lotte continued, "And sure enough, the event organizer also did not know that, when he pressed that button, he'd trigger the device that poisoned your husband. These four clues and the chain of events were carried out by a series of unwitting stooges, each lured into playing a small part in the killing of your husband."

"Four clues? If I counted well, I think you only told us about three so far." Duan, who had cooled off, was following their explanation closely.

"That final clue we received yesterday. An anonymous email pointed us to yet another stooge, who, by following very detailed instructions, was coordinating, in the background, the activities of the other stooges."

She recapped the story of Fred Bongers, his lover Jeannette, and the long list of instructions he had to work through.

Gail looked at Duan in something of a fog. Lisa-Lotte's explanation raised more questions than it answered.

"Do you have a theory of why Luc planned his murder with such a complicated series of events?"

"Actually, we do. Didn't you once tell us on the last evening that your husband whined about being a failure?"

Gail nodded.

"He was so depressed. He also said he couldn't cope with the continuous pressure he was under from his ex-customers. As much as I hated him, I also felt sorry for him. He appeared to see no way out."

Duan excused himself and made everyone another cup of coffee. It was time for a break. The past minutes had been one surprise after another.

Gail was lost in her thoughts and wondered what feeling she now felt for Luc. The anger of all he had done to her prevailed, but she could not resist a certain level of respect for the ingenious way he'd killed himself. These conflicting feelings confused her.

Duan returned with the coffee. She noticed how he observed her and came to sit next to her and put his hand momentarily on her knee as a sign of support. Gail realized he was cautious about displaying too much affection in the presence of the policewoman.

When they finished their coffee, Lisa-Lotte continued, "I have another important update. Our investigations into *CryptoSwap* also had a breakthrough. Yong Chi, your kidnapper, proved how your husband spread a virus that emptied the wallets of his customers and also how he moved the coins through a complex set of transactions all over the world. Finally, he demonstrated how these coins ended up in a bank account under your husband's control."

Duan, as if reading her mind, asked, "With Luc already dead, how will that affect Gail legally? Will she be held responsible for his crimes?"

She was glad he asked.

"Legally, no. You do not inherit guilt. But once this theft becomes public knowledge, the victims are likely to start multiple civil claims against you to regain their losses."

Gail could easily imagine what a nightmare she could end up in.

"Knowing Luc was behind that theft, it now all becomes clear what must have happened in your husband's recent life. Being chased by *CryptoSwap* customers, he must have known they were in their right to threaten him and wouldn't stop. Admitting he committed the crime would put him in a compromising position and cost him his reputation. How would that impact his BionTic business? Would he be able to find new investors once they found out he had robbed his customers? We know BionTic had severe cash challenges and required investments. We believe your husband became desperate to salvage something from his business."

"Our theory is that it got too much for him, so he ended his life but in an incredible fashion, as his last masterwork."

Duan added, "As a farewell, raising his middle finger to all of us, 'See what I can do!"

"Indeed."

CHAPTER 50
MONDAY, 28 OCTOBER, 3:55 P.M.

The press conference at the Zuger Police headquarters was standing-room-only. The crowd of reporters barely fit into the headquarters' largest meeting room.

When some of the case's twists and turns became news, everyone realized the story of Luc Starck's death was unique. The press from all over the country came to Zug to listen to it firsthand and meet the team that had solved it. Three TV teams were positioned at the back and side of the room. All printed press had sent a representative, and several online news outlets found a spot in the packed room. Not just general online publications but also crypto and blockchain blogs and podcasts. Nobody wanted to miss this.

Carl Coppen and Ilse Bamberg from *blogchain.ch* had camped out early to make sure they had a perfect spot in the first row. The rumors Carl had picked up that morning varied from Luc being killed by his wife, Gail, by his partner, a BionTic, to Luc being killed by a crypto whale who'd contracted a killer to eliminate him. When he heard the first rumor, he was about to put them on *blogchain.ch*. Every time he wanted to publish, he'd receive a message with another version and the next one. All in about an hour. He decided to wait until the press conference. He was already well known as the guy with inside information. At this stage, the truth mattered more than speed.

Carl was scanning the audience, trying to spot Gail Starck. He was keen to get a reaction from her after the press conference. Ever since he had heard she was freed, he had been trying to talk to her. With no luck. How hard he looked. He could not find her in the room.

At exactly 4 p.m., the press conference started. The head of Zuger police, Tell Schmidt, opened the event.

"Thanks all for coming today in such numbers. Ladies and gentlemen, we are pleased to inform you we have solved the killing of Mr. Luc Starck. I'm proud of my team. They've been able to get to the bottom of this very challenging case in record time. I'm going to pass the microphone to Detective Lisa-Lotte Berg, who will provide you with all the details."

Rudy and Lisa-Lotte had agreed that Lisa-Lotte would do most of the talking. It would complete her masterclass.

Lisa-Lotte started by introducing herself and acknowledging the hard work of her team, especially thanking Rudy and her father, Bernt, who was in civilian clothes at the back of the room. Pride for his daughter was swelling by the minute.

Next, she described the sequence of events that ultimately led to Luc's death. She built up the tension with dramatic phrasing and paused before revealing that Luc himself had organized his own murder.

All in the room went quiet with surprise and disbelief when she shared the revelation. The only noise came from TV cameras zooming, the photo cameras clicking, and laptop keyboards clacking.

As usual, the Q&A session was full of useless or superficial questions raised by journalists who wanted to justify their trip to Zug and had to ask something to excuse their expenses.

During the conference, Ilse already started writing her story. Once they heard about Luc's self-organized murder, Carl immediately sent out a newsflash from his laptop. *Blogchain.ch* could not miss the opportunity to be first.

> *Crypto King Luc Starck Planned his own killing!*
> *The Zuger police just explained how crypto entrepreneur Luc*
> *Starck planned his own murder in a unique and sensational*
> *manner.*

The rest of the article he'd prepared upfront, so he just had to paste it under the opening. Within ninety seconds after Lisa-Lotte mentioned Luc had planned his murder, it was online on their blog. Being first was king in his business, and it gave him a huge kick. The adrenaline was pumping through his body when he pressed *Publish*. Many thousands of subscribers' mobile phones began beeping with notifications and were directed to the blog.

Before the conference ended, Carl whispered in Ilse's ear. "Let's move and have a chat next door. I think I fully understand what happened. Probably more than anyone else here. This story is way bigger than they realize."

Ilse looked uncertain, but Carl's instinct was never wrong. They moved to a small coffee shop next door.

When they sat down, Carl started.

"Did you hear them say that none of the people involved in Luc's killing knew they were taking part in a murder?" He looked at Ilse.

"Of course, I was there."

"I can't believe it! If there is one person who could come up with this ingenious idea, it must have been Luc Starck."

"Why? That's what that policewoman said, didn't she?" Ilse looked puzzled.

"Let me explain. In blockchain, there is a technique where one party, the provider, can prove to another party, the verifier, that something is true without sharing that information. It's used to validate cryptocurrency transactions securely."

Ilse looked puzzled, clueless about where Carl was going to.

"This is exactly what happened here. Luc Starck, as *the provider*, kept his own murder a secret and passed it on to these unaware accomplishes, *the verifiers*. None of them knew the secret information they were passed on. The murder."

Ilse listened, fascinated, although she had a hard time following the logic.

"It's widely used in cryptography. It's called zero-knowledge proof. It's difficult to explain, but let me try it simply. Imagine I have a closed combination lock. I could simply prove I have the right password by unlocking it without showing you the password. By doing this, you have certified that I know certain information without me disclosing it. That's what a zero-knowledge proof is like."

"Hmm, OK, I get that, but how is that used in real life?"

"Imagine you wish to buy a house, and you need to prove you have sufficient income to afford it. You don't wish to disclose your financial status to the seller. Using a zero-knowledge proof transaction, you can confirm you have the funds to buy the house without having to share your financial details with the seller.

"It is also used in voting machines to allow anonymous voting, where your identity gets confirmed through such a transaction. Whenever someone doesn't want to reveal personal data, a zero-knowledge proof transaction is useful."

"None of these accomplices had any idea they were taking part in a murder. Like blockchain is used in distributed security, distributed finance is based on blockchain using zero-knowledge proof. Luc's murder is the ultimate distributed murder. It is genius! If there's one person who could have masterminded this, it was Luc Starck!"

Ilse felt out of her league.

Frantically, Carl started typing up the story he had just explained to Ilse. Fifteen minutes later, he pressed *Publish*.

> *Blockchain Entrepreneur Luc Starck killed himself with a*
> *unique Distributed Murder…*

Within the hour, his blog reached over one million hits, and in no time, his story was taken over by national and international news outlets. *Blogchain.ch* did it again!

CHAPTER 51
MONDAY, 28 OCTOBER, 4:20 P.M.

Bernt answered his phone.

"Hi, Dad, it's time for our traditional case-closing ceremony dinner. We have loads to catch up on, and I'm eager to hear your insights into what we've learned. Over the past couple of days, almost every hour, something surprising happened. I've had no time to slow down and reflect. Now that you're back on your feet, we deserve a get-together. Shall we meet at *Platzmulhle?*"

This was their favorite pizzeria in town, at the *Landsgemeindeplatz*. It had become a family tradition that after working on a case together, they'd share a pizza. Perhaps ironically, the restaurant was opposit*e Hotel Loewen Am See* and the terrace where it all had started earlier that week.

Bernt was sitting at the large window in front when Lisa-Lotte arrived. The restaurant had made a stab at an Italian decor with scenic posters, red-checked tablecloths, and Chianti-bottle candle holders, but the typical Swiss tidiness and the pizza prices made it obvious this was not Milan.

"Let's first order the pizza," she said with a smile as she dropped her bag onto a chair. "I'm starving. The usual for you?"

"Yes, pizza Napoletana with an extra egg on top."

"You want me to ask them to cut it into four or twelve pieces?"

"Four, please. I'm on a diet!" Bernt answered drily.

She looked at him to check if he was serious, but he was laughing.

"Does it never stop?"

As was their ritual, she raised her glass of Barbera d'Asti in a toast to the case's close.

"To Andi," she said, gazing upward—a tribute to her brother who had left this world far too soon.

They sat in silence, eyes fixed ahead, each lost in memories of the moments they once shared with him.

"OK, let's debrief." Bernt got serious and started a recap.

He peeked through a tent of his fingers and began speaking quietly into it. As the discussion became more animated, his hands mimed a hospital bed, Luc's collapse, and the killer's unwitting accomplices.

"I have been with the police for over thirty years, but this is by far the weirdest case I ever worked on. Did I just call this working? I did so little on this case. I'm proud to congratulate you, darling. You did a marvelous job. Cheers to your success!" He raised his glass of Primitivo, and they toasted.

"The remote support you gave me from your hospital bed was great. You provided essential tips that ultimately helped me uncover the surprising solution and helped me bring everything together."

Lisa-Lotte waited for this moment.

"Dad, but what about Brucker, Minten, Vogel, and Bongers? They killed Luc Starck and almost took you with him. You've been extremely lucky. You think they are guilty?"

Bernt thought for a moment and twirled his wine glass thoughtfully. "Yes, they were technically accomplices, but each of them acted without malice. These men have suffered enough for their unintentional involvement. I'm sure they'll be more careful next time they visit a porn site, kiss a married woman in public, or accept an offer that's too good to be true."

Bernt brushed breadcrumbs from the tablecloth and continued. "You can compare the police to an audience watching a magician perform. We, at the police, are confronted with a mystery, a burglary, an accident, or a murder and must figure out how they did it. As with a magician, you have the desire to solve a puzzle as you watch something occur, but have no inkling of how it's being done and can't relax till you've figured it out."

"What a clever analogy, Dad!" She smiled fondly through a pizza slice.

When they finished their dinner, Bernt paid the check, and they began walking through the darkening streets toward the police headquarters.

As they walked together, Lisa-Lotte started the conversation. "How come you mentioned that analogy with magic?"

"Well, I have been thinking about what to do with my life during my retirement. Playing with trains and trams is nice but not overly exciting. I always was fascinated by magic and started reading about it."

"What a great idea. Any trick you can already show me?"

"No, not yet. I tried to make your mother disappear, but that one only worked half."

"Come on, Dad, be nice to her. For once, try to be serious."

"Okay, I will. At the hospital, I read a magazine interview with a Spanish magician named Juan Tamariz. Tamariz is known for his deep analysis of magic and what transforms a magic trick into a memorable display. He drew an interesting comparison of magic and crime that got me thinking about our case and re-energized my interest in magic."

"Wow." Lisa-Lotte saw a passion in her dad's face she had not seen that often.

"In magic, Tamariz explained, for an audience, genuine miracles happen when the technical magic method is extremely complex but invisible to the audience. The more complex the method, even if not noticeable to the audience, the more impressive and mystifying the effect becomes. For Tamariz, it is a mystery how that works."

Lisa-Lotte listened intensely. She had not seen her father that seriously. "I got it. You mean that even if the public does not know about the method, why is the effect better when the method is more complex?"

"Exactly."

"Hmm, I think I see how that could relate to a crime."

"In our case, Luc Starck's murder plan was so ingenious and improbable that even when we knew he'd organized it himself, we couldn't accept that scenario. I still can't accept that he did it. We heard early on he considered suicide, but because of the complexity of the method, discarded that."

"Only when you told me about Fred Bongers did I accept that Luc Starck planned his own murder. From the beginning, we heard he was depressed and saw suicide as the only way out. He even confessed his death would be a big surprise. He told the world he was going to do it, and then he did it. And yet, we still could not believe it. But it's the only solution that covers all the bases. Case closed. Congrats again," Bernt said with a big grin.

They walked to the police station to pick up some of their stuff before going home.

A few police officers were clearing their desks upstairs. Her father led her into an empty conference room overlooking downtown and an adjoining park where they'd occasionally eaten carryout lunches together. He crossed his arms, leaned against a half-cleared table, and looked seriously at her.

"I need to tell you one more thing. This afternoon, Tell Schmidt called me into his office."

Lisa-Lotte's eyebrows shot up. She knew the police chief never called officers in for idle chats. "Did he want to talk to you about how badly I handled the case?"

Bernt laughed. "No, absolutely not. He asked if I wanted to begin my retirement effective immediately. I only have a few months left anyway. He feels sorry about what happened and is concerned about long-term health repercussions so close to my retirement. Also, he was quite impressed with how professionally you've managed this investigation."

"Thanks to you! And so?"

"Not sure I intend to accept his generous offer. I'll have to think about it."

"You'd better not!" She held up her fist threateningly and noted his small, mysterious smile.

Had he already decided but wasn't ready to tell her? She kissed him on the cheek. "Love you, Dad."

After a few moments with both lost in their thoughts, she exclaimed, "That's it?" Lisa-Lotte looked at Bernt with expectations.

"Why? Did I forget something?"

"No, I'm just waiting for a punchline, a 'Ba-da-bing' or a last corny Berg joke."

They laughed, deep in a shared moment of triumph and camaraderie. It was wonderful.

CHAPTER 52

TUESDAY, 29 OCTOBER, 9:08 A.M.

Gail was with Duan in her bedroom. She couldn't remember ever feeling so challenged yet safe at the same time. Who she'd become since being kidnapped and was hoping to become clashed in a confusion of personalities.

"I'm sorry, Duan, but this is all going way too fast. I'm completely overwhelmed and not sure I'll ever find my comfort zone again. Do you realize it is only a week since Luc died? So much has happened. Too much for me to grasp."

"I know, first the shock of Luc's death, your kidnapping, and serious injury, and now news about his having committed suicide as part of a very complicated plot. Everything's a new challenge for you in the past week."

Duan pulled Gail toward him. "But luckily, I have just what the doctor ordered. I love you."

Their swelling intimacy was interrupted by a beep on Gail's phone. She couldn't believe what had popped up on the little screen. "Oh my God. Look at this!"

The new email's subject was simple, 'Clue Five.'

"I thought Clue Four was the last one?" Gail was suddenly close to tears.

Duan put his arm around her in a show of protection but was also at a loss. Their roller coaster hadn't come to a complete stop.

The sender was *luc@isgone.com.*

Hello Gail,

This is the last clue.

Sorry for making this so difficult for you. I wish I could have saved you from all you had to go through but trust me, I couldn't. Ever since realizing what a gigantic mess I'd made of my life, it became unmanageable.

It all started when I realized I had missed the Bitcoin boat. If only I'd spent a measly one hundred Swiss Francs on Bitcoins when Nakamoto published his paper, I'd be a multibillionaire. Not a single day passed without me feeling depressed about it.

Late in 2017, Bitcoins' valuation doubled in a single week, so I decided this was the moment to make good on that epic missed opportunity. I took a significant loan from investors and bought 15,000 Bitcoins at $15,000 each. In no time, that investment gained 30% in value. Within a few weeks, however, it dropped to under $10,000.

I kept my coins, hoping for a recovery, but instead, their value bottomed at $4,000. I was struggling to pay off my debt and did not want to default on the loan. That would have been the beginning of the end of my company.

I was desperate and came up with the idea of 'borrowing' coins from my customers to repay my debt, but it was not enough to cover my losses.

Since then, I've been under unrelenting pressure. From my bank, unpaid vendors, and potentially violent ex-customers.

Gail, I'm dead tired and cannot handle it any longer. I've decided to end it all, but can't leave everything in this sorry state. This creative, rather cinematic drama is what I want to leave with. Financing my death was expensive but has been the most rewarding thing I've ever undertaken. I may have made a mess of things while alive, but at least I die in style.

*I'm sorry for the pain you've endured, but leaving now is the
best for everybody.*

You will not believe this, but… I love you,

Luc

Gail was once again emotionally torn. Deep in her heart, she pitied Luc but was determined to never forget all the anger and forgive the violence. His grief and pain were obviously real, but so were hers.

Duan read the email over Gail's shoulder.

"I can't understand why Luc never asked for help," Duan murmured. "I feel sorry for him. He suffered so much. It's understandable why Luc called it quits."

Gail stared at Duan. Was this it? The rollercoaster in her head slowly came to a stop. It was all over. No more stress, trauma, and drama.

"What now?" She didn't know how to react to this new reality.

"Get your life back together and sort out what needs to be sorted out. I'll be here to help whenever you need me."

She looked at Duan and kissed him playfully on the tip of his nose. "You're so sweet."

Gail called Lisa-Lotte about Luc's last email. Finally, she could accept that Luc's death had been a suicide. Lisa-Lotte told Gail they'd closed the case and were disbanding the team. The facts spoke for themselves, so they'd officially called Luc's death a suicide.

"We're not sure this was technically suicide, though," Lisa-Lotte said suddenly.

"What?" Gail was stunned. Was this another twist? "How come?"

"Because the literal definition of suicide is *death caused by injuring oneself with the intent to die.* Luc did not directly kill himself. We now classify it as a self-directed murder. I asked around the office, and this is definitely a first."

Duan could only follow Gail's side of the call. When she repeated to him the full conversation, he looked surprised.

"Does this mean they're going to prosecute our Confetti boy, Harry Potter, Federer, and God, the orchestrator?" he asked with a smirky smile growing across his face.

"What's only important to me is that Luc's gone, and I'm free. The future should be our priority."

Next, Gail returned the call from Roberto Giobbi. It felt like a year since they last spoke.

"Hello, Roberto, Gail here. Sorry, I missed your call."

"Thanks, Gail. I read about Luc's suicide and wanted to check if you were OK."

"Well, I can't say I had an easy week. The past few days have been so weird. I simply can't believe it. The evidence the police shared with me was conclusive. We also just received a written confession from Luc. They even found the person who Luc had contracted to coordinate his death."

"Do you know anything more about Luc's motive?"

Gail described Luc's last email, explaining what had driven him to organize his murder.

"Roberto, the reason I'm calling you is that the police informed me that BionTic faces financial challenges, and they believe this played a major role in Luc's suicide. What's going on?"

"We certainly have serious cash-flow issues, but business is good. We couldn't find new investors, which caused stress between Luc and me."

"Gail, we're committed to making BionTic the success that Luc was dreaming of, but I have no clue how to keep going. I urgently need cash. I don't know your financial situation, but if you could help me complete Luc's life work, that would be terrific. We're close to being a commercial success in a new and exciting industry. Please help us finish what Luc started."

Giobbi was so typically Swiss-Italian. His business approach was structured and made lots of sense, but the way he begged her to help him was melodramatic.

"Thanks for being so honest, Roberto. I frankly would not do it for Luc. He has been a real bastard to me, which I'll be happy to explain someday. BionTic is your brainchild, not Luc's, and I'd love to help you realize *your* dream. How much would it take to get the business fully solvent?"

"One million Swiss Francs would help us survive this make-or-break period. It's frustrating and distracting to deal with constant financial struggles, although business is booming. I just need to get through the next couple of months."

"One million is a lot, Roberto. I'm not sure I can cough that up at this moment. I need to get a better view of my current financial situation. But thanks for the transparency. I'll think it over and call you back later this week."

After the call with Giobbi, she looked at Duan. He had followed most of their conversation.

"So, they need money?"

"Yes, one million Swiss Francs. I've always had an excellent impression of BionTic's business potential. Giobbi is talented, and I'm convinced his brainchild has a bright future. As much as I'd like to help him, I don't know where to get that kind of money on such short notice."

Duan sighed. "If only I could solve that last riddle, you'd have that much money and plenty more."

"And I can repay the *CryptoSwap* victims." For Gail, it was all about justice.

CHAPTER 53
TUESDAY, 29 OCTOBER, 3:46 P.M.

Duan returned to Zurich to work on that last riddle. He'd have to clear his mind and focus.

The rest of the key is behind what you see!

He hadn't stopped wrestling with what that could mean since he first read it. He thought about redoing his 'hot bath' method. Then he remembered one of his favorite quotes, 'If you do what you always did, you'll get what you always got,' and decided this challenge called for something new.

This unsolved riddle was extra complex, so he'd need to be extra clever and 'color outside the lines.'

He was back doing what he enjoyed most, solving puzzles. That was the good news. When he pressed *Continue*, Luc's picture popped up with the riddle written underneath. He had no clue where to start. That was the bad news. Which of the countless alternatives would work?

Taking that puzzle literally and trying to find all the photos with Luc got him nowhere.

Every time he tried to focus on the riddle, his attention wandered to how Luc had plotted his murder.

He wondered about Luc's state of mind while he was busy working out his killing. Many suicides happen after a lengthy period of depression and are impulsive. Just planning this distributed murder must have taken Luc ages, and then the execution (pardon the pun) must have taken him even longer. Knowing he'd die soon, what had his last few weeks been like?

He imagined Luc sitting behind his desk with a blank sheet of paper, planning his own murder down to the last detail. When he looked at it objectively as a security consultant, Duan wondered what other scenarios Luc had considered and rejected. Did he have any backup plans prepared? What if that guy with the RF cap had refused to take part, for example? His entire project would have fallen apart. Did an accomplice help him with the organization? He couldn't believe a single person had organized this and anticipated every possible glitch.

Duan used the phrase 'Failure is not an option' often to reassure his cyber security clients. The phrase would forever be associated with NASA Chief Flight Director Gene Kranz during the Apollo 13 Moon landing mission. For the Apollo flight crew, NASA's failure would have resulted in the trio's death on their way to the moon. In Luc's case, to the contrary, failure would have resulted in life!

It was ironic that Luc's loss had eventually brought him and Gail together. The movie *Sliding Doors* follows a character's life as one long concatenation of 'what-ifs.' Such a scenario was pertinent to Luc's case as well. What if Luc was still alive? What if he hadn't picked up the phone when Gail called? What if Mina was still alive? In the end, life was one huge 'If-Then-Else' statement.

Luc's nickname, *Luc the Loony Loner*, was very appropriate. All these riddles he'd been chasing to discover that private key looked almost logical. They could only have been created by a loner, come to think of it.

Understanding the cleverness of Luc's murder/suicide and its parallel with zero knowledge proof, Duan wondered if there might be a more technology-oriented solution to that final complex riddle.

He missed Mina so much. She'd helped him with so many breakthroughs during complex hacking cases he'd completed for clients. He wondered how she would have approached, *The rest of the key is behind what you see.*

He closed his eyes and imagined her sitting next to him, like in the good old days. "Come on Duan, we can do this!" he could hear her saying in that distinctive, low-toned voice.

"Hello, gorgeous, what a pleasure to see you. I missed you." It felt so natural to have her next to him.

"Remember how you told me about various encryption techniques and how most had been developed way before we had computers?" she encouraged him.

He'd always enjoyed teaching her the fascinating history of encryption. It was first used circa 4,000 BC in Egypt. The tombs of kings and noblemen often contained scripts with unusual hieroglyphs to hide the meaning of a text. In ancient Egypt, encryption was used to protect knowledge and as a way for religions to discuss taboos.

Using encryption for military purposes started about 500 BC. The Spartans used a device called the *scytale* to send and receive secret messages. They would wind a strip of parchment over a cylinder and write a text on it. Unwound, it was just a random sequence of letters. The message would remain unreadable unless rewound over a second identical cylinder. It was the first use of a common key, similar to what was used nowadays with a crypto wallet, for encryption and decryption.

Often, during long road trips, he would educate and intrigue Mina with such stories. This made them both feel like more knowledgeable cybersecurity experts and consultants.

Closing his eyes, he could still hear Mina saying from her passenger seat, "Darling, tell me again about that hidden message on the courier's scalp. I love that one, and you tell it so well!"

"It happened in 440 BC. Histiaeus, the tyrant of Miletus under the Persian king Darius I, instigated a revolt of the Ionian Greeks against Darius.

"To send a secret message to his Greek vassal, he shaved the head of his servant and 'inscribed' a message onto his scalp. Then he waited for the slave's hair to grow out again, and the message was hidden. Next, he would send the slave to Aristagoras, who shaved the slave's head to read the hidden message. That type of encryption was called 'Steganography.'"

He looked at Mina's spirit, still sitting beside him. Then he jumped.

"Oh my God, darling!"

He could see a gentle, wise smile warming her face.

"You remember how Luc told me, *If anyone could solve it, it would be me*? He was encouraging me to apply my special skill and knowledge to find the answer. He could only be hinting at my expertise in cryptography."

Duan saw the spectral Mina looking uncertain.

"Don't you get it, Mina? The rest of the key is behind what you see!"

Mina still appeared puzzled.

"'Behind *what you see!*'" He accentuated the last three words.

"Steganography is hiding a secret message in another medium. That can be an audio file, a video, or…." He paused for a moment. "Or an image. An image. Behind what you see – an *image*. You get it?"

Mina finally got it.

Very few messages are written on scalps today, but steganography still has some very useful descendants. In this case, hiding a secret message inside a digital image. Every digital picture is composed of millions of *pixels* or tiny dots. The more pixels, the higher the quality a picture becomes. These pixels are generated by a computer as a stream of zeros and ones called *bits*. A group of bits is a byte, which determines each pixel's color. The more bits in a color byte, the more colors appear in the picture.

With steganography, the secret message is translated into a series of ones and zeros. To code that message randomly in the image, the lowest bit of a color byte is changed from a zero into a one, or vice versa. It doesn't affect the image noticeably and cannot be seen by the naked eye.

The film industry actively uses steganography to tag movies to detect pirated copies.

Decoding a secret message in an image isn't simple. The easiest way is to take an unmodified image and compare it with the coded image. Every image is a long series of zeros and ones, so comparing those, we could tell a modified image from an unmodified one.

With Mina's silent help, Duan was now fully in the flow and was crackling with it.

He looked again at Luc's picture that had popped up online. It was the same picture as the portrait on BionTic*'s* corporate website. He surfed to *www.*BionTic.*ch*, clicked on *About Us*, and selected 'Our Founder.' The photo of Luc on that page was identical to the picture displayed with the riddle. Could Luc have used his own image to encode the last part of his private key using steganography?

The rest of the key is behind what you see!

It made so much sense.

He right-clicked both pictures and saved them to his computer. Without too much hassle, he found steganography decoding software and executed a quick comparison of the two images. At first glance, they looked the same.

He clicked the *Compare* button. After a few seconds, two strings of zeros and ones appeared.

"Bingo!" He translated the ones and zeros into their hexadecimal values. It was thirty-two hex characters, which was exactly the number of hexadecimal values he lacked for the private key.

His hand shook as he moved to the website with the field where he could enter the private key. Mina watched him nervously. The tension was killing.

In his notebook, he found the first thirty-two characters he'd decoded so far, which had given him a fifty percent score.

He entered the first thirty-two from his notebook and added the thirty-two he had just found. He typed them carefully in the required field, double-checking each one before going on. All correctly entered and verified? He took a deep breath and cleared the sweat from his forehead. He pressed *Enter.* After what seemed like ages, he got a response.

100% Correct! Well done!

Below that line, a series of hexadecimal digits appeared, resembling a standard private key.

"I fucking did it!" he shouted impulsively. "Luc Starck, you bastard, I did it!"

He danced a joyful jig around his study.

On a new browser screen, he went to the site with access to Luc's digital wallet. Duan entered the newly gained private key.

It opened! Holy Moly, it opened! It displayed 8,327 Bitcoins!

He had to share this with Gail, so he called her.

"I did it Gail! Holy shit, I decoded the private key to Luc's wallet. Can you believe it? I did it! All 8,327 coins are there! I bloody fucking did it, Gail!"

"Wow, Duan, you're incredible!

When he looked next to him, the astral Mina had disappeared.

CHAPTER 54

FRIDAY, 1 NOVEMBER, 6:08 P.M.

Normal life resumed for Gail and Duan but with vastly different mindsets.

Duan split his time between Zurich and Baar, working on assignments he'd put on the backburners after Luc's death.

Gail offered Roberto Giobbi a management buy-out and ran his own company. After a round of discussions with a bank, he secured a business loan and took full possession of BionTic.

Giobbi contracted Duan to conduct an exhaustive review of BionTic's security infrastructure. He identified several major weaknesses in how the company stored DNA data and designed a new architecture, which applied an original zero-knowledge proof structure so DNALink clients could securely access their DNA data. Luc would have been proud of how smoothly yet securely it prepared the company for rapid growth.

The next issue to resolve was how to complete *CryptoSwap's* closure. Gail was committed to compensating the victims. She had to make good of what Luc had messed up. The last thing Gail wanted was years of nasty litigations, with *CryptoSwap's* ex-customers seeking compensation. As a student in business law, she knew how messy that could get. Even with Yong Chi safely behind bars, she expected him to pursue legal action, with other victims following suit.

To help her prepare for such confrontations, Gail sought advice from a respected local lawyer named Harry Thierry. Harry, originally from Geneva, was a slewed, devilish lawyer. He always dressed immaculately and wore a Parmigiani Masterpiece watch. His specialty was white-collar criminals, who often hired him to buy themselves out of problems. He was the perfect legal eagle to help her bring the *CryptoSwap* case to closure.

Gail told Harry she wanted closure as soon as possible and was willing to compensate the victims for a significant part of their losses. Thierry contacted those who had reported thefts when *CryptoSwap* went bankrupt. Thanks to the embedded transparency of Bitcoin transactions, it was easy to trace the deposits made into *CryptoSwap* and how much. Most hadn't expected any settlement, so they quickly agreed to drop their future lawsuits in exchange for compensation of fifty percent of their loss.

Having quickly put BionTic and *CryptoSwap* behind her, Gail finally felt Luc Starck disappear from her life. It was time to focus on her future – picking up her studies and a bright future with Duan.

That evening, they were enjoying a cheese and wine dinner. Gail had lit all the candles she could find in the house. As she was lighting the candles, she told him how much she was in the mood to let go.

"I want to thank you for your support," she said, languidly raising her glass for a toast. "With BionTic gone and *CryptoSwap* closed, I feel the weight of the world lifted from my shoulders. I could never have done that without you near me."

Over the past few days, he had indeed noticed Gail growing more relaxed. She had picked up her study books, resumed attending classes, and bit by bit found her rhythm. He noticed how her face lost the stress around her eyes.

"You know what, Duan? If it was up to me, I'd prefer to live without Luc's wealth. But thinking back about all the fights and all the emotional trauma, I guess I somehow deserve his money. Am I wrong?"

"Darling," Duan said, taking her hands in both of his. "Things always happen for a reason, and I'm convinced Luc would have wanted you to have his coins. Luc was a complicated person, driven by an enormous inferiority complex. After that CryptoSwap settlement, there is more than enough left for you to have a very comfortable life with no feelings of guilt. Think about it, you deserve it!"

Gail remained silent, lost in her thoughts, and began to run her fingers through his hair.

"I guess Luc never figured out how to care for you and I sense deep inside he must have regretted mistreating you. Like he just lost control, and you were the closest person to strike out at."

"Maybe you are right. I appreciate how much you try to make me feel good."

"I hope it helps." Duan continued. "Luc could have said nothing about his private keys and let the coins be inaccessible but chose not to do so."

She looked up. "I guess that happens a lot with crypto millionaires, don't you think?"

"Oh yes, of the maximum twenty-one million Bitcoins that will ever get into circulation, four million are already lost. Much of that is because the owners of these coins died without passing them on. Four million coins are almost one hundred billion US dollars."

"Wow. I guess I'm lucky."

"While the number of Bitcoins in your wallet has seriously reduced with the *CryptoSwap* pay-out, you cannot allow what's left to go unused. The remaining 516 Bitcoins will provide you with a very comfortable life. There's no need to feel embarrassed or guilty. You should be proud of having paid off all the *CryptoSwap* customers, and for helping Roberto Giobbi to keep his dream alive. You succeeded where Luc failed."

He saw Gail think for a moment. "You know what? You're right. I'm entitled to these Bitcoins. We should just get out of all this crypto shit and exchange them into good old Swiss Francs, hard cash on the barrelhead. When push comes to shove, the old economy wasn't that bad."

Duan laughed. "If only Luc heard you say, 'the old economy isn't that bad', he'd turn over in his grave!"

"I don't care what Luc might think. All that matters to me is that he is gone… and you're here."

Gail reached out for his arms across the table.

"Mina would be so happy to see us like this. I know she approves." She looked at the ceiling and raised her glass in honor of Mina.

Duan smiled and pulled Gail closer. "Yes, ma'am, we're a perfect match."

Later that evening, comfortably on the couch, lying relaxed in his arms, Gail spoke up.

"We should go on a nice vacation. This past year has been rough on both of us, and a relaxing trip would do us a world of good. I hope you can find time for a trip because I've already booked a villa in Tuscany, and we leave in two weeks. Good food, wine, and the sun. That's all we need. Well, and maybe some more."

Gail turned her head around and kissed him on the lips.

The rest of the evening they spent watching TV. They almost were like a normal couple.

Just as they were about to go to bed, Gail's and Duan's phones beeped at the same time. They were surprised and curious by the coincidence. Each had received a new email. When they read the sender and the subject of the message, they get shivers.

It was from Mina!

It had been exactly eight weeks since she died. The subject said *Last and Final clue*.

When they opened the email, it was short.

Hello, my darlings,

I hope you are making the most out of your time together. You deserve each other.

Love,
Mina

CHAPTER 55
FRIDAY, 19 JULY, 11:12 A.M.

15 weeks earlier

Shortly after Mina received the news about her imminent death, she made a calm, rational decision to accept her fate and make something positive out of it. As a born problem solver, instead of panicking and feeling sorry for herself, she would not allow her very serious personal problem to become a problem for anyone else.

She soon realized that her lifelong instinct to fight would not help her this time. The message from her doctor was clear; she was going to die-period. She couldn't change that, but she could choose how she dealt with the news.

In those last months, taking care of Duan was her top priority. He was everything to her. Ever since they'd met nine years ago, there hadn't been a single day without at least one conversation. Their relationship was fusional; every morning, he took her in his arms, and they cuddled for thirty minutes before getting out of bed.

With her help, Duan managed to keep his mood swings and anger fully under control, and her worst nightmare was that, after her death, Duan would fall into a black hole and lose his emotional balance.

She was determined that he'd begin his new life and would help him find his future happiness. She had managed their business and professional lives. Taking the lead came naturally to her, and she noticed how Duan always appreciated that. Most of their business leads had come from her network.

She planned their holidays and handled their finances. How would Duan manage all of that when she was gone?

She knew, eventually, he'd meet someone. But she felt a deep sense of responsibility for Duan's future happiness. Her sickness was already hard enough for him to handle. She had to take care of him even from beyond the grave.

One Friday, Gail was in a crisis due to drama with Luc at home and came over while Duan was away on a business trip. For the first time in many months, the girls could enjoy a few days together.

"So good to have this 'girls weekend.' We used to do it all the time."

"I'll truly miss them," Gail said with a sad face.

"For God's sake, Gail, let's not get depressed and melancholy. It is what it is. Let's celebrate life and have fun."

"So tell me, what happened with Luc?"

"He's become a completely loose cannon. I do not know what's going on or how I can help him. His crises have become more frequent, and I'm so relieved to be away for a couple of days without having to walk on eggshells. This week, he had three giant outbursts, and I had to call the police when he started kicking me. Tonight, he came home completely drunk, and things were about to start again. I just *cannot* handle this any longer."

She lifted her shirt and showed Mina egg-shaped bruises scattered over her torso.

Mina held her breath when she saw her friend's contusions. Her mouth fell open, and she could not get anything out.

"This is just the upper part. I've bruises everywhere. I can no longer stand this anymore. Something has to happen. One of us has to leave. I'm so fucking done with that fucking monster!" The anger in her eyes said it all.

"So why not just stay here? I'm sure Duan wouldn't have a problem with that. He loves you."

"Oh, my God, no. You guys already have too much on your mind to worry about me. Today, you are still okay, but we have no clue how things will develop for you."

"No, Gail, I'm worried for you to be with him, alone in that big house in Baar."

Noticing how she started to refer to Luc as 'him,' Mina recognized that she'd lost all respect for Gail's husband. Men who hit their wives were the lowest form of life.

"However much I'd enjoy being here with you, I couldn't do that to you."

"Is it because of Duan that you could not be yourself here?"

"No, absolutely not. I love Duan. He is a great guy, and you are so blessed to have him at your side. No, I need to sort out my own shit."

The rest of the weekend was like old times, and Sunday came before they realized. Gail's departure was hard for Mina, especially knowing she had to go home. They held each other tight and kissed goodbye. Neither of them dared to say it aloud, but they knew every meeting could be their last one.

After that weekend, two sentences struck Mina and got stuck in her head. *I'm so fucking done with that fucking monster*, referring to Luc, and *I love Duan*. Hearing her say that and seeing Gail's smiling face when she spoke about Duan, Mina realized Gail would be an excellent match for Duan. His sense of humor, his intelligence, his sensitivity, and natural desire to please would be so deserved for her dearest friend.

Mina's thoughts went back to a game she and Duan had played not long before her cancer diagnosis. They fantasized about who could be their ideal partner if the other one died. A gruesome exercise, generating lots of laughs.

Duan blurted out, "I wouldn't mind being with Gail. I'm sure we'd get along very well. It's such a pity she's stuck with that wanker Luc," he said with a cheesy grin.

Mina realized how real that innocent game had become. The more she thought about it, the more she was convinced they'd make a wonderful couple.

Long before Gail had mentioned Luc's violence, Mina already had developed an aversion to him. She just didn't trust him. She couldn't put her finger on her issue with Luc but had always felt it. She told Duan about her misgivings but kept them from Gail, as she didn't want her disgust for Luc to undermine their friendship. Mina had steeled herself to accept Luc the way he was.

Gail and Duan would indeed form a perfect couple; bringing them together one way or the other became Mina's obsession.

With that weekend fresh in her mind and having seen the anger in Gail's eyes and bruises all over her body, Luc began to appear subhuman.

"It's my duty to free Gail. Luc will have to die."

Subconsciously, her thoughts went back to how Duan 'freed' her from the toxic relationship she was in before they met. Now, she was determined it was her turn to free her best friend, Gail.

The more time she spent nurturing this bizarre idea, the less time she had to focus on her pain and death.

It was a devilish but very convenient solution that appealed to her and gave her a chance to end her life on a historically triumphant note.

She wouldn't tell Gail and Duan until it was too late for anybody to do anything about it.

Luc's death would devastate Gail at first, but she knew that deep in her heart, she'd welcome her new life. She'd just have to make sure it would drive Duan straight into Gail's open arms. For a moment, she considered sharing her plan with Gail. Then she realized that if Gail knew she'd killed Luc to bring her and Duan together, it would be a lifelong emotional burden for her friend.

For several days, she puzzled over how it might be done. Contracting someone to kill Luc was doable but wouldn't automatically bring Gail and Duan together. Luc's killing could even make Gail pity Luc.

Then she realized it had to appear to be a suicide. Having Luc take his own life would be more palatable to Gail. She already knew that he was deeply depressed, sorry for all he'd done to Gail, and saw only one way out.

With Luc dead, Gail would naturally turn to Duan for support, and it would only be a matter of time before Gail and Duan began happier new lives together.

So, it had to be suicide! What would that look like, and how could she arrange it to avoid damaging anyone but her target?

Her plan was coming together. Next, she had to decide when Luc would die. To avoid any suspicion of her involvement, it should happen *after* she was gone. That extra wrinkle would make it neater.

Now she had a good general idea of *what* should happen to Luc and *when*. It was time to dive into the *how*.

CHAPTER 56
THURSDAY, 8 AUGUST, 2:14 P.M.

Mina's mind raced, crafting a plan that met all her criteria. It was an exhilarating intellectual challenge, but she regretted not having anyone to collaborate with on the project. Thankfully, her painkillers were working because the coming days would demand every ounce of her focus.

She weighed various options. One was dosing Luc daily with mercury—a known cause of severe depression. Experiments had shown that rats exposed to over-the-counter pharmaceuticals containing thimerosal or sodium ethyl mercury exhibited the expected symptoms. It would be easy enough to slip a small amount into his beer or yogurt. If Luc fell into deep enough despair, it seemed only a matter of time before he'd take his own life.

In the end, she rejected this approach because of the lack of guaranteed results and logistical issues. *Failure was not an option*, as Duan always said.

During one internal brainstorming session, the very creative notion of a distributed murder occurred to her. She would have to gather a group of unwitting accomplices. She'd read about zero-knowledge proof, and with Luc being a crypto entrepreneur, it would make sense for Luc to commit suicide with this blockchain technique. It was the perfect way to apply *Zero Knowledge Proof* in a real-life, or more exactly, in a real-death scenario.

She adopted a new identity for her plan: Fritz Fleming, a nod to Ian Fleming, the creator of James Bond. Whenever she had to call someone, she used a transformer, allowing her to talk with a male voice.

Under the disguise of Fritz Fleming, she easily managed to scam a bank for 250,000 Swiss Francs.

With the funds secured, her first step was to rent a workspace where she could plan in peace. She told Duan she had taken up walking as a hobby and used that as an excuse to slip away for a few hours each day. The garage she rented nearby was perfect—equipped with a workbench and a small desk for her computer. The walls soon became plastered with printouts of her plan, which she had dubbed "Project Zero Knowledge."

Many years ago, Mina dated a magician who performed a so-called electric chair act. Using a remote-control device, the magician caused a sharp pin to pop up through the seat, which would sting the audience member and make him or her jump.

What if, instead of a pin, the chair ejected a deadly gas or liquid? A quick, painless death—Luc deserved at least that much.

Buying the VX gas was tricky, but she managed to pull it off.

Next, she needed the right setting. She decided Luc would die with a view—on the edge of Zuger Lake, in the historic town square at *Landsgemeindeplatz*. After scouting the location, she settled on the terrace of *Hotel Loewen Am See* as the perfect spot. She found identical chairs online to match the ones used at the hotel.

To modify the chair, she contacted her ex-magician boyfriend, explaining she was looking for a chair like the one from his act but with a confetti bomb beneath it triggered by a remote-controlled CO2 canister. She told him it was for a friend's wedding prank. The magician put her in touch with a professional in Switzerland, and she ordered two chairs: one standard and one modified. The job was simple but expensive _ twenty thousand Swiss Francs. Welcome to Switzerland!

Once she received the prepared chair, the modifications to add the VX gas canister and the remote control were not simple, but eventually, she did it. Working with the deadly VX gas was scary. Leaking the smallest bit could result in her death. Although, in her case, that would not be a huge loss.

Her full plan was dependent on the chair to flawlessly do its job. She could not afford this to fail and decided to run a trial execution. In a pet shop, she bought a rabbit in a cage. It was cruel, but it was unavoidable. *FNAO, Failure was Not An Option.*

She placed the rabbit in its cage on the chair, positioned herself at a safe distance, and pressed the button. A few seconds later, the rabbit convulsed briefly, then collapsed. Mission accomplished!

She contracted *Zug Events* to publish a quiz in a local newspaper, followed by a prize ceremony on the square. Mr. Minten, the owner, agreed to the odd request. Helped by the generous fee she offered. Things got tricky when the local government didn't want confetti on the square, but she resolved that easily. Money did miracles in Switzerland.

Unfortunately, her ex was no longer performing, so she asked if he knew another magician who did the electric chair.

On his advice, Mina hired magician Peter Vogel to perform the electric chair act during the event. She provided him with the standard set, matching the chairs of Hotel *Loewen Am See*. She staked out Vogel's house to understand where he stored his props. Eventually, she hired a burglar to swap the chairs the night before the event.

She looked over her planning sheet approvingly. Things had come together nicely. Her project turned out to be the perfect pastime while waiting for her death. Not sure how much time she had left, she hurried through the preparations.

It was essential Luc came to the square at the right moment and sat in the prepared chair.

Tapping into her advanced hacking skills, she sent a phishing email to several single men she'd come across on a popular dating website. Within a day, four of them had clicked on her email, allowing her to install a malicious piece of software on their mobile phones. This malware gave her full control over their phones, allowing her to activate their cameras remotely and start recording them. Within a few days, she'd recorded three men 'pleasing themselves' while visiting porn websites. She decided Brucker would be the lucky one and blackmailed him into meeting Luc at the square. The man with the Roger Federer cap.

The following critical step was making sure Luc attended his fateful meeting. He could not miss it. The more attractive she could make that meeting, the more likely he'd accept.

She knew Luc could not reject an invitation that was part of a transfer coming from a wallet full of virgin Bitcoins, so she had a friend ask a fellow crypto whale to invite Luc to the meeting. He knew Luc's reputation and track record and did it with sincere satisfaction. Boy, was this going to be a surprise!

Finally, she'd need a project manager to flawlessly coordinate all the steps of Luc's killing as if it were an important project at work. She would have loved to have done this herself, but unfortunately would no longer be available.

Outside Zug, on a hill above the city, was a secret lovers' lane. Everybody in town knew what went on there. During lunchtime, the parking lot was full of cars, with ardent lovers enjoying a quick kiss or something more. Mina visited it for several days and noticed a few cars stopping regularly. She discreetly followed these cars and took pictures of the men. She figured out where they worked and, with some help from LinkedIn, identified them. One of them appeared to have the perfect profile.

Fred Bongers was a seasoned project manager who worked and lived in Zug. He was quite attractive: blue eyes, toned body, with white teeth, like a washing machine salesman. When she realized his mistress was the boss's wife, she whooped like a cowgirl. Fred Bongers was the perfect target!

She painstakingly prepared his instructions and left some materials in a storage locker at Zurich's train station.

Everything was moving on all cylinders for her now. She started feeling giddy.

Finally, Luc's death had to appear to be a suicide. For that, Luc had to deliver the envelope with instructions personally to Fred Bongers.

One afternoon, she went to Luc's office at BionTic. Seeing a sickly Mina stepping into his office surprised him.

"Mina, what a surprise. Is there something wrong? Can I help you?"

"No worries, Luc. It's really nothing. I'm finishing a project and was supposed to deliver an important confidential report to *Zug Machines* in town."

"Wow, what a dedication!"

"My contact, Mr. Fred Bongers, insisted I bring this to him personally, but he was out of the office. I just spoke with him, and he'll be home in about two hours. That's in the *Baarerstrasse*. As that's close to your office, would you mind dropping this off? It's highly confidential, so please keep your conversation with him short. Also, it would be best if you didn't even mention our names. Please let me know when you've dropped it off."

She made it sound like a very casual request. Luc had no suspicion at all, and three hours later, he messaged her, "Mission Accomplished!" Never imagining he was now another unwitting accomplice to his own murder.

She had reached the end of her preparations. Mina rewarded herself with a glass of wine and a bowl of cashews. Everything still had to be executed, but her job was done. It felt like she'd been preparing for a rocket launch. All that was left was the countdown! A very long countdown!

Enjoying her wine, she wrote Luc's farewell email to Gail as 'Clue Five.' She wasn't sure it was the wine talking, but the drama in her email was coming across very well. Of course, she had heard about the failure of *CryptoSwap*, so she conjured up the story of Luc taking a loan he could not pay back. Nobody could validate that story anyway. She saved the mail and planned its distribution a week after Luc's death.

Her detailed checklist had it all spelled out.

She went through it one more time.

- ✓ Invitation for meeting with Luc–check.
- ✓ Fred Bongers activated as organizer–check.
- ✓ Brucker set up to meet Luc–check.
- ✓ Prepare draft mail for Brucker to send - check.
- ✓ Magician contracted–check.
- ✓ Event organizer contracted–check.
- ✓ Burglar to swap chair and remote controller–check.
- ✓ Prepare mail with 'Clue Four' hinting Fred Bongers–check.
- ✓ Prepare Luc's farewell mail to Gail as 'Clue Five,' delayed sending–check.
- ✓ Write a note to Duan and Gail with delayed sending–check.

She'd missed nothing and was glad to be working with such a reliable, professional Swiss team.

Hoping it would confuse the police, Mina introduced the clues as misdirection. It was done to condition their mind. Mentioning 'Clue Four' was the last one and adding Luc's farewell as 'Clue Five' would give the impression the end had been reached.

On an impulse, she added a last note to Gail and Duan as 'Clue Six.' She wrote it but was in doubt if it was the right thing to do; they could conclude she was behind Luc's murder. Twice, she deleted it, but only to rewrite it fifteen minutes later. Finally, she kept it. It's like giving a small wink to the happy couple. She had a big smile as she wrote the loving email.

Like all her work, everything was meticulously planned. That last email, 'Clue Six,' would hopefully give Gail and Duan all the happiness they deserved. She was sure they would finally understand what had happened to them. She triple-checked her plan, and once she was one hundred percent convinced all was complete, she could finally plot her own exit.

Preparing for her own death was relatively simple compared to Luc's.

The culmination had occurred exactly one week before she woke up with a smile the morning of her death. She was ready to go.

Five hours later, after some precious moments in Duan's arms, she whispered in his ears. "I'm ready, darling. All that had to be said is said, and all that had to be done is done…."

With a light smile on her face, she peacefully died in Duan's arms.

◆ The End ◆

ACKNOWLEDGMENTS

Zero Knowledge is inspired by my own experiences in Zug during my stint at SEBA Bank, the bank of the new economy. I spent many hours on the terrace of *Hotel Loewen Am See*, which indeed serves a delicious cappuccino while brainstorming about the idea of a distributed murder.

I thank Oliver Deak for being the first one to mention the expression Zero Knowledge Proof when I explained to him the concept of distributed murder. Jeff Schliemann explained steganography, and I'm thankful to many others at the crypto bank who introduced me to various crypto concepts and terminology.

The city of Zug is thanked for making it such a gorgeous, inspiring backdrop for this unique story.

I also acknowledge the many heroes in the world of magic for being a never-ending source for names of individuals in my books.

I'm grateful to Magali and Jean-Luc for the inspiration and years of friendship. Finally, I thank my beta readers, Granny, Romain, Vikki, Allan, Gary, Caro, and Marina.

My editors, Carey Giudici, Tory Hunter, and Brent Howard, have polished this story over and over again, adding color and bringing it to a level where I never could have pushed it. My publisher Mikael Carlson, fully believed in this project and giving it the global audience it deserves.

Finally, I thank my daughters, Lisanne and Charlotte, for always being in my thoughts while writing this book.

Arnaud Pascolo
Zug, Oviedo, New Delhi, Riyadh, 2025

ABOUT THE AUTHOR

Arnaud Pascolo is a Dutch writer currently residing in Oviedo, Spain. His writing is sprinkled with tongue-in-cheek humor combined with an endless passion for stories with unexpected and quirky twists. In each of his stories, he blends elements from his passions: business, IT, magic, and the complexities of human nature.

After pursuing an international career with several executive management roles across the globe, he now dedicates his time to writing.

Arnaud's aim is to entertain you with imagination and a genuine love for storytelling.

Please do reach out to Arnaud on:

Email	info@arnaudpascolo.com
Website	www.arnaudpascolo.com
Facebook	ArnaudPascolo
Instagram	ArnaudPascolo
X	@PascoloArnaud
Bluesky	@IamArnaudPascolo